PENGUIN BOOKS

Tom Clancy's Ghost Recon

Peter Telep is the *New York Times* bestselling author of over forty novels spanning many genres including film adaptations, medical drama and military thrillers. In addition to his writing career he teaches creative writing courses at the University of Central Florida.

D0610895

TOM CLANCY'S HAWX

TOM CLANCY'S GHOST RECON
GHOST RECON
COMBAT OPS
CHOKE POINT

TOM CLANCY'S ENDWAR
ENDWAR
THE HUNTED

TOM CLANCY'S SPLINTER CELL

SPLINTER CELL	FALLOUT
OPERATION BARRACUDA	CONVICTION
CHECKMATE	ENDGAME

Created by Tom Clancy and Steve Pieczenik

TOM CLANCY'S OP-CENTER	TOM CLANCY'S NET FORCE
OP-CENTER	NET FORCE
MIRROR IMAGE	HIDDEN AGENDAS
GAMES OF STATE	NIGHT MOVES
ACTS OF WAR	BREAKING POINT
BALANCE OF POWER	POINT OF IMPACT
STATE OF SIEGE	CYBERNATION
DIVIDE AND CONQUER	STATE OF WAR
LINE OF CONTROL	CHANGING OF THE GUARD
MISSION OF HONOR	SPRINGBOARD
SEA OF FIRE	THE ARCHIMEDES EFFECT
CALL TO TREASON	
WAR OF EAGLES	

Created by Tom Clancy and Martin Greenberg
TOM CLANCY'S POWER PLAYS

POLITIKA	COLD WAR
RUTHLESS.COM	CUTTING EDGE
SHADOW WATCH	ZERO HOUR
BIO-STRIKE	WILD CARD

Tom Clancy's GHOST RECON®

CHOKE POINT

WRITTEN BY

PETER TELEP

PENGUIN BOOKS

PENGUIN BOOKS

Published by the Penguin Group
Penguin Books Ltd, 80 Strand, London WC2R ORL, England
Penguin Group (USA) Inc., 375 Hudson Street, New York, New York 10014, USA
Penguin Group (Canada), 90 Eglinton Avenue East, Suite 700, Toronto, Ontario,
Canada M4P 2Y3 (a division of Pearson Penguin Canada Inc.)
Penguin Ireland, 25 St Stephen's Green, Dublin 2, Ireland (a division of Penguin Books Ltd)
Penguin Group (Australia), 707 Collins Street, Melbourne, Victoria 3008, Australia
(a division of Pearson Australia Group Pty Ltd)
Penguin Books India Pvt Ltd, 11 Community Centre, Panchsheel Park, New Delhi – 110 017, India
Penguin Group (NZ), 67 Apollo Drive, Rosedale, Auckland 0632, New Zealand
(a division of Pearson New Zealand Ltd)
Penguin Books (South Africa) (Pty) Ltd, Block D, Rosebank Office Park,
181 Jan Smuts Avenue, Parktown North, Gauteng 2193, South Africa

Penguin Books Ltd, Registered Offices: 80 Strand, London WC2R ORL, England

www.penguin.com

First published in the United States of America by The Berkley Publishing Group 2013
First published in Great Britain in Penguin Books 2013
001

Set in 12.5/14.75pt Garamond MT Std
Typeset by Jouve (UK), Milton Keynes
Printed in Great Britain by Clays Ltd, St Ives plc

ISBN: 978–1–405–91259–4

www.greenpenguin.co.uk

MIX
Paper from
responsible sources
FSC
www.fsc.org   FSC® C018179

Penguin Books is committed to a sustainable
future for our business, our readers and our planet.
This book is made from Forest Stewardship
Council™ certified paper.

ALWAYS LEARNING   **PEARSON**

Acknowledgments

I'm deeply indebted to the great number of people who contributed their expertise to this manuscript:

Mr James Ide, chief warrant officer, U. S. Navy (Rct.), has continued his work as my first reader, researcher, and collaborator – from idea to polished manuscript. He is a great friend, fantastic writer, and it's my honor to know him.

Mr Sam Strachman of Ubisoft Paris has worked with me on several other book projects and offered his excellent advice, insights, and great sense of humor.

Mr Jay Posey of Red Storm Entertainment fielded my many questions and provided me with an entire unit history of the Ghosts that was invaluable to the writing of this novel. He was an amazing resource, and I hope to work with him again.

Special thanks to Richard Dansky of Red Storm Entertainment, as well as Jean-Marc Geffroy, Michiel Verheijdt, and Julien Charpentier of Ubisoft Paris for their assistance and encouragement.

My agent, Mr John Talbot, and editor, Mr Tom Colgan, have supported and encouraged me for many years, and I'm truly grateful for the many projects we've shared together.

Finally, my wife, Nancy, and two lovely daughters, Lauren and Kendall, went above and beyond the call of duty on this one. If you only knew what I put them through . . .

He who conquers others is strong; he who conquers himself is mighty.

— Lao Tzu, *Tao Te Ching*

The bravest are surely those who have the clearest vision of what is before them, glory and danger alike, and yet notwithstanding, go out to meet it.

— Thucydides (460–395 B.C.)

One

You cannot apply to become a Ghost.

They find you . . .

And find him they had, recruited him right out of the Navy SEALs so he could wind up here, in South America, on a search and rescue mission for a CIA operations officer abducted only hours ago by Fuerzas Armadas Revolucionarias de Colombia, more concisely known as FARC.

During the past year, this revolutionary group had violated their cease-fire agreement with the government. They were back to drug smuggling, acts of terrorism, and kidnapping, which was why former Command Master Chief, now *Captain*, Andrew Ross was crouched beneath a thick canopy of palm fronds, about to order his Ghost team to attack –

When a gunshot cracked to the east. Remington MSR. Sniper rifle. Fired by one of the AFEUR guys.

The Agrupación de Fuerzas Especiales Antiterroristas Urbanas was the Colombian Army's special forces group that had first responded to the abduction. They had twelve operators working with Ross's four-man squad, and one of those boys had just blown their ambush.

'Pepper, SITREP!' Ross cried into the boom mike at his lips.

'Hey, it wasn't me,' answered Master Sergeant Robert 'Pepper' Bonifacio.

'He's in your zone. You got eyes on him?'

'Negative!'

The sniper rifle boomed once more, echoing across the valley and sending chills ripping up Ross's spine.

'Ghost Lead, this is Kozak. I got the drone on our sniper. He fired in reflex 'cause he's dead. They cut his throat.'

Ross lifted his voice: 'All right, Pepper? 30K? We're moving in. Kozak, you hold back with the drone. Let's go!'

As he sprang to his feet, Ross switched to the command net and spoke in Spanish to his counterpart, an AFEUR captain named Jiménez. 'One of your snipers is dead. We need a squad in there to take out those troops on the west side.'

'Roger, Captain. I'll send them now.'

The FARC outpost where the CIA officer was being held lay on Colombia's southwest coast, between the ramshackle villages of San Antonio, Las Juntas, and Aguaclara, all captured like insects within the web of Valle del Cauca's mountainous jungle and the coca fields hidden within.

A storm system had just passed through, and the jungle's hot breath rose and hissed from the damp earth as Ross sprinted toward the collection of tin-roofed shacks and lean-tos, partially obscured by enormous fronds. The stench of mold, rotting wood and gasoline grew thicker as he rounded the next knot of trees then hunkered down just twenty meters away from the clearing. Ahead lay five mud-covered jeeps, along with three flatbed trucks probably manufactured in the 1960s, an automotive graveyard if you didn't know better.

Automatic weapons fire flashed and resounded from behind those trucks, drawing a string of short-circuiting wires in the late-afternoon gloom. Ross reached into his web gear, reared back and let fly a sensor grenade.

Once the grenade hit the ground behind the vehicles, the exact positions of the hostiles appeared in his Cross-Com's heads-up display, targets marked by flashing red outlines of the figures, with data automatically sent to the other Ghosts, their own combination monocle-earpiece and microphones allowing them to mark the targets, hear his reports, and respond in kind. What's more, the Cross-Coms weren't the only technological trick up their sleeves. The team's initial recon of the outpost had been conducted by Staff Sergeant John Dimitri Kozak, the youngest operator and self-professed technophile who loved commanding their Unmanned Aerial Vehicle (UAV). More sophisticated than its predecessor, the Cypher drone, this new UAV's quad rotors rotated downward and turned into wheels so it could land and rumble along for an even quieter and stealthier approach on targets.

At the moment, though, Kozak had the drone in the

air for overwatch, and his voice cut through the team net, burred with anxiety: 'No movement from within the shacks. Something's wrong. They're not moving the package.'

Before Ross could comment on that, the AFEUR men, along with Pepper and 30K, returned fire on the rebels behind the vehicles, the barrage of rounds thumping and ricocheting off the jeeps, windows shattering and tires whooshing flat. The AFEUR troops were fielding TAR-21 Israeli bullpup rifles using standard 5.56mm NATO rounds. That distinctive thunder stood in sharp juxtaposition with the FARC rebels' Chinese-made AK-47s that popped in reply.

Noting the hostiles IDed by the sensor grenade, Ross peered out from behind the trees, and the images of his teammates now shimmered in his HUD, green outlines superimposed over the surrounding jungle, along with blue outlines representing the Colombian SF squads.

Well, Major Scott Mitchell had been right. This sure as hell was an 'interesting' first mission for Ross, who'd just gone through the selection and qualification phases of becoming a Ghost, even after surviving the rigors of a career in the SEALs, beginning with preindoctrination and the infamous Basic Underwater Demolition/SEAL training (BUD/S).

Ross recalled the welcome letter from Mitchell, the explanation of how the D Company, First Battalion, Fifth Special Forces Group had been deactivated, with the Ghosts reassigned to the newly formed Group for Specialized Tactics (GST) and Mitchell promoted to serve as its commanding officer. There'd been some mention of a Joint Strike Force that would one day comprise all branches of the service, with test operations beginning at the unit level, mostly notably within the GST. In fact, Ross was one of the first non-Army operators to become a Ghost, and it was with some trepidation that he took on the role of a Ghost Lead to command three members from the US Army's Special Forces. In the field it was all business, but during downtime, well, he feared their interservice rivalry would reach new heights. So far everyone had been cool, utterly professional, but he was waiting for the bomb to drop and for the team to give him a nickname that he would hate more than terrorists, reality TV, and Cupcake, his ex-wife's ferocious white Chihuahua.

'I'm moving up,' he announced. 'Cover me now!' With that, he sprang from the mushy ground, weaving a serpentine path along the perimeter, elbowing past vines and ducking beneath low-hanging branches with raindrops threatening to fall from them like hot wax dripping from a candle. He was drenched in sweat now, his mouth salty, his eyes burning. He ignored his pulse ringing in his ears and was all about the course ahead, cutting, weaving again, sidestepping, and bounding over two fallen logs whose bark was flaking off like sunburn. His boots made sucking noises in the mud, and for a moment his vision blurred and returned as he blinked away more sweat and crossed beneath a stand of wax palms.

He broke from there to a small clearing and the nearest shack, where three of the FARC rebels had assumed defensive positions beside a wall that resembled a quilt of cannibalized sheet metal with fading soda company logos.

One of the rebels glanced back.

Ross lifted his HK416 assault rifle, the same one he carried as a member of the United States Naval Special Warfare Development Group, also known as DEVGRU. Like the AFEUR team's rifles, his thirty-round magazine was loaded with 5.56mm NATO rounds, and he was about to express deliver some flaming hot lead to these rebels –

When Kozak's voice buzzed through his earpiece: 'Ghost Lead! Get down! Got three behind you!'

Ross hit the deck. Craned his neck.

And his HUD lit up like the Vegas strip.

Two

Kozak was perched about halfway up the mountain overlooking the FARC outpost, and he had a clean line of sight on the shacks and trucks.

With the drone crawler's remote clutched in his hands, he gaped at the LED screen showing the drone's point of view: Ross had just hit the deck and activated his optical camouflage. The team's fatigues, boots, gloves, scarves – everything – were made of a meta-material specially engineered to reflect the current environment. The drawback was that you had to remain perfectly still; movement produced a visible distortion as the system's microprocessor attempted to catch up. Moreover, the report of your weapon would send reverberations through your body that often deactivated the system.

'Ghost Lead, I have you covered,' Kozak said, taking the drone into a nosedive, then flying in and out of trees until he reached an opening in the brush. He brought the drone down, the quad rotors rolling into tire position, and thump, she was on the ground, speeding up behind the three FARC rebels who were jogging toward Ross.

Kozak switched on the drone's speaker and spoke into the remote's built-in microphone: *'Oo ti blya, golova, kak obezyaniya jopah.'*

If the FARC rebel who spun around had grown up in Little Odessa, Brooklyn, and been the son of Russian immigrants, then he would've understood Kozak's words: *Your face looks like a monkey's ass.*

But the rebel did not share Kozak's background. And getting his attention was all Kozak needed. The bearded rebel took aim at the little 'toy' rolling toward him –

And that's when Kozak thumbed the touchscreen and launched the drone right into the man's face, knocking him to the ground, a triplet of gunfire erupting from his AK, his two comrades crying out and turning back to see what had happened.

'Get 'em now, boss!' Kozak cried.

It was, in Kozak's young mind, a perfect marriage of technology and tenacity, with the drone diverting the rebels and clearing the way for Ross to attack. Indeed, Ross fired three rounds – perfect head shots that dropped the targets nearly in unison, as though they were androids controlled by a single power supply that had suddenly been cut.

'Get that drone back in the air,' Ross ordered, bolting off toward the shacks.

'Roger that.' Kozak flew the drone straight up above the canopy and once more began sweeping the entire perimeter. 'The Colombians have their squad attacking in the west,' he reported. 'I got eyes on about ten guys around the shacks, marking them now. Still no sign of the package.'

The drone's computer picked out and highlighted

each of the targets and updated their positions every one-hundredth of a second. Kozak wasn't sure what he liked more: providing overwatch and intel with the drone (which in his youthful twenty-six-year-old mind gave him major baller status) or actually being in the shit and firing the guns (which was equally awesome). He figured he'd catch hell from Ross later for that stunt with the drone, but he'd argue that he had just been improvising, not trying to show off, not trying to perform some feat of heroism. They had the technology – why not put it to good use with a little old school demolition derby?

A rustle of leaves from behind, followed by the sudden rhythm of footfalls, had him turning, tucking the remote into his web gear, activating his camouflage, and holding still –

Just as two dark-faced rebels wearing boonie hats approached from the east, one grunting in Spanish, 'I heard him up here, somewhere.' The other used his free arm to hold back some fronds while he and his comrade drew closer.

Kozak adjusted his grip on the rifle, a Remington ACR with suppressor, well suited for jungle ops like this one.

He held his breath. Time slowed. Sounds congealed into one another like pieces of clay to form one constant: the beating of his heart. The men drew closer. He could ambush them now, but in the second he killed one, the other could get off a shot.

Don't move, he ordered himself.

'Being a great warrior isn't just being a good killer. It's knowing when to pull the trigger, and when to shake a hand. It's doing what it takes to win.'

Kozak's father, Leonid, who'd remained behind in Russia, had said that after learning his son wanted to join the Army. And while Kozak hadn't realized it then, he understood now that being a successful Special Forces operator required just that: knowing when. And the only people who'd ever witness his decisions, good and bad, would be his teammates. They were, in truth, the audience he needed to please. You didn't become a Ghost to get famous – that was for sure. *'Credit is failure,'* Major Mitchell had told them time and again. You became a Ghost because you wanted to serve, you wanted to make sure that all those kids who'd suffered through 9/11, those kids who'd lost their families, would never, ever have to go through something like that again. Someone had to do the job, someone who would not lead an ordinary life. Kozak had always known he would be a soldier. He had the Russian fighting spirit in his blood and the love for America in his heart and soul. He was a Russian-American. He was proud.

'There he is! Right there!' cried one of the rebels.

Whether he'd been shaking unconsciously or his optical camouflage system had malfunctioned, Kozak wasn't sure. That he would die in the next heartbeat was absolutely certain –

Unless he sprang up, took his chances, and fired.

Three

Pepper had a feeling the two rebels who'd broken off from their buddies on the east side of the outpost were aware of Kozak's position. He also noted that the drone was now on autopilot, conducting a series of slow passes along the perimeter out to the river, wheeling around like a lost buzzard without a meal, which all meant that Kozak's attention had been diverted.

Pepper's teammates didn't call him 'Old Reliable' because he was a self-indulgent slacker; no, when he had a hunch, he paid attention to it because years of combat experience had taught him to 'read the signs' and 'watch the skies' in order to better sense danger. These were a hunter's instincts, forged over decades in the field.

His Remington M24A2 sniper rifle was now trained on the mountain behind him, and his Cross-Com's HUD picked out the two men, with Kozak huddled across the clearing, presumably under his camouflage.

Pepper adjusted his aim, the reticule now floating over one rebel's head.

The moment was before him, the moment he liked most about the job. 30K had once asked him to explain it:

'*You know, that moment just before you take the shot. When it's all lined up and perfect. When you know everybody did their part just right, and you own that battlefield. Then you pull the trigger, and it all goes to hell anyway.*'

They'd never laughed so hard because they'd both been there, done that, understood the blood, sweat and tears the way only other brothers in arms could. And 30K appreciated Pepper's fatalistic sense of humor the way others did not.

And here it was, once again, that perfect moment.

He took in a deep breath.

Yep, it looked like the skinny Russian kid from Brooklyn was a goner if old Pepper didn't loan him some lead.

Why Kozak was crouching there and letting them get so close in the first place was beyond Pepper. Was he just taunting them or hoping not to give up his location? Damned brave or damned stupid. Hard to tell which. Maybe some new-school tactic that the kid had invented, a tactic that Pepper's old-school head just couldn't wrap around.

For just a second, the enormity of the task struck Pepper. Maybe he was just getting old (thirty-nine was certainly north of spring chicken territory), or maybe he was just appreciating his life a whole lot more . . .

As a kid, he'd never been sure what he wanted to do. He did know he did *not* want to own a gas station like his pop had, and he certainly did *not* want to be a construction foreman like his stepfather, Connor. By the time he was eighteen, Pepper figured he'd do a stint in the Army, since no one at home was volunteering to help pay for college and an education was the only way to escape.

The rest was history, his life in perfect order now: the feel of the trigger beneath his gloved hand, the bullet drop calculated, the body as silent and still as any predator.

Thor's hammer struck the mountainside as the rifle went off and a .300 Winchester Magnum belted bottle-necked rifle cartridge removed the boonie hat from the FARC rebel, along with most of his head. At the same time, Kozak was up, cutting loose a salvo into the chest of the second rebel, who staggered drunkenly back until he crumpled in the underbrush.

'Dang, Pepper, nice shot,' said Kozak.

Pepper was about to open his mouth, when a barrage of small arms fire ripped into the trees around him, sending him to the deck hollering, 'Little help!'

Four

There was no man that Sergeant First Class Jimmy '30K' Ellison respected more than Pepper. He was ferociously loyal to his friend and teammate and had sworn a personal oath to always have his back.

So the second that Pepper sounded the alarm, 30K broke off from his position near the shacks and hauled ass toward the combatants behind the trucks, the ones laying down heavy fire on Pepper's position.

Now you couldn't blame his youth (he was just twenty-eight) on what he was about to do. And you couldn't blame it on him being some crazy farm boy who hailed from Alma, Arkansas, although the latter was true. This wasn't something rash or reckless, over the top or insane, no.

It was just him being him. Not a reckless kid whose father had abandoned him. Not a warmongering maniac with a Stoner 63 light machine gun clutched in his grip, although, once again, the latter was true.

'Ain't no such thing as style points, kid,' he'd once told Kozak. *'You do what you gotta do to get it done. The rest is just details.'*

30K's Cross-Com pinpointed the locations of the four rebels strung out near the trucks, cutting loose with their rifles then dropping to cover like carnival targets.

Man, these were off the shelf, generic brand cowards, the kind that 30K neither feared nor respected. Worthy adversaries needed to prove their mettle, and these clowns couldn't even earn his pity. He raced up behind them and hollered, 'Hey, *pendejos!*'

He gritted his teeth, leveled his rifle on them as they turned, then the rat-tat-tat of his Stoner delivered their last rites more powerfully than any trailer park preacher 30K had ever seen or heard.

'Learn how to fight like men,' he spat, then spoke into his Cross-Com. 'You're clear, Pepper.'

'Thanks, bro.'

'Guys, this is Ghost Lead. Rally on the biggest shack out back, near the river. Got four targets holding there, with a fifth inside, not moving. Could be the package.'

'Ghost Lead, 30K here. I can see the shack from my position. I'm going in.'

'Roger that.'

One day 30K would learn some humility. Probably wouldn't be today. Or tomorrow.

Pepper said he hated going to bars with him because there'd always be a fight, but when there was, 30K was the guy you wanted around. Hey, it wasn't his fault. If someone called him a hick or a redneck, he'd turn up the Southern accent, flex his hands into fists, and set them straight the hard way. He wasn't an evil guy, just evil-minded for the sake of saving lives. He hadn't spent a lifetime blowing up mailboxes and frogs, only most of his childhood. He knew the names of every principal from every school he'd been kicked out of because he kept the list in his wallet. These were the men who'd doubted him, who'd thought he didn't have what it took. They were just like his father. They didn't want him around. Was he psychologically scarred? Was he mentally and emotionally handicapped? Hell, no. He was just pissed off. But when he'd joined the Army, he'd learned order and discipline and had earned the respect of the men in his company. His colleagues and superior officers would often ask why he carried that chip on his shoulder, why he was so angry at the world. And he'd say, 'Hey, it ain't me! It's the world!' Damned fate had dealt him a shitty hand as a kid. He'd never win the Mr Personality Award. But look where he was now.

Was he too cocky? Too confident? Well, if he were writing the Special Forces training manuals, he'd start every chapter with the reminder that you must believe in yourself and your team. You had to visualize the victory and make it real before it happened. And if that was being too cocky, then he was guilty as charged. If you were going in for brain surgery, which doctor would you pick: the one who said she was pretty sure she could help you. Or the one who said, 'I'm going to fix you.'

Enough said.

30K chose a path that wound eastward along the mottled, oily waters of the river. He remained about ten meters from the tiny continents of lily pads clustering along the shoreline as he closed in on the shack that Ross had identified. The structure was about ten meters wide, forty long, built like an old barn or shed with wide gaps between the wall beams, certainly not a living structure but perhaps a heavy equipment storage house or repair shop or something. The tin roof was alive with crawling vines, and they reminded 30K of an earlier observation he'd made – that there had to be more than a thousand shades of green in this jungle. There were greens the color of baseball fields, greens the color of flak jackets and Christmas trees and berets. He saw a bird so green that its feathers seemed made of crystal backlit by LEDs. Sure, he'd been in South America on several other ops, but never in this part of Colombia. Too bad he didn't have more time to hike up the river, find some local girls and have a beer.

A familiar whirring at his left shoulder sent his gaze skyward: the drone. Kozak had his back now and even reminded him of that. 'Come on, big brother, move it!' With that, the drone raced forward. 30K cursed and stormed after it. He'd been calling Kozak his 'little brother' for a while now because he knew the string bean didn't like it. Hey, if it made the guy with the funny accent work a little harder to prove himself and step out of his big brother's shadow, then rock on, that was fine with 30K. He'd appointed himself the team's morale officer, pushing everyone to new heights because he enjoyed the hell out of annoying them, and the better they were, the better he was – meaning they all had a better chance of staying alive.

With the tables turned now and 30K sprinting madly to prove himself, he had red-zoned his heart by the time he reached the edge of the forest to spy on the four guards posted near the back of the shack. They had crouched down, rifles raised, their eyes intently panning along the clearing and probing farther out, into the deep maw of tangled branches.

'Marked four,' said Ross.

30K's Cross-Com shimmered with the targets. He lifted his rifle. Took a breath. He had a bead on the first one and practised panning right to the second. No scope on his Stoner. Just experience and instincts. 'Got two, just right of the door,' he told Ross.

'Gotcha. On three.'

30K would remark later that, yes, it had been his fault. He'd been a little too eager.

Ross never made it to three. By the time the word 'two' left his lips, 30K had already opened fire.

'Damn it, I said three!' cried Ross not a second after 30K had taken out his two guards.

30K saw them now, the other two FARC rebels, the ones Ross was supposed to drop. Both charged inside the shack, where that unmoving third target had remained.

'Uh, sorry, boss, not much of a math guy.'

'Great,' said Ross. 'Now it gets fun. Pepper? Kozak?

You cover the exits. 30K? Get over here. You're taking point.'

Oh, well, he was in trouble now. He rushed up to the shack's wall, then shadow-hugged the wood, slipping his way to the corner, wary of more contacts. Every footstep was measured, his gaze flicking between the ground and the wall, making sure he didn't do something stupid like trip and give up his location. He turned and met up with Ross near the main door, which was actually a pair of doors, cracked open a few inches.

Ross raised an index finger with one hand, cupped his hand to his ear with the other. He nodded over something, then reported over the team net. 'AFEUR guys report the rest of the rebels have fled back into the jungle. Hold fire.'

After that, Ross nodded and rolled left beside the door, rifle at the ready. He gave 30K the hand signal: *Go!*

But 30K frowned as he drifted closer to the doors, stealing a look inside.

What he saw made him recoil. 'Whoa . . .'

Ross had tugged free a flash bang grenade, and 30K turned back, put his hand over the boss's, and shook his head.

'What?'

'Take a look.'

Five

'Aw, hell,' grunted Ross.

At least fifty plastic gasoline containers lined the shack's rear wall. To the right were bushel baskets brimming with almond-shaped coca leaves, stacked as high as refrigerators. Six or seven wheelbarrows filled with what might have been salt or limestone were parked across from the stacks, and at least twenty or more oil drums formed two rows down the center of the shack, as though they were stacked on the deck of a cargo ship. Still more containers with labels that read SULFURIC ACID and SODIUM PERMANGANATE sat on wooden shelves buckling under their weight. Beneath them were piles of brand-new microwaves still in their boxes.

'Well, they ain't making burritos,' said 30K.

Ross knew all about the infamous cocaine labs of Colombia and how these guys needed about 1,000 kilos of coca leaves to yield just a kilo of paste or 2.2 pounds. That's why they needed so many bushels of leaves, and the process for making cocaine was painstaking, the materials highly flammable. Drawing gunfire, let alone tossing in a grenade, might send them all into low earth orbit.

'Kozak, get the drone over here, crawler mode.'

Even as the UAV came over the rooftop, quadrotors humming, a rustling along a rise to their south had Ross scanning the tree line, where his Cross-Com showed the blue silhouettes of the AFEUR troops, establishing a perimeter. Nothing would leave the shack, nothing that remained alive anyway.

'Ghost Lead, Pepper. We're secure out here. Clear to do your thing.'

The drone landed not a meter from Ross and rolled toward the doors. 30K opened one door wide enough for the crawler to roll through.

'Show it to me, Kozak.'

A window opened in Ross's HUD, and the camera view and data bars from the drone crackled to life. Superimposed over the video was a wireframe representation of the shack, with dimensions displayed and the drone's coordinates scrolling below as it advanced.

'Good,' said Ross. 'Put me on the speaker.'

'In three, two, one, and you're live,' announced Kozak.

Ross cleared his throat and spoke in Spanish. 'Listen up, boys. Your comrades have gone home for dinner. We have this area secured. You can't run. So you know the drill. Put down your weapons and come out slowly with your hands behind your heads. You do that, and you won't get hurt. You play games, and I'll kill you.'

The crawler rolled farther into the shack, past the stacks of oil drums to an open area beyond, where in the light of a single flashlight sitting on the floor appeared a figure sitting in a chair, hands bound behind the back, a cowl of some sort pulled over the head. The image was too grainy to make any further distinctions. At either side of the prisoner were the guards, one with a pistol to the man's head.

'Ghost Lead, Kozak. What do you think?'

'Get in a little closer.'

Kozak complied, advancing another meter with the drone.

'Hold on a second,' said Ross, getting a better look at the prisoner.

'Don't come any closer,' shouted one of the rebels, a clean-shaven man with thick eyebrows and several missing teeth. 'You know what we'll do!'

'Kozak, get the drone out of there.'

'Say again?'

'You heard me. Back off.' Ross faced 30K and shook his head. 'That's not our guy. Too small. This is a bull-shit diversion to stall us. Our package is already on the move . . .'

'Either way, they got a prisoner. Intel said our CIA guy wasn't the only one in the car.'

As the drone rolled out of the shack and past them, Ross knew they were out of time.

'Ghost Lead, Pepper. I dropped another sensor just outside the shack. Signal's clean. I can take out the guy with the pistol – right through the wall.'

Ross smiled inwardly. This was why he'd become a

Ghost – to work with aggressive, creative operators from all branches of the service who could teach him their tactics, techniques and procedures, the good old TTPs of any good operation. Like him, Pepper was an old salt who'd mopped up bloody operations in Sangin, hunted bomb makers in Waziristan, and danced around the conflicting orders between higher and intelligence offices like the CIA. His experience had taught him to always be thinking ahead and keep the mission tempo high by not succumbing to the deep bitterness and cynicism that could easily rule your life.

'Pepper, this is Ghost Lead. You're the man.'

'Roger that.'

Ross looked at 30K but continued speaking to Pepper. 'Now can you count to three?'

Pepper gave a snort. 'No problem, boss.'

'Okay, then. Here we go.'

Six

Pepper steeled himself and was just a breath away from firing. The target's head was perfectly centered beneath his crosshairs, and the M24A2 felt magnificent in his hands.

Unlike his trigger-happy colleague, 30K, Pepper floated on waves of calm and silence – until Ross counted down . . .

And then it was game on.

He pulled the trigger. The round left his rifle at 990 meters per second and with an awe-inspiring report that woke something primitive inside, as though the spirits of his ancestors – those warring tribes in Europe who had worn leather plates for armor and who had fought with spears and halberds – were lifting their battle cries within the echoing shot.

Before Pepper could take in his next breath, the rebel holding the pistol fell back and away.

'Target down,' he reported.

Ross sighted the second man as Pepper's target thumped to the dirt floor. Two rounds leaped from Ross's HK and drummed the rebel into the back wall as Ross rushed forward with 30K in tow. They charged across the shack, reached the prisoner, and Ross immediately pulled the cowl from the man's face.

Nope, not their guy.

'Who are you?' Ross asked in Spanish.

The middle-aged man with the thick mustache and the paunch hanging over his belt looked sweaty and terrified, his thinning hair flying in all directions. 'Don't kill me, please!'

'Answer the question!'

'I'm Raul Morales. I drive a taxi in Bogotá.'

Ross softened his tone. 'Well, Raul, we're the good guys.' He pulled from his pocket his Ghost Recon skull patch and reverse-print American flag. 'See?'

'Sir, this one's still alive,' said 30K, hovering over the soldier Ross had just shot. 30K grabbed the man by the jaw. 'Where did they take him?'

The rebel's eyes were tearing, his fatigues darkening with blood. He sounded as though he were breathing through a straw, and his head began jerking involuntarily as his lungs began to collapse.

Ross moved in beside 30K and stared hard at the man. 'Listen to me. You're going to die. If you believe in God, then maybe he'll forgive you – if you help us. Now, where did they take him?'

The man opened his mouth. 'Timbiqui.'

'What?' 30K asked.

Ross and 30K exchanged a frown.

'Timbiqui is a town about eighty kilometers south,' said the cabdriver. 'I ought to know. I was born there.'

'He could be lying,' said 30K.

'I don't think so,' said Raul. 'Los Rastrojos do a lot of shipping out of there. They use the rivers. If they wanted to keep him on the move, it's a very good place to take him.'

Los Rastrojos. Ross had heard that name before. They were a neo-paramilitary organization, basically a private army commanded by a warlord. During the FARC's cease-fire with the government, Los Rastrojos had moved in and struck up a deal. Some called them a 'narcogang,' others a fully-fledged cartel. They were now allied with the FARC to produce and export cocaine and heroin to the international markets. Initially, the group and the FARC had fought against each other; however, like many criminal organizations, their mutual enemy was the government. Like Colombia's own military, they fielded the Galil assault rifle, originally made in Israel but produced under a license by Indumil, a Colombian weapons manufacturer headquartered in Bogotá. The standard assault rifle's 5.56mm cartridge would make it hard to distinguish between them and friendly forces – not exactly welcome news.

'The man you were driving . . . was he ever here?' Ross demanded.

'Yes, he was with me. Then we were separated maybe an hour ago. I heard the trucks leaving.'

'Hold here a minute,' said Ross, then he sprinted out

of the hut, calling Captain Jiménez along the way. The SF officer met him near the front doors.

Jiménez narrowed his gaze and backhanded sweat from his bald pate. 'He's still on the move, isn't he?'

'Timbiqui. Can we get some air assets to cut them off?'

'Pretty remote. No LZ in the mangroves, and I'm sure they're nowhere near the local airport.'

'Fast rope some guys in there?'

'We'd need exact GPS coordinates first.'

Ross cursed.

'Look, Captain, even if there was an LZ, it'd take them a couple of hours – if the weather holds, which it won't. There's another storm moving in.'

'What else we got? Coast Guard?'

'The Marine commando teams, along with some of your DEA advisors, are always running patrols through there. I could call them in, but I think we'd scare off our boys. They could panic and kill your man.'

'So then we just drive.'

'Yes.'

Ross considered that. The Ghosts and the AFEUR team had left their Humvees and the old M35 cargo truck a few hundred meters south of the main trail leading into the valley. Kozak could put the drone up ahead, depending upon how much battery life he had in the main and spare cells.

Then again, the rebels would have at least a couple of hours' head start. They had probably reached Timbiqui about now, if Raul's estimates were correct, and they could already be moving yet again, perhaps smuggling their package down to a boat.

Time to call higher for a little backup – but no, they would not break off the pursuit.

'Do you agree?' Jiménez asked.

Ross nodded. 'Let's get back to the trucks and saddle up.'

Seven

The Group for Specialized Tactics had a streamlined organizational structure to ensure that communication was swift and clear. As Ross and every other Special Forces operator well knew, intel could go stale in a day, an hour, a minute, so it was vital for the group's command structure to stay lean.

To that end, Major Scott Mitchell was Ross's sole commander, and Mitchell reported directly to US Special Operations Command/Joint Special Operations Command. Colonel David Evans was the primary liaison between JSOC and Mitchell, ensuring that budgets and bureaucracy did not interfere with the operational arm. To a former command master chief SEAL like Ross who'd spent the better part of his career navigating through a gauntlet of bureaucracies to get his job done, this was, in no uncertain terms, a dream come true.

While Pepper drove and the caravan of four Humvees and the M35 headed south along a heavily rutted dirt road for the town with the semi-pronounceable name, Ross had a tablet computer with satellite link balanced on his lap. He'd established a secure link to GST headquarters at Fort Bragg, North Carolina, and a window had opened to the major's desk. Mitchell had a touch of gray at his temples and a few wrinkles and scars on his face; otherwise you'd swear he was still a twenty-five-year-old operator, as hard-core and gung ho as his first day with the Ghosts. Ross had seen pictures of Mitchell when the man was younger, and the major resembled the type of guy you'd see on a baseball card, youthful and intense. A few of the Ghost trainees had shared stories of the major's exploits, rumors mostly, but there was an early mission in the Philippines where Mitchell had been stabbed with a unique, multibladed sword constructed in the shape of a Chinese character, and Mitchell had a scar of that same character on his chest. Someday Ross would ask him about that.

'Hello, Guardian,' Ross said, using Mitchell's call sign for the mission, even though this was a video call. Better to be too formal than too casual with superior officers.

'Good to see you, Delta Dragon,' Mitchell said with a knowing grin. 'Our Key Hole satellite from the NRO is still out of range. They'll need at least another fifteen minutes. Some pretty dense canopy down there, though, so I'm not sure what kind of images we'll get.'

'I know, sir, but it's worth a shot. Just need to get that bird in position before the storm moves through. After that, all bets are off.'

Mitchell nodded. 'Now I understand it got a little *loud* down there.'

Ross winced. 'One of our AFEUR teammates was compromised and inadvertently fired a round.'

'You put that very carefully.'

Ross shrugged. 'I'm the new guy – and this wasn't the first impression I wanted to make.'

Mitchell steepled his fingers and sighed. 'So the shot went off, and it all went to hell from there.'

'Not exactly.'

'Ross, the Ghosts are about maximum impact with zero footprint.'

'Absolutely, sir.'

'You told me this was exactly what you wanted, that you needed to be a Ghost more than anything right now. I believed you. I *still* believe you – and I'm counting on you to get this done. So are the Secretary of Defense and the National Command Authority.'

Ross's breathing grew shallow. 'I understand, sir. I won't let you down.'

'Good.'

'Sir, we get anything more on Delgado?'

Mitchell made a face, that same one he'd made during the first briefing in the isolation chamber back at Fort Bragg. 'Langley won't confirm a damned thing. Unfortunately there's no love lost between us.'

Ross repressed his grin.

It was no secret that one of Mitchell's operations in southern Afghanistan had got him caught between his orders and a clandestine operation being carried out by the CIA. He'd almost gone up on murder charges until the spooks' little conspiracy backfired in their faces. And here they were now, trying to bail out the same agency that had almost hung Mitchell.

Trying not to sound as though he were prying, Ross said, 'Sir, Langley could've sent in their own S and R team for this. So I'm still asking the same questions I had before we left: What was Delgado's mission? Why is he so important? I mean, come on, they owe us that much, don't they?'

'He's a spy working in Colombia. What more do you need?'

'With all due respect, sir, it's never that simple.'

A gleam lit Mitchell's eyes, as though he were proud of Ross for prying. 'All right. It's not much, but Delgado's been in South America for the past ten years. He's one of the Agency's most valuable agents in Colombia. This, of course, I got off the record. Colonel Evans says there might be something more because the secretary made a point of requesting us to get this job done.'

'Fair enough, sir.'

'I'll be in touch when the NRO has our bird ready.'

'Roger that, sir. Thank you, sir.'

Ross nearly lost his grip on the tablet as they hit a pothole and he thumbed off the link.

Pepper looked at him and cocked a brow, hazel eyes flashing beneath his salt-and-pepper crew cut. 'Mitchell's a good guy, a straight shooter.'

'He would've been a great Navy SEAL.'

'Somehow I don't think that bothers him.'

They exchanged a grin, then Pepper said, 'That was some good work back there.'

'Good work?' Ross snorted. 'It never goes as planned, does it?'

'Why should it? That'd be boring.'

Ross had to agree with that. 'Well, thanks for the backup.'

'That's why I get the big bucks. So hey, you served with Matt Tanner?'

Ross glanced at Pepper and frowned. 'Yeah, Tanner and I go pretty far back, SEAL Team Four in Little Creek. Great guy. Saved my ass more than once.'

'He said the same about you.'

'He's talking about bar fights. So how do you know him?'

'Tanner was part of an operation in China, and he'd worked with the major. Mitchell brought him to the Liberator to meet the gang.'

Ross's eyes widened. 'Tanner never told me that. So you're saying that Mitchell brought a Navy SEAL to an Army bar?'

'Hell, yeah, he did. And your boy Tanner actually survived. Good guy. I kept his e-mail. And when I heard you were coming over, I gave him a shout to see if he knew you.'

'Spying on the new guy?'

'No, I was actually glad you were coming. It'll take

Kozak and 30K a while to warm up, but you know how that is.'

'Yeah, you gotta earn it.'

'Kozak will come around pretty quickly. 30K? He's another story. That guy needs some 550 paracord to tie down his ego.'

'I like him.'

'Really?'

'He'll keep me honest.'

Pepper stared through a thought. 'Oh, that he will. And, sir, I . . .' He broke off.

'What?'

'It's nothing.'

Ross frowned. 'Better spit it out now, or I'll be thinking about it the whole drive out.'

'I didn't want to say anything.'

'What's bothering you?'

'Okay. It's just . . . Tanner told me about your boy. I wanted to say I'm really sorry about that.'

Ross stiffened, and his blood turned cold. 'That's not something I talk about.'

Pepper grimaced and shook his head, as though embarrassed. 'No problem. I just wanted you to know that I'd heard, and if you ever want to vent or something . . .'

'I wish he hadn't told you.'

Pepper took a deep breath. 'Me, too.'

Ross closed his eyes and rubbed the burning sensation. For the past two years he'd done everything he could to move on, to purge all the guilt from his mind, to avoid dwelling on it so he could perform his job. But it – 14 August – always found him, no matter where he was, even deep in a South American jungle.

He snapped open his eyes and quickly activated his Cross-Com. 'Kozak, what do you got for me?'

Eight

Kozak and 30K were in the lead Hummer, with 30K at the wheel and Kozak handling the UAV's remote. One of the AFEUR troops stood behind them in the roof-mounted weapons station, manning the M2 Browning .50-caliber machine gun (aka 'Ma Deuce'). Rain poured off the gunner's legs and boots and puddled on the Hummer's floor. Kozak wished they could just call the man back inside and seal the hatch because he was getting soaked himself.

At the moment, the drone crawler darted just above the treetops, skimming like a flat rock across an emerald-colored pond. The drone's sensors were reaching out into the jungle ahead, data piped back from thermal and optic cameras, along with Forward Looking Infra Radar (FLIR) images indicating that the jungle on either side of the dirt road was still clear.

Bad news was that the drone's satellite link was beginning to deteriorate as the storm neared the coast, with even heavier rain on the way and wind gusts up to sixty miles per hour.

'Ghost Lead, this is Kozak. Secondary battery on the drone down to thirty minutes. Doesn't matter anyway. Gotta reel her in once the big rain hits.'

'Roger that. For now, though, get her up as high as you can and focus on the rivers ahead. They might try to move our package by boat. We have a Key Hole coming within range, but I need something now.'

'I'm on it. Taking her up. Kozak, out.'

The drone crawler had been designed to remain on a fairly short leash, with a 1.5 to 2 kilometer range and sixty to ninety minutes of battery life, depending upon its power state: high drain occurred when in crawler mode, medium drain when quadcoptering, and low drain when stationary and just transmitting. Their load out included this UAV plus one backup, and while the UCAV – a tri-rotor drone with variants that included fragmentation grenades, missiles and a 5.56mm light machine gun – would've come in handy, they usually reserved that bird for interdiction, direct action and other assault-type missions, not hostage rescues.

Kozak fought with the controls as yet another gust buffeted the drone. The images coming in turned grainy, occasionally popping with static like his mom's old Sony TV wired up to that rooftop antenna. He caught sight of two intersecting rivers, where the tree line seemed to fold in as though the ground were plummeting into a fault line. Farther out, the sky had turned gunmetal gray, with a wall of black clouds approaching from the west like an invading mother ship. There wasn't much time.

'So how you liking the new boss?' asked 30K.

'Good.'

'What do you mean *good*?'

Kozak refocused his attention on the drone's monitor. 'I like him.'

'Better than Ferguson?'

'They're two completely different operators.'

'What does that mean?'

Kozak thought a moment.

Captain Cedrick Ferguson, a thirty-eight-year-old African-American from Minneapolis, had formed a deep bond with them and had served successfully as their Ghost Lead on some highly volatile operations in Zambia, Nigeria, the arctic, and even Russia. Ferguson was a family man with two young sons and was married to a school principal. He was arguably the most levelheaded and decisive man Kozak had ever known, with both his professional and personal lives balanced in a way that only few soldiers could manage. The bullets could be flying, people could be dying, but Ferguson's cool and curt commands would put you at ease. His absence was actually part of the larger Group for Specialized Tactics' team availability and organizational structure.

The GST had four operational detachments of between eight and twelve operators each. The detachments, known as A, B, C, and D squadrons, fielded four-man teams, and very often Ghost Leads would rotate through several teams before a kind of natural selection took place and they settled in with a consistent group of operators, developing a shorthand forged only through time and experience.

Teams rotated through three status levels: Ready, Standby and Hold, with two detachments always in the ready status to immediately deploy, one on standby, and one on hold. Ferguson had temporarily rotated to a team on hold so he could enjoy some well-deserved R & R and spend time with his family. And yes, news of a new Ghost Lead taking them out, one who wasn't even an Army SF operator, had unnerved Kozak. The rumors had run rampant, the reservations so tangible that Kozak actually had a bitter taste in his mouth a few hours before he'd met Ross. But when he'd learned of the man's credentials and listened to Major Mitchell speak so highly of one Captain Andrew Ross, Kozak was put at ease. What's more, Ross said he had a grand-father on his mother's side who'd been born in Saint Petersburg, Russia.

Unsurprisingly, 30K had a problem with new Ghost Leads – especially those who were, as he'd put it, 'members of Uncle Sam's Canoe Club.'

'Well, I get the impression Captain Ross thinks he's above us. He was a Navy SEAL, serving with operators I'm sure he believes were the very best. You know, the SEALs got all the Hollywood hype, so now as he gets older, he's just slumming with us, putting in his time.'

Kozak glanced incredulously at his teammate. 'When did you get that impression?'

'First time I laid eyes on him.'

'Or maybe after he corrected you for jumping the gun?'

'I don't like any of this. I don't think bringing in people from other branches is a good idea.'

'You afraid to learn something new?'

30K snorted. 'So if we watch the Army-Navy Game, who do you think he'll root for?'

'Who cares?'

'Aw, I'm talking to the wrong guy.'

'I think Pepper likes him. And if Pepper is good to go, then so am I. Besides, when we're out here, none of that shit matters.'

30K muttered something under his breath, then said, 'You're in awe of the guy, aren't you?'

'Hey, you read his record. Silver Star, three Bronze with V, too many commendations to remember, and even the Presidential Unit Citation.'

'We ain't here for medals.'

'He was DEVGRU – Naval Special Warfare Development Group. It's not like they killed bin Laden or anything, right?'

'Why don't *you* join the Navy?'

Kozak shook his head and sighed. 'If you're looking for hard-core proof that the guy is legit, then there it is.'

'You're just another fanboy.'

'Give him a chance.'

'Oh, I'll work with him. I'll show him how *we* roll. He might look like Mr Perfect on the outside, but something doesn't sit right with me. I want to know his weaknesses. His baggage. Then I can work around them – to keep us both alive.'

Kozak hardened his voice. 'Do you trust me?'

'I will. I'm not done training you yet.'

'You amaze me.'

'And one day when you grow up, you'll amaze me, too, little brother . . .'

The narrow dirt road began to jog to the left, and 30K hit the brakes to roll into the turn. As the Hummer began to fishtail slightly to the left –

Fireflies twinkled beside the rubber trees lining both sides of the road.

Only they weren't fireflies.

Nine

Raindrops the size of golf balls – or at least 30K swore they were that big – blasted into the windshield, blinding him for a second before the wipers cleared the glass –

And there they were: muzzle flashes accompanied by the thudding and pinging of rounds off the Hummer's front end.

'You gotta be kidding me!' 30K shouted. 'How'd you miss these guys with the drone?'

'It's too high, too far ahead,' Kozak cried. 'And the rain's screwing me up! Heat sources gone cold!'

30K hit the accelerator and barked into his Cross-Com, 'Ghost Lead, ambush! Pushing on through!'

Kozak had already set down the drone's remote and was lowering his window to get his rifle pointed in the right direction. At the same time, he shouted to their gunner, who was already directing a broad bead of suppressing fire on the trees. 'Hey, dude, get some fire right in the road ahead of the truck,' Kozak told him in Spanish. 'Right on the road!'

30K knew exactly what Kozak was talking about. The odds were high that the rebels had planted a pressure-activated IED in the road; perhaps they'd missed the first one and the rebels had opened fire anyway, but there could be more, and the man on the .50-cal could trigger the next bomb before they struck it. If the rebels had set up a trip wire, it'd be more difficult to spot in the rain.

30K juked right, keeping the Hummer tight to the trees, sideswiping a few branches that scraped across the side mirror and door with a screech that sent Kozak hollering and yanking his rifle back inside. 'What the hell?'

'IEDs, man,' 30K answered. 'Trying to stay off the path!'

'Little heads-up first?' snapped Kozak, who then set down his rifle and picked up the drone's remote. 'Shit, shit, shit! Signal's gone!'

Ross had an elbow balanced on the door and squeezed off three bursts with his HK, driving two rebels standing beside some trees back into the brush. He estimated the ambush force at no more than fifteen or twenty, and they rolled past them within a handful of seconds.

He ducked back into the Hummer, closed the window, and got back on the team net. '30K, you guys all right?'

'We're good!'

Ross switched frequencies to Captain Jiménez, who was up in the cab of the M35, and asked if his people were okay.

'Two men were hit, one seriously. We're very lucky. There could be more ambushes ahead.'

'Roger that. Stay sharp. Ross, out.'

'Don't get closer than that,' said Pepper, pointing to a bullet hole in his side mirror. 'That guy was looking to trim my sideburn.'

'No shit,' said Ross, his heart still wrenching in his chest.

'They're calling ahead to their buddies, saying we're on our way.'

'Maybe not,' countered Ross. 'First thing I did was hit 'em with an EMP grenade.'

'I thought that was a frag.'

'Nope. Pulse wave should've knocked out their radios and cell phones, and maybe even deactivated any IEDs they'd planted ahead.'

'Let's hope so.'

'Ghost Lead, Kozak. I've reestablished contact with the drone. Good thing is, I got something. Have a look at this.'

Multiple images appeared in both Ross's Cross-Com and his tablet computer, grainy footage taken by the drone's camera along with FLIR images that showed the outlines of dozens of personnel strung out near the mangrove-fringed riverbank, along with several flatbed trucks and old jeeps whose engines still glowed. Behind them stood several structures, no larger than the shacks they'd encountered at the first outpost, but these had satellite dishes mounted on their roofs. Range was about four kilometers away.

Then something else caught Ross's attention. He did

a double take, and Kozak, seeing it too, zoomed in with the camera.

'Boss, you see that?'

'Can you zoom in even more?'

'Trying.'

Ross drew his head back. 'Oh, yeah, Kozak, I see it now.'

Ten

Fully submersible and semi-submersible narcosubmarines were being built beneath the triple canopy in some of Colombia's most remote, jungle-infested regions. Narrow waterways shrouded by vegetation cut through the mangrove swamps and led to dry docks constructed along the rivers. Within these often sophisticated structures, fully operational subs were produced from parts cannibalized from around the world and often under the supervision of 'freelance' Russian engineers being paid handsomely for their knowledge. The subs cost upwards of four million dollars to build and carried literally six to ten tons of cocaine to Mexico and elsewhere, with much of it eventually bound for the United States and Europe.

This particular boat, whose diesel engine had warmed enough to be spotted through her hull, shimmered like an albino crocodile drawn by the drone's FLIR. She was more than thirty meters long, Ross estimated, and nearly three meters high from deck plates to ceiling. Assumedly, she had twin screws and cruised at more than twenty kilometers per hour, judging from her size. Once out in the ocean, she'd submerge to thirty meters, and her fiberglass construction would make her virtually undetectable to radar. If she was like other narcosubs Ross had studied, she'd be manned by a crew of four: a captain, a navigator, and two machinists, who'd keep the engines and other devices in good working order. Even with a full load of cocaine, her range was probably about three thousand miles, well within the reach of the United States. Conditions aboard the sub would be horrible. The men would be confined to a space no larger than ten feet by ten. They would live off junk food and breathe in diesel fumes all day and night. They would work in shifts, and with every miserable hour that passed, they'd think about the half-million dollars they were earning as a team to transport product with a half-*billion*-dollar street value.

Presently, the hatch was flipped open on the sub's two-meter tall sail, and a rifleman stood in the conning tower. Above him rose some kind of video periscope protected behind a clear glass dome, a kind of home-made, off-the-shelf-looking device that struck Ross as both bold and ingenious.

'Locking in the GPS coordinates now,' said Kozak. 'Sending them back to higher if I can. Wait, damn!'

'What is it?'

'Lost contact again.'

'Kozak, bring in the drone before we lose it.'

'Might be too late.'

'Do what you can. 30K, find us some valet parking about half a klick north, thank you.'

'Roger that.'

Ross shared their discovery with Captain Jiménez,

who was less than enthusiastic about attacking this new outpost. 'The FARC rebels are tough, Captain, but Los Rastrojos are very highly trained. Some of them defected from my group, and others come from the Sinaloa Cartel in Mexico. Others are former Los Zetas, the most ruthless of all. I'm sure this camp is very well defended.'

'I'm sure it is. But we have the storm on our side. You're not bailing on me, are you, Captain?'

'Of course not. I just wanted you to know that if there is a hell in Colombia, then this is it.'

'I appreciate that, Captain.'

'I hope you do, because one of my men has just died.'

Ross hesitated. 'I'm sorry about that. I really am. Stand by. Ross, out.'

'He ain't thrilled, huh?' Pepper asked.

'One of his guys died. He says we're going into hell.'

Pepper shrugged. 'Just another day in paradise, but I'll say this – we need to hit that camp from both sides of the river. Let's assume they know we're coming. They don't know exactly when . . . or how . . . so that's how we get 'em.'

Ross smiled tightly. 'I think I know what you have in mind.'

Pepper hoisted his brows and nodded.

Ross's tablet beeped, and Major Mitchell returned to the video link window. 'Delta Dragon, you want the bad news? Or the bad news?'

'It's all right, sir. Storm's here. Eyes in the sky aren't much help, I know. But it's not all bad. Here's the latest intel we've received from the drone.'

Mitchell glanced away to study the images. After a few seconds he looked up and asked, 'You got a plan?'

Kozak was a heartbeat away from throwing the drone's remote out the window. 'I think it's stuck in a tree,' he cried, still unable to regain a link. He'd managed to lock on to the UAV's locator beacon, an emergency provision if she lost power or was damaged in battle. The beacon had an independent battery and could broadcast the drone's GPS coordinates and elevation, which it was doing at the moment.

'You'll have to get your little toy later,' said 30K.

'You know what the major says – no footprints. So we gotta go back.'

'Yeah, dude, whatever, we'll do that later. Hey, that looks good up there, what do you think?' 30K pointed to an opening in the forest on their right side where the trees seemed to part like a doorway.

'Do it,' said Kozak, clutching his seat as the Hummer jostled up, off the road and on to the slightly higher ground off the path. They sliced through the underbrush until 30K believed he'd traveled sufficiently far to allow the whole convoy to pull off the road.

'Check the range,' he told Kozak, who compared their current coordinates with those of the narcosub camp. 'Half a klick, on the money. Who's the man?'

Kozak looked at 30K and in a deadpan answered, 'Captain Ross. But then again he said that Pepper was the man.'

30K rolled his eyes. 'Get outta here.'

Kozak opened the door –

And stepped into the torrential rain, the wind suddenly whipping him away from the Hummer and toward a cluster of trees. 'Holy –' The rest of his curse was drowned out by another gust that sent him leaning forward at a forty-five-degree angle.

Toto was already road pizza. The wicked witch was somewhere in Siberia, plucking waffles, iPods and family photos from her hair. This was, in Kozak's expert opinion, friggin' nuts and a far cry from the good old days on Brighton Beach Avenue, chasing after those cute girls from Long Island who'd come down and act like tourists.

'Team, this is Ghost Lead. Listen up,' said Ross.

Kozak had to turn up his Cross-Com's volume against the howling wind and thrashing of branches.

While the captain went over the plan, a computer-generated map of the base appeared in their HUDs. The map had been created via intel gathered by the UAV. That was the kind of spot-on, up-to-the-second intelligence analysis they needed, the kind of data that kept them one step ahead of the enemy. Ross designated all of their targets and presented the AFEUR troops with their own overwatch and attack orders.

There was one word that Ross used twice, a dirty

word that Kozak never liked to hear prior to a mission:

Booby trap.

Triggering one would blow the team's cover and get themselves killed without permission. 'Don't do that,' Ross had said. They'd all seen too many good men lose their lives or get maimed because the enemy wasn't man enough to face them.

When Ross was finished, Kozak called him and said, 'Ghost Lead, I have one more idea. I think our primary drone is stuck in a tree – which gets me thinking: let me park the secondary up in a tree near those buildings.'

'I like your style, Kozak. Do it,' he ordered.

Kozak grinned inwardly, then reached back into the drone holster attached to his utility belt and hanging from his right hip. The secondary UAV's rotors were folded inward, shrinking the craft into a Frisbee-size package that was deployed in nearly the same fashion.

'Okay, baby, don't let me down,' he whispered.

And with that he tugged out the UAV and tossed it into the air. The quadrotors automatically expanded and activated, and the drone lifted off, veering chaotically into the night. Kozak plugged in the target zone, and now the drone would fly automatically to that area and hover, awaiting its next command – if it didn't crash first.

'Ghost Lead, the drone's deployed,' he said, then he jogged up behind 30K, who was already slipping furtively into the jungle. 'Hey, bro, you ready for this?'

'What do you think?'

'If anything happens —'

'Dude, now you sound like Pepper,' said 30K. 'We only need one prophet of doom on this team.'

'Pepper's not like that.'

'You ain't been around him long enough. Trust me.'

'Well, if anything happens to me —'

'Look, we're going in there to get our package and get out. These punks with water pistols don't stand a chance. They're waiting on line to get some from the United States Army. You read me?'

'Hell to the yeah,' said Kozak.

He knew exactly how to draw a pep talk out of 30K, one that always made him feel better before the first shot was fired.

And speaking of first shots, Ross had been emphatic about that. No screwups. The captain had even painted the post-op picture for them:

Later on, after the raid, when the rebels found their dead and dying comrades, one of them — about to die himself — would look up into the burning eyes of his commander, shudder, and say, 'We never saw them.'

Eleven

Ross and Pepper were tucked so tightly into the tangled roots and thickets of the mangroves that their optical camouflage could remain off.

Recon time.

En route to this position, they had encountered two trip wires and had quietly avoided them while marking the surrounding trees with tiny, LED-lit sensors that transmitted each trip wire's location via the Cross-Coms. Those coordinates were placed on the team's operational map. They had then spotted a series of planks creating a path through the jungle, one assumedly used by the drug gangs, but Ross and Pepper kept about three meters to the left, sticking to the mud, noting and marking yet three more trip wires at ankle height, above the aforementioned path. Several more calls came over the Cross-Com, with more booby traps IDed and avoided, and then, each team called in to report they were in their recon positions.

Their approach had gone down by the numbers – and while that should have comforted Ross, it didn't.

The dry dock warehouses were situated on the north side of the river, about ten meters from the shoreline, and they must have been there for some time. The vines, shrubs and other aggressive weeds had moved up along their walls and were spreading across their roofs like a dark green rash, while other vines hanging down from the trees and draping across the warehouses helped disguise their man-made angles. Ross was certain that the FARC and Los Rastrojos troops had given Mother Nature a helping hand, shifting foliage so that it would help with the overall effect, and the outcome was impressive. You had to stare hard to discern the buildings.

Opposite the warehouses stood a rickety-looking dock, about a meter wide and ten meters long, with a few of the pilings leaning unnervingly to the right. The narcosub, whose hull was painted a flat olive drab, sat moored to the dock, bobbing as the wind whipped waves up to her sail.

Ross switched to night vision, and the lens mounted on his helmet turned his Cross-Com's HUD to phosphorescent green. He confirmed the locations of the four guards standing at the larger dry dock, and the two others huddling beneath a small awning near the second.

The rain was magic and had driven a larger contingent of the Rastrojos and FARC troops inside, seeking cover, and if they'd moved the package into the submarine, there was no clear evidence. Ross deployed a sensor, noting more than twenty individuals inside the structures. The sub was here. The package was most likely here . . .

So what the hell had they been waiting for?

His answer came in the next breath.

Two late-model SUVs appeared from another trail leading down from the north, and they rolled up alongside the warehouses, the beams of their headlights filled with rain.

'Well, look at that,' muttered Pepper. 'It's a real party now.'

Ross called the team: 'All right, everybody, listen up. Two vehicles just arrived. Hold your positions.'

A storm would hardly delay the departure of a submarine; in fact, the sub captains preferred to launch at night, with no moon, and in bad weather to help cloak their exit. While it was true that high seas could wreak havoc once the sub hit open water, the real reason for the delay became unsurprisingly clear:

The drivers of the SUVs jumped out, ran around to the backs of their vehicles, lifted the tailgates, and after a loud whistle, they were joined by about a dozen men from the warehouses. These men formed two lines and began moving plastic milk crates stacked with bricks of cocaine from one man to the next, a 'brick brigade' to deliver the cocaine from the trucks and across the dock, where the gunman from the submarine had jumped down to receive each crate and hand it back to another man standing in the sail. The bricks themselves were about the size of a trade paperback book, and the crates were square and small enough to squeeze through the sub's tight hatch.

'They're killing two birds,' said Pepper. 'Figured they'd move their hostage along with their drugs, but they were waiting on these guys.'

'And waiting for the second storm to move in,' said Ross. 'Bad move all around.'

Pepper snorted. 'Yeah, it's almost Biblical. Greed gets you every time.'

'Amen,' said Ross. He took in a deep breath to clear his thoughts. 'Okay, we gotta move now. If he's in the warehouse, they'll bring him out as soon as they finish.'

'No doubt,' said Pepper.

Ross called the team and the AFEUR troops: 'This is it, guys. Point team is moving out. Get into your secondaries.'

The river's surface was alive with a billion dimples from the falling rain as he and Pepper drifted out from the gnarled roots and submerged. With their heads just a few inches beneath the surface, Ross suspected they were already well hidden. Being in the water felt perfect, natural, and holding his breath was a skill he'd honed for more than twenty years, beginning with the old drownproofing test during his BUD/S training. Hands bound behind your back, they tossed you into a pool, and the fun began. No reason to panic, right? He'd done well. Some of his colleagues couldn't make it that far, had freaked out, and had rung the bell to drop.

For his part now, Ross took the lead, and the muddy

river bottom quickly fell away. He kicked hard, and they headed toward the opposite shoreline, some forty meters away and about fifteen meters east of the dock and warehouses. Their target was an especially thick section of roots that offered ample cover and allowed a breather.

If all was going well, then Jiménez had divided his group into four teams, with two spreading out to the narrower flanks to ford the river and move in from the north, with another pair, the captain included, remaining on the south side, closer to the narcosub. From these secondary positions the men would launch their ambush.

Ross tried to relax as he swam, fighting against the obvious and gut-wrenching fear that any one of those men could make a simple but grave error. Any one of them, like that sniper had during their last raid, could allow himself to be caught and/or killed.

No, he told himself. *Not this time.* They would attack swiftly, with audacity and purpose, standing on the shoulders of all the SF operators who'd come before them. No fears now. Only the mission. Moving . . . communicating . . .

On target.

The rain was cooling the river's surface, but farther below, the water still felt warm, and his boots began dragging through the silt and finally pushing deeper into the mud. He reached out and felt a thick root, and then he slowed, sensing Pepper's hand on his boot, and together they rose up within some lily pads, clearing their eyes and noses, but keeping their chins beneath the surface.

Ross glanced up at movement in the canopy. No, he wouldn't tell Pepper about the coral snake up there, highly venomous to be sure. It slithered beneath two branches and was surrounded by a cloud of mosquitoes, trying to hide from the storm.

In the next second, shouts from the dry docks and flashing lights near them cut through the downpour and seemed to be right there, right there . . . a breath away.

He gave Pepper the signal and they scaled the roots, shifting behind the trees and settling down along the brush opposite the larger building, where two guards were posted on this, the west side.

'I'm the bait,' he whispered to Pepper.

'Roger that.'

Ross activated his camouflage and ran out of the tree line, directly toward the two guards. He dropped down to his haunches and waited as they noticed something weird in front of them, a strange fluctuating silhouette, as though an extraterrestrial had dropped from the roof and was about to confront them. They both frowned, aimed their guns at Ross, who just stood there, the rain playing havoc with the camouflage's system, flickering and shimmering.

And then, another apparition appeared behind one guard, and an arm that looked as though it were made of water came around the man's torso and plunged a knife into his heart.

As the second guard turned, bringing his rifle to bear on Pepper, Ross put his Cold Steel SRK knife to work, driving the black, Tuff-Ex–coated blade into the hollow between the man's collarbone and the top of his sternum. Using the collarbone as a lever, Ross worked the blade in a circular motion, shredding everything inside.

Neither of these men would die instantaneously, as it took several knife wounds to produce results you only saw in movies; instead, Ross and Pepper dragged their victims back behind some trees, where both were zipper cuffed, their socks removed and forced into their mouths, their lips taped shut. The operation took less than sixty seconds.

'And this is why I still bring a knife to a gunfight,' said Pepper with a wink.

Ross dragged the flat sides of his SRK along his hip, cleaning the blade. He resheathed the knife, than gave Pepper a nod. 'Clear to move in.'

Twelve

With trees now thrashing against one another, and the rain falling so fiercely that it felt more like pellets of titanium striking his back and shoulders, Kozak was at once surprised and shocked to find himself wearing one of the biggest shit-eating grins of his life.

No, he wasn't a glutton for punishment.

He was a glutton for intel –

And boom! He'd hit the jackpot!

In fact, he was almost too excited to speak, but he made the report nonetheless. 'Ghost Lead, the drone's in place. And I think I've spotted the package!'

'Good job, we're moving in. Keep that drone quiet.'

'Roger that.'

Kozak and 30K had found a cover position at the base of two long rows of bamboo that towered into the canopy like the bars of some colossal prison, the shoots groaning and creaking as they bowed in the gale. The mud smelled more pungent than ever because Kozak had spread some on his face and cheeks the way 30K had, a couple of ancient barbarians ready to pounce. They'd applied the bug spray liberally but didn't trust the stuff in all this rain, which had probably washed it off. Easier to just grab mud and drag it across your face and neck, than blind yourself with the spray. So there they were, old-school low and good to go.

'Hey, thanks again for spotting that wire,' Kozak said.

'Just another one you owe me, little brother.'

Kozak rolled his eyes and zoomed in once more with the drone's camera, past an opening in the rear of the larger dry dock building through which they'd probably rolled out the completed submarine. There was no door here, with heavy chains hanging from the ceiling that had either suspended the entire craft or had been used to lower its diesel engine into place during construction. Worktables ran along both sides of the dry dock. Battery-operated power tools were stored in crates or lying near cutting stations. Cans of marine paint, sections of fiberglass and paintbrushes were piled high near one corner station, where a row of gas-powered generators sat beneath coils of extension cords. PVC pipe of various lengths and thicknesses hung from racks above the workbenches, and above them, cobwebs draped in dust spanned the rafters.

Kozak adjusted the drone's camera angle so he had a clean view deep into the structure, where he once more spied the man who matched Delgado's description: just over five feet, with dark, curly hair and a full beard. He didn't look like a CIA paramilitary operations officer. Then again, what did those guys look like? A combination of James Bond and G. I. Joe? Or were they the wiry little guys with snake's eyes, sunken cheeks and raspy voices you found behind the counter of a ghetto liquor store?

In point of fact, Delgado better resembled a rather nondescript drug mule from Colombia charged with swallowing seventy-five or so latex-and-wax-wrapped capsules of cocaine and praying he wasn't X-rayed at the airport. The man's wrists were bound behind his back with nylon cord, and a pair of FARC troops stood beside him. More troops, both FARC and Los Rastrojos men clutching their Galils, stood near the entrance closest to the dock, shielding themselves from the rain.

Kozak sent the images out to the Cross-Coms, and 30K offered his color commentary: 'Well, there's our little geek. Glad to know he's here. He's saying, "Oh, Mommy, please come get me from these bad guys. I wanna go home . . ."'

'Damn, here we go,' said Kozak, panning with the drone's camera to the dock and submarine.

'What is it?' asked 30K.

'Looks like they're done loading the drugs.'

'Pepper and Captain Ahab better be ready.'

'They're not. Ghost Lead, this is Kozak. Are you getting this? That's our package. They're moving him now.'

It had all unfolded perfectly in Ross's mind's eye:

The AFEUR troops flanking and encompassing the perimeter . . .

He and Pepper slipping into the dry dock and, utilizing their optical camouflage, taking out as many thugs as possible before slipping away with the package – after not a single shot was fired . . .

And then, once they were clear of the dry docks. . . . Ambush.

They'd trap the enemy soldiers in a gauntlet of fire so horrific, so impregnable, that all they could do was cower until a round finally silenced their hearts. And even if a few men posted on the perimeter pulled off the small miracle of escape, they would succumb to malaria or dehydration or the wildlife within a few days as they tried to reach the nearest town.

The AFEUR troops would move in and claim victory, the government would issue them medals, and the newspapers would report of their triumph. The Ghosts would take no credit. They, of course, were never there.

It was all so beautiful.

And it would've been –

If they weren't late.

As in eleven seconds late.

Delgado was being dragged toward the submarine, and Ross had to make one of those imperfect choices in a universe that now laughed at him.

'Hold fire! Hold fire!' he whispered loudly into his Cross-Com.

He and Pepper were inside the largest dry dock and hidden beneath one of the workbenches, their camouflage active. 'Let them load the package into the submarine.'

'Ghost Lead, 30K. Say again?'

'I said, let him get on the submarine.'

'And then what?'

Ross ground his teeth. 'Stand by.'

He could almost feel the heat of Pepper's gaze on his back, even though the man lay hidden beneath his camouflage.

Decision time. The entire team – along with Jiménez and his men – were now waiting for Ross to issue orders, to deliver a revised plan that would make them grunt, 'Nice,' and drive them on with a ferocity that would overwhelm these enemy troops.

But for a split second –

Despite all his years of experience.

Despite all the training.

All the medals and commendations.

All the situations just like this one . . .

Ross had nothing but a hollow feeling in his gut.

He took a deep breath, did a mental inventory of everything in his pack.

And then it came to him.

Thirteen

'Back in Vietnam, you know what they called this?' 30K asked Kozak, and without waiting for the man's reply, he added, 'Screwing the pooch.'

'Just focus, man.'

'Popeye the Sailor has just run aground.'

'I don't think so.'

'He'll need the Colombian Marines to interdict the sub. We're out of this fight.'

'Not yet.'

'We'll see . . .' 30K shook his head and watched as Delgado was shoved down the pier.

The two guards helped him up, into the hatch, and he almost slipped and fell overboard while trying to get down the ladder, a man from inside trying to help.

If 30K could've had his way, he would've leveled his Stoner on these rebels and 'Los Chuckleheads' and muttered, 'For those about to rock, I salute you.' Then he would've hammered them until the barrel of his machine gun melted off. The proper application of overwhelming firepower was the first step toward spiritual enlightenment. This was a law of physics that Newton had invented back in the day, when he was playing with guns in the schoolyard with Leonardo da

Vinci. This was the eleventh commandment, written right there in the Constitution near the signatures of John Wayne and Charlton Heston.

Everyone knew that.

For now, though, their fearless captain wanted them to lie on their bellies with their bras undone so they could work on their tans during a tropical storm.

Was 30K frustrated? Nah. His damned suntan was coming along nicely . . .

He balled one hand into a fist. Shit. He had to do something.

And then he saw it, an opportunity sitting there like a Ferrari with the keys in it.

A sudden gale-force wind ripped into the jungle and had the men lifting their arms to shield their eyes. At that second, 30K fished out a sensor grenade from his web gear and hurled it across the river, the device thumping into the mud on the opposite shoreline.

Bingo. His Cross-Com's HUD turned into the bridge of a starship, targets identified, marked, tracked, ready to die. *'Please come shoot me,'* they begged.

He lifted his Stoner. 'Sensor out, marking,' he reported.

And then he saw them, Ross and Pepper, rushing from the dry dock, then stopping to allow their camouflage to catch up with their movements – but the rain was giving up their position, and 30K cried, 'Ghost Lead, 30K, they can see you, man! They can see you!'

'Easy, buddy,' said Ross. 'They don't see us yet.'

The captain was right. Some of the men were running back toward the SUVs, while the cocaine loaders jogged in a group toward the dry docks.

'Roger that.'

'Everybody, keep holding.'

30K cursed under his breath and glanced over at Kozak. 'So how much longer do we sit on our asses?'

'Not long,' answered Kozak. 'I know what he's doing.'

'Well, that's amazing, General Schwarzkopf, you mind filling me in, because as far as I'm concerned, not only are we letting the package escape, but these FARC losers and Rastamen dudes will be out of here in a second. Lose-lose for everybody.'

'Rastamen? You mean Rastrojos.'

'Whatever.'

'Okay, okay, here we go,' Kozak said, pointing toward the river. 'Watch. And learn.'

Ross left Pepper hidden beneath the dock while he swam up behind the submarine, just as the twin screws were beginning to turn. He maneuvered himself along the hull, to where the shaft passed through the thrust-bearing seal. He attached one charge there, the magnet holding fast, then he did likewise on the second shaft, both charges in place.

During his long tenure in the Navy, Ross had been taught how to expertly disable vessels, including submarines. He'd learned that the thrust-bearing flange and seal were pressurized from inside on subs because there was no way to make a watertight seal and allow enough room for the shaft to rotate. All submarines controlled the pressure on the thrust-bearing seal, ensuring the pressure inside the sub was greater than that of the sea pressure pushing in from the outside to, of course, prevent flooding.

In theory, Ross's C-4 charges would damage the watertight integrity of the thrust-bearing seals and distort the shafts. The sub couldn't submerge because the thrust bearings could no longer be pressurized, and the sub couldn't move because the shafts would not turn, or if they did turn, within a few spins they'd tear the ass end out of the sub.

Ross swam hard and away, back toward the riverbank, the timers set for twenty seconds. He paddled around, reached into his holster, and produced a 9mm Glock with star-patterned maritime spring cups on the firing pin. The cups allowed water inside to equalize the pressure, which in turn made the weapon more reliable in wet conditions. He could even fire it while submerged.

He'd been counting the seconds till detonation. And *three, two, one* . . .

The muffled explosions were followed by a pair of fountains behind the sub, and as the craft began to slow and the blast wave struck Ross, he gave the long-awaited order: 'The sub's disabled. Pepper and I are on the package. 30K? You and Kozak suppress any fire coming at us near the sub. The rest of you – do it! Open fire!'

Even before 30K could respond, the AFEUR troops took out the warehouse guards and began moving up. 30K's own Stoner beat a vicious rhythm, the entire riverbank now flickering with gunfire, the fronds spitting as they split apart, the Rastrojos troops near the SUVs dropping behind the cars to return fire.

At the same time, Kozak put the drone back up, wheeling in a steady pattern above the submarine, the drone's rotors coughing up rain.

'Got you covered, Ghost Lead,' he said.

Ross grinned to himself as Pepper swam out from beneath the dock and joined him at the sub, just as the hatch flipped open and a man emerged, bringing his rifle to bear.

Pepper had his own modified Glock in his fist, and the submariner, probably the captain, barely caught a glimpse of Pepper before two rounds drilled into his chest. He slumped in the sail as Ross climbed up and – before dragging the man's body out of the way – he popped a smoke grenade and dropped it down the hatch. As the canister rattled somewhere inside the sub, Ross tugged the dead guy out of the sail, let him collapse into the water, then slipped back along the deck, covering with his own pistol.

'Here they come,' cried Pepper.

One by one they emerged, three more crew members gasping and coughing, their eyes burning, hands raised in the air. They appeared unarmed, just straining to see Ross.

'Get in the water, right now!' Ross shouted in Spanish. 'Right now!'

However, as they obeyed, Ross caught movement from the corner of his eye. He craned his head and suddenly lost his breath.

Two guys up on the shore broke from behind the SUVs, and before 30K could adjust his fire, the Rastrojos troops cut loose with a barrage.

'Get back!' Ross shouted to Pepper.

They rolled off the deck, into the water, while the still-disoriented crew members were left there, swimming right into the maw of fire.

As Ross went under then came around, putting the hull between himself and the gunman, the sub began listing badly, the sail coming straight down at him, with smoke still billowing from the hatch.

He kicked to get out of its path, but it was too late, and all he could do was raise his hands, steal a breath, and let the creaking sail crash on top of him, driving him down toward the river bottom with a rush of bubbling water.

Fourteen

Pepper should have seen that coming, and he cursed himself for missing it. Knowing their sub crew was being captured, those Rastrojos infantry had had no choice but to kill said crew members. Dead men tell no tales about drug smuggling.

Between the torrents of rain and cracking of gunfire, it was hard to judge how close those incoming rounds were getting, but it was easy to decide his next move: get his old-timer butt out of there. He dove under the submarine, swimming hard until he came up on the other side —

Just as the sail crashed into the water and the wave knocked him backward. No, the river didn't taste like Campbell's Soup — more like algae and mud. He coughed, nearly choked, and glanced around, searching in vain for Ross as a fresh spate of gunfire ripped across the submarine's hull, rounds punching fiberglass in a triplet of dull thumps.

Pepper tugged free a fragmentation grenade from his web gear, grimaced, then let it fly in a high arc toward the SUVs.

Eat this, mis amigos.

He imagined the sound of the explosion.

Where was it?

He was about to curse when the frag detonated, lifting the front end of one SUV, its engine compartment igniting. Pepper couldn't see the second car because more withering gunfire drove him back behind the sub. There was an eerie rhythm to the battle, automatic weapons booming at one another one second, followed by an absolute silence . . . and then a shout, more fire, and then a more distant explosion.

He craned his neck. Where was Ross?

Was he – holy shit – inside? Hell, yeah, he was. The package was everything.

Pepper dove beneath the rippling surface and toward the hatch. He slipped a penlight from his web gear, thumbed it on, and pointed down as the sub drifted away from him, toward the bottom nearly seven meters below.

He was no Olympic swimmer, no Navy SEAL, that was for sure. But the rigorous cross-training he'd endured during phase II of his recruitment as a Ghost had had him rescuing trapped pilots from downed and sinking aircraft, along with several other water rescue scenarios that had sent him to the edge of a liquid oblivion and back again. He paddled down toward the hatch and pulled it farther open.

The silhouette of something *large* passed nearby. He repressed a chill. No, he wouldn't dwell on what else was in the water . . .

*

Ross hadn't wasted a second after the sub had rolled and begun to sink. He'd pushed up, clutched the rim of the hatch, and had allowed the rushing water to carry him inside the cramped confines. He turned slightly to his right, a light pen in his hand, and saw a control station on one side with radar screen and navigation controls and GPS. Farther back was a series of modified water heaters and jerry-rigged air compressors, three on each side of the hull. They were used to control surfacing and submerging. The captain would fill the heaters with water to dive, then he'd use the compressors to blow out that water and surface. A label on one of the air compressors caught Ross's attention, but he had to keep moving.

Beyond the heaters were four bunks, the blankets floating up near the ceiling now, where the smoke grenade still bubbled and hissed. Still farther back was an actual toilet and air-conditioning unit.

Ross shifted his light, pulling himself deeper into the sub, and there he was, the package, Delgado, captured in the small light's beam and floating motionless, eyes closed, cheeks swelling, some bricks of cocaine surrounding him and turning end over end, as though he were caught in a slow-motion tornado and this was a snapshot captured by a daredevil photographer.

Ross pushed through them and seized the unconscious man by the shirt. He glanced forward where Pepper was just now entering the compartment. Seeing Ross coming with the package, Pepper immediately turned around and headed back outside, holding open the hatch for Ross, who forced Delgado through and into the open water. Pepper took over, seizing Delgado and dragging him up.

It had been a cumbersome and irritatingly slow process at best, and Ross quaked with the fact that every second counted. Just as he was running out of breath, his head beginning to spin, they broke the surface –

To the sound of so much gunfire that Ross wasn't sure if they were pinned down yet again. He coughed and spat, then shouted to Pepper. 'Gotta get him to the shore. He's out. Need CPR! I'll be right back.'

Pepper was already on it, his arm draped beneath Delgado's chin as he began a hard paddle away from the sub. 'Where the hell are you going?'

Ross waved him off and dove back down, paddling hard toward the sub.

Fifteen

You took the good with the bad, and you should expect a little ugly as well when you are behind the trigger of a Stoner.

Yes, you dished out superior firepower the way a heavyweight world champion dishes out right hooks.

But you weren't exactly stealthy, sacrificing the possibility of being shy or coy regarding your feelings for the enemy.

And once you expressed those true feelings in the form of an unrelenting and vicious stream of superheated lead, those sons of bitches would, unfortunately, know exactly where you were – which 99.9 per cent of the time meant things would get ugly real fast.

All of which explained why 30K loved the weapon. You needed some serious brass in your shorts to play with the big guns and draw enemy fire. If you weren't up for a challenge, then you shouldn't be a Ghost. Go wear the banana suit outside the frozen yogurt place. Applications being accepted now.

With his boy Kozak in tow, he reached the next group of trees and set free another twenty rounds into the SUVs, driving the guys firing at Ross and Pepper back toward the dry docks. Before a self-satisfied grin could split his lips, multiple whooshing sounds rose from the jungle behind him.

And not two seconds after the men firing at Ross and Pepper reached the dry dock, not one, not two, but six rocket-propelled grenades streaked through the air, half targeting the first dry dock, the rest screaming in toward the second, and it was all 30K could do to hit the deck and shout into the Cross-Com, 'Incoming! Get down!'

A young SF lieutenant, fresh out of school, with absolutely no combat experience had once asked 30K, 'In the heat of the battle, do you ever get, like, post-traumatic stress disorder or flashbacks to other battles? Do you ever just sit there and freeze, you know, the whole thousand-yard stare thing?'

30K had thought about that for a long moment – or at least he had pretended to do so. In truth, he was repressing some serious laughter. Poor guy. He didn't have a clue. After an appropriate amount of time that might've had the lieutenant's imagination running wild with what 30K had seen and done, he answered, 'When you're in the fight, you don't think about anything. You shoot, move and communicate. You kill anything in your way. And you protect your buddies at all costs. Like I said, you have no time to analyse it. As a matter of fact, you don't even have time to be scared.'

Sure, that was one man's opinion, but 30K had hoped that he could clean out those dirty fuel injectors between the kid's ears and get him thinking about real life instead

of the way things unfolded on TV or in his imagination. Dialing into the ebb and flow of the battle put
you in a place both mentally and physically that was
much safer. He'd once compared it to riding his mountain bike. You never looked around as you rumbled
across hair-raising terrain; you always looked forward,
out there, beyond the bike, past that narrow bridge that
was barely wide enough for your front tyre. You looked
where you wanted to go. Same thing in battle. Keep
looking out. Not within.

The blast wave from all those grenades hit 30K hard
enough to wrench his head back, and when he dared
steal a look up, his face warmed as twin mushroom
clouds of flames haloed in black smoke roared up
through the storm, past the canopy to points beyond
the gray sheet of clouds.

He allowed himself another second to enjoy the
bonfires before bolting to his feet and triggering
another barrage with his Stoner – cutting down a half
dozen troops scattering like insects toward the road
leading north.

'Ghost Team, this is 30K! They're on the run!' he
cried. Off to his right, four of the Colombian SF guys
broke from cover to pursue the escapees.

The battle had taken a quick turn in their favor.

Or so 30K had thought.

The Ras-whatever-they-were-called dudes had re-
grouped about twenty meters down the river, near
where the submarine had just met its watery grave, and

30K marked at least ten of them strung along mangroves, laying down fire on the shoreline, trying to prevent Pepper and Ross from getting the package to safety.

Hadn't he just cleared that area?

'Don't even think about it,' said Kozak from behind him, bringing in the drone above their positions.

'I'm going, bro. Get the drone in there, draw their fire. On three. One, two –'

Kozak cried for him to wait, but he just grinned to himself and took off jogging across the riverbank, rushing up past the dock and alongside the dry docks – now flaming skeletons of timber and smoking debris.

A secondary explosion lifted from the smaller building, probably some diesel fuel igniting, and then came the fireworks show of ammunition the drug runners had stored there, now beginning to cook off like popcorn on the stove, rounds bursting, ricocheting and sparking skyward.

All right, Jimmy Boy, he warned himself. *Don't screw this up . . .*

He juked right, and even as he moved, the Cross-Com showed him the targets ahead, the ground at his feet thumping with rounds that either paralleled his steps or cut through his boot prints. You play with fire and you will get burned, the old saying went. He was going to need cover in about two seconds.

Holding his breath and still running, he opened fire on the first target, panning away not a second after that guy went down. He struck the second guy and the third before he broke left now, heading toward the river. To hell with cover. He was on a roll now . . .

Three more guys accepted his free bullets before he had the remaining four all shooting at him as he reached the muddy bank. He answered with one more salvo, then abandoned the machine gun and dove beneath the waves.

As he swam, sensing they were tracing his path with their shots, he drew his FN Five-seven from its holster, then came up on his hands and knees, firing one, two, three, four 5.7mm rounds, striking two men. He stole a look back at Ross and Pepper dragging Delgado onto the shoreline. Their CIA operative was not moving.

Two guys left, with only 30K standing in their path. The captain needed time.

He scowled at the mangroves within which hid the last two soldiers. *Get out here and fight like men . . .*

The razor's edge between bravery and insanity was a place few operators visited. 30K had bought several acres there, planned to build himself a house, three-car garage, have some horses out back. It was all about location, location, location, right? If you wanted to save your buddies, you had to be in the right place at the right time. You had to make your own luck. You had to stop thinking in clichés and start firing your weapon –

Which was exactly what he did. Took out the ninth guy with a single round. Missed the tenth guy with the first shot but got him with the second.

But shit, he didn't realize he'd been nicked in the arm until the needles took hold and his sleeve grew bloody. He cursed again, jogged back toward the captain and Pepper.

Only then did he realize that Kozak had never brought in the drone to draw their fire. He glanced up in the kid's direction –

And realized why.

Aw, no. No, no, no . . .

Delgado was turning blue, and Ross was trembling with the desire to save this guy.

They each carried a medical kit, but those were mostly stocked with supplies to treat wounds you'd expect in battle: trauma, gunshot, etc. Automatic defibrillators were a bit too cumbersome to pack along, and Ross seriously doubted that Jiménez's team had one.

So it was up to him to perform CPR on Delgado, who was still unconscious, not breathing, looking DOA. Two breaths followed by the chest compressions. Over and over. Ross knew the routine, had his CPR cert refreshed every year, but after the first round of compressions, he couldn't go on.

Memories . . .

He looked at Pepper, his eyes burning, and said, 'Take over. Do it!'

Pepper jumped right in – just as 30K ran past them, crying, 'Kozak! Kozak!'

Sixteen

Kozak knew he was lying facedown in the mud, and he understood that his brain must be short-circuiting like a laptop left in the rain, but he didn't care. He was ten years old again, up in South Canaan, Pennsylvania, and he'd just tossed his Heddon Torpedo lure into the lake, hoping to catch a bass. He slowly worked the reel, drawing in more line, and the lure's forward prop created a perfect bubbling noise and ripple across the surface. Pepper, a fellow bass-fishing aficionado, would've been proud of the city boy's technique, but it wasn't Pepper who'd been proud:

'That's really good, Johnny,' said David, the college guy with the funny beard who'd served as Kozak's camp counselor.

Behind them lay the lush grounds of Saint Tikhon's Monastery and Seminary, and Kozak was there attending the annual one-week summer camp sponsored by the Diocese of Eastern Pennsylvania. Russian Orthodox Christians like himself attended services and learned about courage, good sportsmanship, and how to raid a girl's dormitory to steal their pyjamas (the older boys called it a 'panty raid').

Suddenly, a bass came up behind the lure and exploded

on it. Kozak's line pulled taut, and he screamed, 'I got one!'

But now he wasn't pulling on a line; he was clutching Amy Weismann's arm after she'd just shoved the engagement ring back into his hand.

They stood in her parents' Manhattan duplex on the Upper West Side, near the window, and Kozak was trying to convince her that this was for the best, that he'd be gone for too long, that they were from two different worlds and had somehow fallen in love but it probably wasn't meant to be.

'How could you do this to me?' she said through tears and clenched teeth. 'You just led me on.'

'No, I didn't. But I know what'll happen.'

'How do you know?'

'It's not fair to you.'

Kozak sensed pressure on his shoulders, and for a second, he was floating, but then there it was, the feeling of the ground on his legs and rump, and when he opened his eyes, he realized he'd been propped up against a tree, and this wasn't the duplex or even Central Park . . .

'I didn't mean to leave you, buddy! I know, I know. I shouldn't have done it. But you're okay! You're going to be okay!'

He knew the guy talking to him. 30K. 'Where's Amy?' he asked.

30K frowned. 'Who's Amy?'

'My fiancée.'

'Her? You dumped her a while ago.'

'Oh, yeah. That's right.'

'Look, you're good, dude, you're good.' 30K's gaze swept over Kozak's fatigues. 'Don't see any wounds. Probably just got the wind knocked out of you.'

'What the hell happened?'

30K shrugged. 'Grenade maybe. Looks like that tree hit you from behind.'

Kozak craned his head, the motion making the world turn sideways for a second before his vision cleared and he spotted the tree, cracked in half like a piece of balsa wood from a toy glider. 'No, look –'

Near the broken tree lay a jagged piece of tin roof that had blown off one of the dry docks. It had struck the tree like some oversize ninja dart and knocked it down, into Kozak.

30K's eyes widened. 'Damn, that thing could've taken your head off.'

Kozak nodded as a chill rushed up his spine.

A sudden cracking of more fire sent 30K groaning to his feet. 'We gotta go.' He seized Kozak by the wrists and hauled him up.

'I got this,' said Kozak, but then a realization sent him into panic mode. 'The remote? Where's the remote?' His eyes probed the mud, past the rotting brown fronds, until he spotted the slight trace of something rectangular barely peaking out from the sludge.

He wrenched the device from the ooze, wiped it off, and breathed a sigh. The drone was still wheeling overhead on autopilot, the signal full strength. 'Okay. Ready.'

'I'm sorry, Captain, but he's not coming back,' said Pepper, removing his palms from Delgado's chest and letting his gaze sweep the jungle as Jiménez's men charged up, forming a perimeter around them.

Ross stared at Delgado, cursed, then began shaking his head in disgust.

Captain Jiménez himself hustled up to them and dropped down beside Ross. 'The area's secure. I'll have my men search the bodies.'

Ross glanced at him. 'Good.'

'Will he make it?' Jiménez asked, his gaze riveted on Delgado.

Ross practically leapt on the CIA agent and began doing more compressions. 'Come on, you, you son of a bitch!' he screamed. 'I didn't come all this way for you to die on me!'

Pepper shifted around and put his hand on Delgado's neck, checking for a carotid pulse. He waited, then held up his palm.

After a few more compressions, Ross finally surrendered and glanced up at Jiménez, who shared an equal look of helplessness and frustration.

No, this wasn't the first time Pepper had been on a search and rescue mission only to have the package expire on them. And it wouldn't be the last. The anger was always palpable. You'd spend months going over every decision you made, second-guessing yourself, considering all the what-ifs, then finally trying to justify why you had failed so you'd do better next time.

Ross was a good man, and he didn't need this shit. Not now. Not when he was just starting out . . . *It was just bad luck,* Pepper thought. *That was all. Bad luck.*

Seventeen

After retrieving his Stoner, 30K ran a sweep of the perimeter with Kozak at his side. The HUD was clear of enemy contacts. The dry docks continued to burn and sizzle, and the stench of gunpowder and gasoline was heavy in the air. The rain had tapered off to a drizzle as they headed back to link up with Pepper and Ross, who'd moved Delgado to some cover beneath the trees.

'Look at him,' grunted 30K as they approached. 'He's dead as a doornail. Mission fail. Shit.'

'Hey, we got him,' said Kozak. 'The fact that he's dead could be considered just a detail.'

'Yeah, a real inconvenient detail.'

Kozak called in the drone, catching it like a trained bird, then tucking it back into its holster. 'I've got the location of the first drone,' he said, studying his remote. 'We need to go get it.'

'Yeah, yeah . . .' 30K had been hoping for a feel-good, kick-ass mission, one for the record books. What he got was a minor gunshot wound and a failed rescue attempt. Not exactly a world-class memory.

They reached the captain and Pepper, and Kozak's tone grew a bit more somber as he made his request.

Ross glanced back at him. 'Take 30K. You got ten

minutes. Marine patrol boats are on their way to mop up, and we need to be out of here by then.'

'Lead the way,' 30K told Kozak, and once they were out of earshot, he added, 'Ross sounds bummed. What did I tell you?'

Kozak scowled. 'I'll give you a dollar to shut up – because you couldn't have done any better.'

'Oh, yeah?'

'Yeah. 'Cause they'll never put you in charge.'

'Why's that?'

'Because in five minutes you'd cause an international crisis.'

30K chuckled over that. 'Yeah, I guess I would.'

Ross was watching Pepper search the bodies around the SUVs as he put in the dreaded call to Mitchell. 'Guardian, this is Delta Dragon, over.'

'Delta Dragon, Guardian. SITREP?'

'We've scuttled a narcosub and destroyed the dry docks.' Ross took a deep breath. 'Unfortunately, our package has expired, over.'

Mitchell's hesitation was enough to make Ross vomit all the stress and anger. *Some first impression, huh?*

'Delta Dragon, you're to recover the body and have it transported back to Bogotá. The Agency will take over from there.'

'Roger that, sir.'

'Now listen to me carefully. On board one of the Colombian patrol boats is an operator call sign Adamo.

He's a US State Department advisor and an old friend. Stay put till he arrives. He's got some updated intel for you. Guardian, out.'

Updated intel? Ross thought. What did this guy know that Mitchell didn't? Why wasn't Mitchell conveying this information himself? The major had said that there was no love lost between him and Langley . . . so what was this about?

Pepper's body searches had come up empty. When he passed this on to Ross, the man reached into his pocket and handed him a metal plate. 'I ripped it off one of those air compressors. That's why I went back in the sub.'

'Nice . . .' Pepper used his Cross-Com's camera to snap a photo of the air compressor nomenclature plate, then he used voice commands to upload that photo to GST headquarters, where intelligence analysts would better identify it.

'Delta Dragon Two, this is Guardian Base, over,' called the intel analyst. Woman's voice. Sexy. But then again they all sounded sexy to him.

'Guardian Base, this is Delta Dragon Two. That was fast.'

'Roger that. Farsar Tejarat comes up as an Iranian medical air compressor manufacturer. The Model 06 doesn't show in their sales listings. Looks like they're moonlighting. Serial number 02769 came up on a bill of lading – along with serial numbers 02770, 02771 and

02772 – shipped from Fadakno Piping Company in Tobruk. The phone number on the plate matches a local number for the Fadakno warehouse, over.'

'Roger, received. Where's Tobruk, over?'

'It's a Libyan deep water port on the Mediterranean, over.'

'Roger that. Need to brush up on my geography.'

'Sending e-mail copy to your team now. More specific intel to follow. Guardian Base, out.'

Kozak found the primary drone wedged between two branches about six meters up, and he activated the secondary drone to fly up there and knock the first one free.

The plan was ridiculously simple and should have gone down by the numbers.

However, after several attempts of squinting through the rain and deepening gloom and trying to maneuver the secondary drone just right to force the first one free, the thing just wouldn't budge, and he feared he'd damage both drones if he continued.

'It's not working. Can you climb up there and get it?' he asked 30K.

'Are you serious?'

'Look, man, I still don't feel good,' said Kozak, feigning dizziness. 'Come on, do me a solid.'

'Hey, my arm hurts,' said 30K, showing Kozak where he'd been grazed. 'My monkey skills suck right now.'

'Are you dizzy?'

'No.'

Kozak nodded. 'Then come on.'

After reciting a string of epithets, 30K shoved his reloaded Stoner into Kozak's hands, then he reached up and grabbed the nearest branch. 'You know when's the last time I climbed a tree?'

'When you were a kid?'

'No, when I was regular Army back in the 'Stan. Kids were always flying those kites, you know? One kid's got stuck in a tree. He cried for me to get it down. So I went up there, but some Taliban assholes took advantage of that and started shooting. Got two in the plates before my buddies took 'em out. I mean, how do you like that shit? I'm trying to save a kite for some kid, and those bastards decide to engage me. I mean, I hate fighting against cowards like that. Got no respect for them at all.'

'Man, that sucks,' said Kozak, feeling the guilt of pressuring 30K work into his throat. 'So now you have an aversion to trees.'

'You could say that.'

'You get the kite?'

30K gave him a look. 'Yeah. I got the kite. But it was full of holes.'

'Swiss cheese.'

'Don't talk about food.'

'You hungry, too?'

'Dude, I could eat an entire tray of lasagna right now.'

'And wings. Fifty wings.'

'At least.' 30K reached the branch where the drone was stuck and began to inch his way toward the end like a clumsy caterpillar, the branch bending more sharply with each move. 'Dude, I can't reach it.'

'Don't give up. You're almost there.'

30K's attention was diverted away, over Kozak's shoulder. 'Aw, hell,' he said. 'The Marines are already here.'

'Then hurry up!'

He shifted forward once more.

And the branch snapped.

Eighteen

Four Colombian patrol boats from the Naval Base *ARC Bahía Málaga* in Buenaventura came whirring down the river, their pilots throttling down as they drew closer. A half dozen heavily armed Marines stood in each vessel, and the barrels of .50-caliber machine guns extended from bow and stern. The lead boat slowed enough to bump the dock and allow a man wearing a black baseball cap, fatigues and a heavy Kevlar vest to hop out. He strode down the dock, undaunted by the wind or rain, and marched across the shoreline toward Ross and Pepper as, behind him, the rest of the Marines prepared to come ashore.

Why he wore aviator sunglasses in a rainstorm was beyond Ross, but if you stayed in the military long enough, you got used to the eccentricities and superstitions of operators who were all, admittedly, just a little off center. That came with the territory.

The man stopped before them and tugged off the sunglasses to expose the deep scar running from his nose, beneath his right eye, and down toward his earlobe. His mustache and soul patch were patterned after the old rocker Frank Zappa but were pure white, and his eyes were a brilliant blue. Whether he was bald or not would remain a mystery, as his baseball cap remained fixed on his head. He proffered a hand and said, 'You're Captain Ross, aren't you?'

'That's right,' said Ross, taking the hand. 'They call you Adamo?'

'Yes, sir. And don't let my present company fool you. I'm an old ex-Army colonel. Seems like a lifetime ago, but I was on an ODA team myself. Maybe you heard of them: Triple Nickel?'

Ross's eyes widened. Hell, yeah, he'd heard of them. ODA-555 was one of the first Operational Detachment Alpha Special Forces teams to deploy in Afghanistan after 9/11, and their work there had become legendary among all SF operators. 'Well, then, sir, it's an honor,' Ross answered. He introduced Pepper and Jiménez.

'I already know Captain Jiménez,' Adamo said with a knowing grin. He added quickly in Spanish, 'The captain and I have been working these mangroves for a long time.'

Jiménez gave a weary grin. 'Too long.'

Adamo finished shaking hands, then regarded Ross. 'Mitchell needs good people like you. Don't get discouraged. Now, let me see what you got here.'

Adamo turned away and crouched down over Delgado's body. He muttered something to himself, studied the man once more, then lifted his voice. 'Just what I thought. This ain't him.'

'What?' asked Pepper.

Adamo got to his feet. 'That's *not* Delgado.'

'Bullshit.' The word came out of Ross's mouth before he could stop it. 'We got intel. That's our man.'

Adamo shook his head.

The branch had cracked, sending 30K sliding forward, but he managed to maintain his grip, even as his legs came swinging around. Now the branch acted like a vine, and he crashed into the trunk with a heavy thud.

When he looked up, he realized he was dangling by a splintering thread, and if he didn't find better purchase, he was going down the hard way at a rate of 9.8 meters per second squared, according to the math guy who had invented gravity – what was his name, Carl Sagan?

Wise-ass thoughts like that kept him from panicking, he assured himself, but Kozak wasn't helping matters, screaming for him to hang on. Yes, his 'little brother' had an absolutely keen eye for the obvious.

'Reach out and grab that branch right there,' hollered Kozak.

30K saw the second branch in question, tried to grab it, couldn't. 'Get under me,' he ordered.

'What?'

'I said get under me!'

'Why?'

''Cause I'll let go, and you'll catch me.'

'Are you nuts?'

No, he wasn't. Those were just more wise-ass remarks to punish Kozak, whose eyes threatened to explode.

'Dude, wait a minute. Wait a minute.' Kozak worked

the controls on the remote, got the secondary drone back up in the air, and brought it close to 30K, the quadrotors humming loudly in his face. 'Grab hold in the center.'

'That thing can't hold me up,' 30K shouted.

'No, but it'll slow your descent. You ready?'

30K felt the branch begin to give way, and he suddenly dropped another half meter. 'Oh, shit. Here goes nothing!' He reached out, seized the drone, then let go of the branch.

The quadrotors whined in protest, fighting against his considerable weight, but lo and behold, his descent slowed enough so that when he hit the ground, the reverberation that rose through his legs was mild. He fell back, on to his rump, and released the drone.

And not a second later, the primary drone plummeted from the tree and crashed to the ground, practically in his lap.

'Sweet!' cried Kozak. He policed up both drones, then quickly offered his hand. 'Nice work, bro.'

30K snickered and ignored the hand. 'You know how much beer it'll take to pay me back for this shit? More than you can afford.'

Kozak switched on his Russian accent. 'What is it with you, country boy? Always beer? Drink vodka! For good health.'

'All right, Sulu. Let's go.'

'Chekov was the Russian guy.'

'Whatever!'

*

Ross had some hard-copy photographs of Delgado tucked into his pack, and he produced them for Adamo.

'See, have a look,' said Pepper, hovering at Ross's shoulder. 'He fits the description. He's the guy!'

Adamo thumbed through the photos, his frown deepening. 'Gentlemen, we got ourselves a bit of a mess here.'

Pepper threw up his hands. 'Oh, here we go. I don't believe this.'

Ross hardened his voice. 'Sir, I hope you can clarify, because we're all about to have some anger management issues.' Ross felt his cheeks warm.

Adamo returned the photos. 'Take it easy, Captain. This intel was supplied to your group by Langley.'

'Meaning it's not worth shit,' snapped Pepper.

'Meaning it was deliberately altered by someone,' Adamo corrected. 'Here's a picture of Delgado.' He reached into his pocket.

Pepper shifted in beside Ross and cursed as he glimpsed the photo. 'Well, ain't that something. That's the cabdriver we rescued. What the hell was his name? Raul?'

Ross turned to Jiménez. 'What did you do with him?'

The man winced. 'We let him go. He said he'd walk back to the village and get a ride back to Bogotá. We had no reason to hold him, and I couldn't afford to leave anyone behind with him. I called the local police to see if they could pick him up, but no one answered at the station.'

Ross and Pepper looked at each other in disbelief.

Adamo slapped a hand on Ross's shoulder. 'Don't beat yourself up, Captain. Your mission was a success. You rescued Delgado. You just didn't know it – because *he* didn't want you to know it. I've been here for nearly ten years myself, and I've worked with the guy quite a few times. Never trusted him.'

'Does Mitchell know about this?'

'I briefed him on what I know. My mission here is to work with our own DEA and the Colombian Marines to interdict these narcosubs coming out of the mangroves. Delgado was a good source of intel. Then, about six months ago, he dropped off the map. I thought they'd killed him, chopped him up, fed him to the sharks. But then he turns up, working some kind of operation with the FARC and Los Rastrojos. One of my DEA guys gets a picture of him in Bogotá meeting with a guy named Saif Hamid.'

'That name sounds familiar,' said Ross.

'It should. Hamid is an old-school al Qaeda bomb maker, a High Value Target we've been after for a long time. He was also working behind the scenes in Afghanistan, supplying weapons to the Taliban in the Wardak Province.'

'Are you serious?' Ross asked, his voice dropping to funereal depths.

Adamo gave a reluctant nod. 'The RPGs and other ordnance Hamid supplied to those bastards were used to kill your teammates from DEVGRU.'

On August 6, 2011, thirty Americans – including twenty-two Navy SEALs – had been killed when their Chinook helicopter was ambushed and shot down in Wardak Province. The SEALs had been part of a QRF, or Quick Reaction Force, en route to support an Army Ranger unit.

What was more, Ross had served with every single operator who'd died that day, and there was, in his mind, no act more evil. Some accounts noted that US forces had been tricked into the area via false intel and that the Taliban had set up a trap for the helicopter, knowing there was only one good approach into the valley. An RPG strike to the aft tail rotor assembly resulted in an entire troop of SEALs being wiped off the face of the earth. If Ross had been upset five minutes ago, he was seething now.

Adamo went on: 'Hamid has formed a new group called *Bedayat jadeda*, which means "new beginnings" in Arabic. We think Delgado was acting as a liaison between all three groups.'

'So Delgado went rogue?' Ross asked.

'We don't know. The fact that they captured him would argue against that. I think his cover got blown, and I think the Agency realized they couldn't contain the mess down here – but as always, they're never telling us the whole truth.'

Ross squinted into a thought. 'It can't be that simple. Why would the FARC drag a cabdriver all the way out here unless they wanted us to believe he was Delgado?'

'Maybe they were like us,' said Pepper. 'Maybe they didn't know what he looked like. Maybe only a few of the officers had actually met him. They had their orders and just followed them. They thought they had Delgado, and so did we – and that's exactly what he wanted.'

Ross thought back to the cocaine lab. 'Maybe you're right. I mean, for a cabdriver, he was pretty forthcoming, wasn't he? He wanted us out of there so he could take off.'

'And you know how those spooks are. They will never give up their cover,' said Pepper. 'Even to the good guys.'

'We oughta know about that,' said Ross.

Pepper rubbed the corners of his eyes. 'I still can't get my head wrapped around this. So whose side is that little bastard on?'

Adamo grinned crookedly. 'I'd ask that of his entire agency. Anyway, I need to mark the location of that sub, since we plan to salvage it for study. These Marines will finish with the bodies.'

'What about Delgado now?'

'I'll put out my own feelers with AFEUR and the DEA, but if Delgado doesn't want to be found, then trust me, we won't find him.'

'And Hamid?' Ross asked.

'I think the Agency was tracking him, but I haven't

heard anything more. Maybe they lost him. Who knows?'

'We need to find Delgado,' said Pepper.

'That's up to the major,' Ross said.

Adamo lifted his hand for a farewell shake. 'Well, Captain, Sergeant, maybe someday we can all get together for a beer. Until then, stay sharp.' Adamo gave them a curt nod as he shook hands, then faced the Marines and cried in Spanish, 'What kind of disorganized dumb-ass bullshit is this? Bag up those bodies and get 'em loaded. Let's go, Marines!'

Nineteen

As they humped back through the jungle toward the trucks, minding their steps and the booby trap markers they'd set in place, Kozak asked Pepper to go back over the intel they'd received from Adamo:

'So the guy who died was the cabdriver.'

'Correct.'

'And the guy we let go was really the package.'

Pepper sighed. 'There it is.'

30K, who was standing beside Kozak, said, 'That sneaky little runt. He was right there all the time. Son of a bitch!'

Pepper closed his eyes. 'I'd like to get my hands on him for just ten seconds.'

'Hey, it ain't all bad,' said Kozak. 'Mission accomplished. The package was rescued. Our cover remained intact. And the Colombian special forces guys get credit for bringing down a cocaine lab, a narcosub, and the dry docks. Woo-hoo.'

'Yeah, woo-hoo,' said Pepper darkly. 'But this ain't over. I just hope the major agrees with me.'

'Oh, he will,' said 30K. 'And when we're done with that little lollipop kid, he will *definitely* believe in Ghosts.'

Kozak had heard enough of the chest drumming, so

he drifted back toward the captain. 'What do you think, sir? You think we'll be going after him?'

'Not sure yet,' said Ross. 'No word back from Guardian. For now, we deliver the cabdriver's body.'

'Do we know what really happened?'

'I've been playing it over and over. We've got the FARC, Los Rastrojos, and some new Islamic terrorist group in a possible alliance. We've got a missing CIA agent who was either trying to expose this alliance or was part of it. We have a connection via the sub's parts to a port city in Libya.'

'Man, it all sounds very actionable to me.'

'Me, too.'

Kozak braced himself. 'You mind if I ask you something?'

Ross gave him an odd look.

'Oh, it's nothing personal. Just curious. How'd I do?'

'What do you mean?'

'Out here.'

Ross almost smiled. 'Let the After Action Report reflect that Staff Sergeant John Kozak performed his duties admirably and in the best interests of the United States Army.'

Kozak didn't hold back his grin. 'Thank you, sir. Just want you to know that I, uh, I really believe in this. You know, what we're doing. I'm always thinking about all the people who came before us, the guys who died for our country. What we're doing is important – even if we're getting screwed over by the CIA.'

Ross finally beamed. 'I appreciate that, buddy. I really

do. And I'm glad you're not too pissed off having to take orders from a Squid.'

'No, sir.'

'You think I'm a Squid?'

'Sir, I didn't say that, sir.'

'Relax, I'm just messing with you.' Ross lowered his voice. 'Only guy I'm worried about is 30K. He's got an issue with me, doesn't he?'

'He's cool, sir. I wouldn't worry.'

'You don't sound like you believe that.'

Kozak hesitated. 'He's got some trust issues with everybody. Sometimes I think he'd rather operate alone. Funny because he's one of those guys who's always had a problem with authority figures, and he winds up in a place full of authority figures. Ironic, huh?'

'Yeah.'

Kozak thought a moment. 'You know what? You should ask him about his nickname.'

Ross chuckled under his breath. 'Are you serious?'

'That'll get you talking.'

'Okay, but I have to be honest. I figured you guys already had a name for me.'

Kozak shrugged. 'Not that I know of.'

Once they had reached the Hummers and the M35, Ross told Pepper he was riding with 30K, and that drew the man's curious stare.

'It's not that you smell, but I want to talk to him,' Ross whispered to Pepper.

'Ah, gotcha. Good idea.'

Ross climbed into the passenger's seat of the lead Hummer, settled in, then looked over at 30K. 'What's wrong?'

'You're riding with me?'

Ross nodded. 'Yeah, Pepper smells.'

30K smiled. 'He does, doesn't he?'

'Seriously, I thought we should talk.'

30K swore and said, 'What'd I do now?'

'Nothing. Start the engine. Let's go.' Ross leaned back and tapped the leg of the Colombian SF guy manning the fifty. 'Stay frosty, big guy. They get another chance to ambush us, they will.'

'No problem,' said the gunner.

30K led the convoy of vehicles out of the clearing and back down the jungle road, the potholes now filled with water, the cab rattling like Ross's father's old '68 Ford pickup. The once gray sky had washed off into streaks of gray and white as the storm's feeder bands passed through.

They sat in silence for a few minutes, then Ross cleared his throat and asked, 'Why don't they call you Jimmy?'

'They could, but everyone calls me 30K.'

'Where'd that come from?'

'If I tell you, sir, you have to promise you won't share the story with anyone – and you won't turn me in.'

'Are you about to confess to a crime?'

'Sort of.'

'Maybe you shouldn't tell me.'

'No, I think you'll like it. It involves the CIA. See, when I was in Afghanistan, this CIA ops officer I knew was paying off this warlord to get intel. But the warlord was a real dick and screwing everyone over. He was storing all this cash – I'm talking about American dollars – in his compound. So me and a few guys were out on patrol and got wind of this. We broke in there one night and stole the money. We split it up. We each got 30K. It was my plan, so the guys started calling me 30K. And ever since then, the name stuck. Later on, I felt bad about it. I was telling myself that the CIA was wasting American tax dollars and we were doing a service by saving the money and pumping it back into the economy. But that still didn't feel right. I spent about a thousand bucks on booze, then I gave the rest to charity.'

'Wow, that almost sounds like a plot from a movie.'

'I know, right? But that's how I got my nickname.'

'So how elaborate will the story be this time?' asked Pepper, who was behind the wheel of the second Hummer.

Kozak shrugged. 'He's a pretty amazing bullshit artist.'

'Maybe he'll tell Ross the truth.'

'The truth? I wonder if *he* even knows the truth. Every time someone asks him about his nickname, he comes up with a different story. He told Ferguson he won 30K in the lottery so his friends started calling him that. He told me an old girlfriend gave him the name, that it was also the name of a mom and pop bar where they'd met.'

'And he told me his father said he'd never amount to anything, that the most he'd ever make in his life was 30K a year, which you told me is bullshit because his father left when he was a baby, so he never met the guy.'

'Yup. So who the hell knows why they call him 30K. But there it is . . .'

Pepper nodded. 'So, you had a little talk with Ross.'

Kozak nodded.

'And how'd that go?'

'Very well.'

Pepper's voice softened. 'I want to share something with you, just so you don't get into trouble with him.'

'What is it?'

'I found out some stuff about Ross through a mutual friend. Before he joined the Ghosts, I'm talking about a couple of years ago, there was an accident. His little boy was killed. Broke up his marriage. Nearly ruined his life. You know it's hard, but if you try hard enough, you can get past the deaths of your buddies in combat. We all know what we signed on for. We know the risks. We go on in their name, their memory.'

'That's right,' said Kozak.

'But losing a child . . . how do you let that go?'

Kozak pursed his lips. 'You don't. So what're you saying? You think Ross is messed up?'

'No. I just get the feeling that he's still torturing himself over it.'

'You said it was an accident.'

'I don't know the details, but I just got that feeling. Anyway, I think he jumped at the chance to become a Ghost so he could get away from it all. New job, new people, you know, not be around everyone saying, "I'm so sorry." Trouble is, I screwed up. I told him I knew. I told him I'm sorry, and he really locked up.'

'Then don't talk about it.'

'Damned straight. Don't bring it up.'

'Unless he wants to talk about it.'

'Yeah. Leave it up to him.'

Twenty

30K sensed that Ross didn't believe his story, but he didn't care. The captain was trying to have a feel-good moment, and 30K figured he'd be cordial but wouldn't go out of his way to be buddies. He'd rather maintain a professional relationship until Long John Silver proved himself –

And the only way that would happen was over time, over blood, sweat and tears.

The record was one thing. The 'show me in the field' was another, and while Ross had earned himself a few points during this operation, he had a long way to go, and 30K would be there every step of the way, keeping score.

'Anything you want to know about me?' Ross asked.

'Not really, sir.'

'I see.'

A particularly awkward silence followed, then suddenly 30K blurted out, 'You married?'

'Divorced.'

'She got sick of the long deployments?'

'Not exactly.'

'I don't care what they say. If your wife is hot, and you're gone more than half the year, she's going to cheat on you. It's not a physical thing for them, it's an emotional thing, and they need that. If you're not there to give it to them, then they find it someplace else. It's nature. No one can stop it.'

'So yours cheated on you?'

'Cheated? I never let it get that far. I like a nice twenty-four-hour relationship. Doesn't give 'em much time to cheat.'

'Sounds like you keep a tight schedule.'

'Hell, yeah.'

'Works for now, but when you get to be my age, you start thinking about a family.'

'Damn, that's the last thing I want. My mother raised me alone. My piece of shit loser of a father walked out when I was a baby. I'd kick his ass now if I saw him.'

'That's too bad.'

'Yeah, I guess I got some daddy issues. Not sure I'd ever know how to be a father.'

'Maybe one day. That kid looks into your eyes and calls you Dad. That's hard to beat.'

'How many you got?'

'I had one. A little boy.'

'She got him in the divorce?'

Ross didn't answer at first, and when 30K looked over at him, he had his eyes closed.

'Sir, you all right?'

'Yeah, man. Let me call the major back. Harass him a little. See if he's got new orders.'

'Cool.'

30K swallowed and adjusted his grip on the wheel. Whatever happened to the captain's little boy didn't sound good. Mental note: Don't go there again.

Still, the captain's honesty regarding his personal life had just scored him a few more points. Not many. But a few.

Twenty-One

Ross was preparing several arguments as to why he and the Ghosts should remain on this mission, not the least of which was because Saif Hamid was involved. Second, Ross planned to remind Mitchell about the SEALs who'd died in Wardak Province and add how the SecDef and National Command Authority had undoubtedly known that the Agency was involved in something borderline illegal in Colombia – and that's why they wanted the Ghosts involved instead of allowing the CIA's own paramilitary officers to conduct the rescue. Admittedly, the latter was speculation, but he'd offer that opinion nonetheless.

Ross placed the video call to Mitchell, inserted his earbuds, and to his mild surprise, all of his potential arguments were for naught – because not sixty seconds into the conversation, he realized he would have been preaching to the choir:

'We IDed one of the dead at the sub dry dock as Juan Marquez, a lieutenant with Los Rastrojos and a liaison between his group and the FARC,' Mitchell explained. 'Turns out he used one of his known aliases to do business with Fadakno in Tobruk, but he wasn't just buying compressors for narcosubs.'

'Oh, really? So what's up with Tobruk?'

'The port might be a distribution hub for Colombian cocaine being smuggled into Europe. Hamid's group, the *Bedayat jadeda*, may be using their old al Qaeda contacts to reopen those markets. Obviously we want Hamid, but let's see how deep the rabbit hole goes. The SecDef and National Command Authority aren't getting straight answers from Langley, and we've been ordered to find out what the hell's going on out there.'

'Roger that, sir. Any word on Delgado? He report back in?'

'Nothing. And even if he does contact the Agency, once again, they're tight-lipped about everything.'

'I hope we're returning the favor and keeping our operations compartmentalized. If Delgado's gone rogue –'

'No worries there, Captain. Colonel Evans knows how to deal with them.'

'Good. Your friend Adamo told me about Hamid's connections in Afghanistan and the link to Wardak Province.'

'Hamid's a scumbag of the highest order, and I can't think of a better Ghost Team to bring him in.'

Ross made a face. 'You want him alive?'

'C'mon, Captain, you've been down this road before.'

'With all due respect, sir, I have. We often assume they have valuable intel, that we need to bring them back alive and question them. Maybe even use creative interrogation techniques. But in the end, most of them don't know shit, don't give up shit, and need to be put out with the rest of the garbage. Sir.'

Mitchell paused to consider that. 'Take him alive. If possible. Terminate his command.'

'Roger that, sir.'

'All right then. You and your team will proceed to Tobruk. I've contacted Mohammed Darhoub. He'll meet you at the airport. Darhoub's from the Transitional National Council, their military council rep. I've worked with him before. He's a good guy. He's already offered a platoon of NLA troops.'

'NLA? Is that the National Liberation Army?'

'Exactly. They're the guys who took over after Gaddafi's army fell. Most of them come from the original Free Libyan Army, and I'd say more than half of them are officers who defected from Gaddafi's forces. I wouldn't say they're the highest-caliber operators, but they've got courage in spades. Trust me on that.'

'I will, sir.'

'And oh, yes, in regard to the Fadakno Company. They're an Iranian distributor/wholesaler of valves, flanges, fittings and pipes to the Tobruk Refinery. Their home office is in Tehran.'

'So Hamid is supported by the Iranians?'

'We can't confirm that. The office may be just a front for his operations, and he might've bribed the management team, leaving the Iranian government out of it. That's what I'd do if I were him. Bringing in the Iranians and the Quds Force opens him to security leaks.'

Ross nodded.

Mitchell went on: 'The Tobruk office includes two large warehouses out near the piers. The place is manned by five employees who may or may not be aware of Hamid's operations. Darhoub sent a few men over there, and they'll keep a safe distance for now. He just called to say there's been no unusual activity thus far, just the regular trucks coming to and from the airport, along with cargo being loaded on to ships. They could be smuggling cocaine right now.'

'That's good. Maybe they haven't been tipped off, which means we'll need to move quickly.'

'And we will. I also called the ISA for HUMINT and SIGINT support.'

Mitchell was referring to the United States Army Intelligence Support Activity (aka 'The Activity' or ISA), an Army Spec Ops unit that gathered actionable human and signals intelligence in advance of operations like theirs. They worked for both the regular Special Forces like the Rangers, Delta Force, and SEALs, as well as the GST. They changed their code name every two years, and currently they were known as WOLF'S EAR. Anyone who'd ever worked with them would confirm that they were the unsung heroes of countless operations, providing crucial information and pathfinding in some of the most hostile regions on the planet. They were, arguably, the most underrated, least known group within the Army.

'I'll take all the help I can get,' Ross told the major.

'Good. I'll have transport waiting for you in Bogotá.'

'We won't be late.'

'If there's any change, I'll update you ASAP. Try to get some sleep.'

'Thank you, sir.'

'And Captain, one more thing. I almost forgot to ask. How're you getting along with your new team?'

Ross smiled thinly and stole a look at 30K, who was concentrating on the road. 'These guys are top-notch. Proud to be here, sir.'

Mitchell cocked a brow and scrutinized Ross, who finally crumbled under the major's gaze:

'All right, sir. They don't hate me that much. But honestly, like I told you, this is exactly what I need.'

'Very well then. Good hunting, Captain.'

Ross ended the video call and glanced over at 30K. *'Hal tatakallam al-lughah al-'arabīyah?'*

'Of course I speak Arabic,' 30K answered in English. He then rambled on in what he called 'the ancient tongue,' talking about the weather, the long drive, and even demonstrated that he knew a long list of curse words and vulgar expressions, laughing through them. The GST's language school and his twisted sense of humor had not failed him, he said.

'Good man,' Ross told him. He let his head fall back on the seat. 'I'll be glad to get out of this rain.'

Twenty-Two

The flight from Bogotá to Tobruk, Libya, was approximately 5,600 nautical miles, with a seven-hour time change. The Group for Specialized Tactics had been issued their own dedicated aircraft and pilots, mostly for Close Air Support, but there were always two or three Ospreys or C-130s at their disposal.

Waiting for them in Bogotá was, indeed, a CV-22B Osprey – the US Air Force variant for the US Special Operations command. The tilt-rotor vertical takeoff and landing (VTOL) military transport was primarily used for long-range missions and was equipped with extra fuel tanks and terrain-following radar, along with other special operations equipment such as the AN/ALQ-211, a system that provided detection against radar-guided threats and the cueing of countermeasures like chaff dispensers via integration with the CV-22's entire self-protection suite.

During the interminable flight that involved several midair refueling operations, Pepper scanned through all the intel they'd received on the new target. He reviewed the locations of the airport, the warehouses, the connecting roads (both paved and unpaved), along with a more detailed map of the city. After that, he familiarized himself with the broader area of operations. He'd once had a high school instructor who'd taught American history through scandals and conspiracies, and ever since then, he'd been fascinated with the past.

As it turned out, Tobruk was steeped in military history, most notably at the beginning of World War II, when it had been an Italian colony. The city was strategically important to both the Axis and the Allied powers because of its deep water port. You could bomb the hell out of the place, and yet makeshift piers could be quickly erected to maintain those vital supply lines for the desert warfare campaign. Additionally, the escarpments and cliffs to the south provided a natural bulwark against invaders, allowing the peninsula to be defended by a minimal number of troops who, even if overrun, could more easily cut off an attacking army's supply lines. Finally, just twenty-four kilometers away from the port was the largest airfield in eastern Libya. It was plain to see why so many countries wanted control of the city, its port and the surrounding territory.

Tobruk was indeed captured by British, Australian and Indian forces, then wrenched away by famed Lieutenant-General Erwin Rommel, whose forces held the city for more than a year before they were driven out during the Second Battle of El Alamein. There were a number of World War II cemeteries in Tobruk, including the Commonwealth Cemetery, the English Cemetery, and the French and German Cemeteries.

It was quite a different world now. For some, the port's strategic importance rested squarely on drug smuggling and terrorism instead of military conquest.

Now weary of his studies, Pepper closed his eyes and turned up the volume on his iPod. Johnny Cash's 'God's Gonna Cut You Down' began with its heavy downbeat, quivering guitar, and gruff admonishments from the man in black himself.

Less than forty-eight hours later, that same song was playing in Pepper's head as he raced west toward Tobruk along Libya's main coastal highway toward a heat haze rising like the devil's breath in the distance.

The motorcycle between his legs was a Kawasaki KLR650 with single-cylinder carbureted engine that whined like a lawn mower, but its simplistic design allowed most third-world mechanics with limited means and skills to repair it. The bike had been around since the late eighties, and parts were abundant.

Was Pepper a motorcycle aficionado, well versed in the history of bikes from around the world? Hell, no. He wouldn't have known those obscure details were it not for the garage owner who'd rented him the machine. For some reason, the short, yellow-toothed grease monkey felt the need to 'sell him' on the bike, but Pepper had reassured him that it was perfect and they'd pay double to rent it for a few days. He'd been dropped off at the garage, which was just a kilometer from the airport, and was now headed back toward the port, following the exact same route of the motorcycle courier the team had observed arriving at the warehouse office in the morning, about six hours prior.

Although he still wore the ache of jet lag behind his eyes, the old Ray Bans felt sweet, and the dry desert air was a welcome change from that Colombian rainforest, which had been like walking through loaves of warm bread. He eased on the throttle, checked his rearview mirror, and watched as a truck shimmered up from the black plains behind him.

Ross sat at a small desk, studying satellite images of the warehouses.

Their contact, Darhoub, had provided the basement of an old Italian church within which they'd set up a small command post. The church had peeling plaster walls, a single spire, and was only a five-minute drive from the pier and the Fadakno complex. Once their satellite dish was safely concealed behind the spire, Ross had established communications with Mitchell and had received another set of intel files.

A knock came at the door.

'Come on in.'

'Here he is, sir,' said one of the NLA troops, a lieutenant who escorted the lean, broad-shouldered man into the basement. He was about Ross's age, had wavy, coal-black hair, a week's worth of beard, and wore a T-shirt beneath a dress shirt stained near the buttons. Dust rose up his black pants to the knees, and a cheap

Casio watch hung loosely around his wrist. He looked like one of Darhoub's NLA soldiers out of uniform, but when he opened his mouth, his English was perfect, that of a native speaker, with a slight Southern accent. 'Captain Ross, nice to meet you, sir. I'm Captain Abdul Maziq, ISA.'

Ross turned away from the desk, rose and shook hands. 'Good to see you, Captain.'

'I've just put three observers on the warehouses in addition to Darhoub's men. My local contacts here in Tobruk tell me the warehouses have been here for about five or six years. Trucks come back and forth from the airport; some parts are shipped in and offloaded at the dock, but there are always a number of motorcycle couriers making the airport run. Could be delivering company mail or small parts orders to other customers . . . or at least that's what they want us to believe.'

'One of my operators is on a bike right now.'

Maziq grew wide-eyed and nervous. 'You're sending him in? What's his cover story? What's he look like? Can he —'

'Take it easy, Captain. He's not doing anything. Just following the run. If we need him to pose as one of their couriers, we'll be good to go.'

Maziq sighed deeply. 'Please, Captain, let me do my job first before you make a move.'

'I know the drill. I worked with a few of your buddies in Waziristan.'

'You know Halitov and St Andrew?' Maziq asked.

'I know those guys well.'

Maziq grinned through a thought. 'Damn, it's been a long time since I've seen them.'

'We went through a lot together. Bottom line is they trusted me, and so can you. I'm not here to steal your thunder.'

'Good. Because I'm here to make sure you have yours, so give me some time. I'm working with all the three-letter agencies on signals intel, and that takes a while.'

'Not Langley, though, right?'

He nodded. 'The major was very specific about that, but they've got a man here. I've known about him for a while. We've IDed him as Tamer Abdel Kahlek. They just call him Tamer. I'd like to temporarily shut him down while we conduct our operations, if you understand me correctly.'

'I do. Just get me the intel on him.'

'It's already being sent over. Now, if I'm correct, you have two more operators. Where are they?'

'You getting nervous again?'

Maziq snorted. 'I'm afraid of ghosts, especially the ones who like to shoot first and apologize later.'

Ross's mouth fell open. 'We're, uh, just an ODA team . . .'

'Okay, whatever you say.'

'They told you who we are?'

'I spoke to Mitchell myself. I used to be a Ghost, before you guys became the GST.'

'Wow. He never said anything.'

'It's really not important.'

'So if you don't mind me asking, why'd you leave?'

'The group was changing, there were politics involved, and I just needed something different,' he said with a deep sigh.

'Politics? In the military?' Ross asked, beaming through his sarcasm.

Maziq grinned crookedly. 'I was always good at this part of the job. Couple of guys I knew on ODA teams were recruited by the ISA and ran ops in the 'Stan, so I went for it. Haven't looked back. And I'm happy to support your operations.'

'We're happy to have you. And I understand what you mean about needing something different. I really do.'

'So about your other guys . . .'

Ross checked his watch. 'If I'm right, they're a few hours away from heat stroke, and they're about to call and remind me.'

Twenty-Three

Kozak and 30K had established an observation post on the roof of an old British aircraft hangar at Tobruk Airport. They had donned NLA desert fatigues and were carrying the same weapons as those local troops: AK-47s and Russian TT-30 pistols. The hangar beneath them had been buffeted so severely by the wind and sand that most of its surfaces had been worn smooth, while a thick layer of sand had caked along its sides, allowing it to vanish into the landscape, as though it were some desert animal's burrow rather than a World War II storage facility.

Tobruk Airport was one of many small, third-world airstrips Kozak had visited during his travels. The single main terminal was a meager rectangular box, and of course, if you took a commercial or business-class flight, you had to disembark via roll-up stairs and hike your butt across the tarmac to get out of the heat. Apparently, there had been plans for a big renovation and modernization of the airport before the civil war. Now it might take years before that project was put back on the table. The Libyans had more important things to consider first – such as rebuilding and reinforcing their government.

For his part and much to his satisfaction, Kozak was operating the drone crawler and had flown it over to the end of the runway, where several emergency vehicles were parked. The drone was parked atop the cab of a fire truck, and from there he watched close-up images of the incoming flights, while 30K checked them against the terminal data being sent from Fort Bragg. Analysts there had 'accessed' the terminal's system and drawn the flight data because, wouldn't you know, that data wasn't available on the web, even though it should be public knowledge. Third-world airport to be sure.

'Can't we just leave the drone, have its signal sent to the web, and pick it up from there? This way we can go back to the church and cool off?' asked 30K.

'And if something goes down?' Kozak challenged. 'Our response time would be like what? Twenty minutes? Nah. We gotta be here. Come on, you know you love it. You just like to bitch and moan to pass the time.'

'Yeah, well, even my sweat is sweating right now.'

A dark brown bird with a pale red neck wheeled overhead. Was it a vulture? Yes, it was, waiting for them to keel over.

'We ain't dead yet,' 30K grunted while hoisting his middle finger at the vulture, giving the bird the bird as it were.

Kozak blinked sweat out of his own eyes. 'Whew. Yeah, you're right. It's hot. Ten million sunblock ain't enough. But if you can't take the heat –'

'Hey, remember how I said I'd find Admiral Nimitz's baggage?'

'His name's Ross.'

'Yeah, well, I found it.'

Kozak's eyes never left the remote's screen. 'It's his son.'

'How do you know?'

'Pepper found out. Just drop it.'

'What happened?'

'You told me you knew.'

'Sounded like a bad divorce.'

Kozak shifted over and slapped a palm on 30K's shoulder. 'His little boy died. I don't know how, but I'm asking you as a friend and a colleague to let this go.'

'I'll let it go if I'm sure his head's clear.'

'Are you serious? You think Mitchell would have given him a Ghost Team if he was a basket case? Come on, dude, get real. Ross is as squared away as they come. He's just had bad times – like everyone here.'

'I'm not so sure. Some guys hide it good. But then, when it all goes to hell, they lock up because they weren't clear.'

'It kinda went to hell back in Colombia, and as far as I'm concerned, the captain rocked it. Maybe I should be worried about you. Maybe you're, like, OCD about Ross. Paranoid. Maybe you're going to spend more time watching him instead of keeping your eyes on the primary target.'

30K spoke through his teeth. 'We're trusting that

man with our lives. I want to know – I deserve to know – that his head is in the right place.'

'I could say the same thing of you.'

The sound of plane engines drew Kozak's attention skyward, and there it was, a medium transport with high-mounted wings, boxy fuselage, and a conventional tail. As the drone recorded its final approach, those images were automatically sent to one of the GST's aircraft databases, which automatically scanned them until a match was found, the file displayed in Kozak's HUD:

ID confirmed. CASA C-212 designed and built in Spain for civil and military use. Also manufactured under license by Indonesian Aerospace. Non-pressurized, low-flight-level. Turboprop used in a variety of utility and paramilitary roles due to low cost, large cabin, rear loading ramp.

'I've seen those planes in Afghanistan,' said Kozak. 'I think Blackwater used them for dropping cargo.'

'Yep, looks familiar to me, too. We might want to get down there and put a tracker on it.'

'Why?'

''Cause it ain't on the list. No flight plan filed. Just came in. Landed. Just like that. And you don't see security rushing out to meet the plane, do you? Like they've all been paid off and know about it.'

'Well, that's red flag city right there. I'll call it in.'

After a few words with Ross, Kozak received permission to move in and plant a GPS tracker, along with a listening device (if they could get inside the cabin).

They crawled back to the edge of the hangar's roof and descended a rusting maintenance ladder clinging to the hangar's side wall by only three of the original twenty bolts.

Below lay their dust-covered Tacoma pickup truck, and with sighs of relief to be out of the sun, they both plopped into the cab, wincing over hot seats. Of course there was no air-conditioning, the unit having died some years ago, according to one of the NLA troops who'd loaned them the ride.

They'd counted a total of six airport security guards near the terminal, and several more near the main parking field. Before the war, the Army had a detachment here, but now, with everything in transition, a private firm had taken over, at least temporarily, but they were poorly staffed and probably even more poorly trained.

Nevertheless, Kozak and 30K had still chosen a stealthy approach, coming in from the south, along a low-lying dirt road with the old British hangar and a few scattered fig trees shielding them from view.

As they followed the same path out, Kozak recalled the drone while 30K steered them toward a row of seven Quonset-shaped hangars situated on the north side of the runway. The hangars were large enough to house medium-size aircraft like the C-212, were constructed of aluminum, and were, like the old British hangar, heavily weathered by the sun and sand. The C-212 was already taxiing along a road leading out to them, and its pilot would, they assumed, pull inside one of the hangars or park in the lot behind.

'That security team will see us now,' said Kozak. 'No way around it.'

'I'm not worried about them.'

'Well, let's see what they do.'

After a few seconds, 30K blurted out, 'Hey, before we leave this country, remind me to get us some magrood.'

'What is it? Libyan whiskey or something?'

'No, you Cossack. It's a date-filled cookie. They're so good. Probably the only good thing in this whole shitty sandbox.'

'You've been here before?'

'Been to Tripoli a couple of times. Got 'em in the airport. Hey, look, he's turning inside.'

The C-212 slipped into the last hangar on the right, and 30K veered suddenly off the road to park beside the first hangar. Whether it was the time, the heat of the day, or even the day of the week, Kozak wasn't sure, but the place looked dead. No activity at all, all the other hangar doors shut tight, no cars around, nada.

He and 30K were about to get out when a black airport security jeep rolled up and out hopped the puppy patrol. They must have been waiting for them behind one of the hangars to launch their 'ambush.'

The fatter guard with a button missing at his navel

shook his head, three chins wagging, and said, 'Who did you piss off to get assigned here?'

'No one,' said 30K in Arabic. 'Mohammed Darhoub, military advisor of Transitional Council, asked us to come out here and observe you. So far your security is bullshit and your men are filthy whores. We were up on that old hangar all day, and not one of your stupid bastards spotted us. What kind of sorry-ass shit is that?'

The fat man's eyes grew glassy, and he regarded his partner, a guy who looked like he hadn't eaten in a month. 'We got no reports of this?' he cried.

'I'm sorry, sir.'

'I'll tell you what,' said 30K. 'You guys look like you're trying your best, and it's really hot out here, so why don't you head back? I'll tell our boss you picked us up at the hangars and were right on it. But you can't tell anyone we were here or that I'm cutting you a favor, okay?'

The fat man rolled his eyes. 'Okay. Just promise me. Don't say shit.'

30K smiled. 'Get out of here.'

They climbed into their vehicle and, with a fart of exhaust, rumbled off.

'Dude, that was crazy,' Kozak told him.

'You spend enough time in bars, talking to people, bullshitting, practising how to intimidate people, and it all pays off.'

'I thought you did most of your negotiating with your fists.'

A gleam came into his eyes. 'Sometimes the negotiations break down. Let's roll.'

Kozak followed 30K along a path behind the hangars. They kept tight to the walls and avoided the windows mounted within a few of the back doors. When they reached Hangar 7, the sound of a diesel engine rumbled past the thin walls, and before they could react, the vehicle pulled out – a nondescript twenty-four-foot-long cargo truck, not unlike a U-Haul rental.

Out of reflex, Kozak reached into his holster and let fly the drone. He immediately got the bird in place behind the truck to get a tag number and description, sending real-time video back to Ross.

The words *Al jamahiriya*, which were used by Gaddafi to refer to Libya and to argue for his ideologies, were embedded on all vehicle registration plates, and they were present on this truck's tag as well.

'Good work, Kozak. Keep that intel coming,' said Ross.

Before the driver or anyone else was the wiser, he recalled the drone, then he and 30K shifted furtively to the front of the hangar, whose main doors had been left open. Kozak peered around the corner, holding his breath.

Inside lay the plane, and along the left wall were parked four more cargo trucks identical to the first.

Suddenly, voices echoed from inside, and from the corner of his eye Kozak spotted an airplane mechanic in greasy coveralls striding across the hangar toward the airplane, with a second mechanic in tow. Kozak gave 30K the hand signal, and they fell back behind the open doors.

'We're putting a lot of time into this hangar,' Kozak said. 'You sure about this?'

'They got the plane, the trucks, no flight plan, come on, dude, what do you need? A sign that says, "We Smuggle Cocaine for Less"?'

'Okay, you're right.'

'Of course, I'm right. Now they'll track that truck with the satellite. If it arrives at the warehouse, bingo, we're good to go,' said 30K.

'What now?'

'Can you get the crawler in there so we can eavesdrop?'

Kozak hoisted his brows. 'I got a better idea.'

Twenty-Four

Pepper pulled up behind the old church, switched off the motorcycle, then headed down the back staircase to the basement entrance. He knocked twice, then said, 'Delta Dragon.' The door opened and one of the NLA troops allowed him inside. He passed through a narrow, dimly lit hallway toward an office on the right, where Ross glanced up from his desk.

'I thought you signed on to see the world, not sit behind a computer.'

Ross chuckled under his breath. 'Can't say I mind a little recon, though. More boring but less dangerous.'

'No doubt. What do we got?'

'30K and Kozak spotted a small cargo plane at the airport. Pulled in a hangar. Pilot seems to have taken a truck. Might be headed here.'

'Good deal. Cargo traffic to and from the airport is fairly high, so that's nothing unusual. We need to see what's inside that truck.'

Ross nodded. 'How's the bike?'

'Pretty sweet for an old girl. You link up with the guy from the ISA?'

'Yeah, Abdul Maziq.'

Pepper grinned in recognition. 'Hell, I know Maziq. We go way back.'

'Yeah, he told me he was a Ghost.'

'Where is he?'

'He's tracking down a problem.'

'What now?'

'Old spooky's in town.'

'How many?'

'Just one for now. Once Maziq locates him, you and I need to address this. Let's call it a security leak.'

Pepper lifted his brows. 'Sir, I can't wait.'

'We need to be careful. Just take him out of the equation temporarily until we're long gone.'

'How you wanna do it? Old school or new?'

Ross frowned. 'Do I look new school?'

'That's what I thought.' Pepper showed Ross his best evil-minded grin.

'However,' Ross quickly added, holding up an index finger. 'We're gonna have to do this new school. I won't break the law or violate the rules of engagement.'

Pepper nodded. 'That'll make things a little more difficult . . . and dangerous.'

Ross smiled broadly. 'I was going to say more *interesting*.'

Kozak was trembling with excitement. 'Dude, this is the first time any Ghost Team has fielded this baby. This is one small step for a kid from Brooklyn, one giant leap –'

'Man, kill the theatrics. That thing looks like it'll break from just staring at it too hard. How much it cost? A million bucks?'

'I don't know. Why are you so negative?'

'Because we fight with guns – not shit you find on Aisle 5 of Toys "R" Us.'

'Oh, this isn't a toy,' Kozak argued, staring wide-eyed. 'Say hello to my little friend.'

In his palm sat a MUAV, or Micro Unmanned Aerial Vehicle. Shaped like a dragonfly, the battery-operated ornithopter remained aloft for ninety minutes by flapping its translucent wings as its tiny camera transmitted sound and images back to Kozak's cell phone. A smartphone application allowed him to pilot the craft and record its operations. Kozak considered the Dragonfly a 'close quarters drone,' and with the push of his right thumb, the MUAV hummed softly and flew away toward the roof of the hangar, then descended to zip inside.

'Those geeks got too much time on their hands,' said 30K, his mouth falling open as Kozak showed him the camera images piped in from the tiny craft:

The two mechanics were discussing something near the plane, while Kozak flew the drone past them and into an office area cordoned off with cubicle walls. There on the desk were inventory lists and shipping manifests with the Fadakno logo at the top, everything written in Arabic. Kozak hovered over them and began taking snapshots.

'You know what's even more cool?' he asked 30K. 'The fact that there really are dragonflies here in Libya, so even if these guys spot the drone, they'll just think it's a bug.'

'So you're a bug pilot. That make you feel proud?'

'Yeah, it does. Now shut up.'

Kozak worked his thumbs on the screen, and the Dragonfly ascended and wheeled back toward the mechanics, who were now standing atop a rolling ladder and gaining access to the plane's starboard side engine. Kozak kept a safe distance and decided to have the Dragonfly alight on the fuselage just above them.

Once the drone was in place and stable, he zoomed in on the men and turned up the cell phone's volume.

The conversation was so dull that Kozak fought to keep his eyes open. They said nothing that would betray them, argued over who'd last serviced the plane, and then got to work.

'I'm going in with the blanket,' 30K said. 'Or if you like, I can just walk in there with another story.'

'Whoa, whoa, whoa. Slow down,' Kozak began. 'You're going in? What're you going to say?'

'I'll feel them out. I'll say how pissed off Hamid is, that this poor aircraft maintenance is ridiculous, and Hamid was mad enough to send us here with orders to kill them if they don't fix it.'

Kozak gave him a look. 'Why don't you run that idea by Ross?'

30K frowned.

'If you're talking to them, how're you supposed to plant the tracker?'

'That's where you come in.'

'I don't like it.'

30K threw up his hands. 'The blanket it is.'

'Let's just wait.'

'Wait here all night?'

Kozak narrowed his gaze. 'They'll be done soon.'

'In the time it's taken to have this conversation, I could've been in and out.'

30K breathed deeply and cursed as he slipped off his pack. He tugged out their Cross-Coms, handed one to Kozak, and donned the other headset. Next he removed the optical camouflage blanket and computer, which was about the size of an external hard drive and communicated wirelessly with the blanket. He slipped the computer into his breast pocket, then pulled the blanket over his head. He now resembled a weird Libyan Jedi Master.

'Camouflage active,' he said. The computer read his voice command, and he vanished, save for his face, now a sweaty, disembodied mask floating beside the hangar.

'If they spot you,' Kozak warned.

'If they spot me, they ain't gonna be around long enough to sound the alarm.'

'Oh, and that's zero footprint, huh?'

30K rolled his eyes. 'Hey, they *won't* spot me.'

Kozak's breath shortened as his teammate shifted toward the entrance, the blanket flickering.

'Jimmy,' Kozak whispered.

30K turned back.

'Be careful.'

30K smirked and rounded the corner, the air where he'd just passed bending like a rift in the space-time continuum.

Twenty-Five

It was an old Libyan fishing trawler moored at the marina for who knew how long, and when Ross lowered his binoculars and glanced over at Maziq, the man was typing furiously on his laptop computer. Pepper, who was hunkered down beside Ross on the church's rooftop, gave a curt nod and said, 'If you want to go new school, then Kozak's our man for this. Pair him up with Maziq and cut 'em loose. I can use one of the drones and run surveillance on the trawler. I'll give them the signal if and when he leaves.'

Ross thought about that plan as he raised his binoculars and zoomed in on the boat once more. She was a medium-size trawler, about eighty feet, with a meager boom and dark red stains running down from her hawse pipe. Her pocket-shaped nets lay piled on her deck, and judging from their faded appearance, they hadn't been used in some time. Perhaps the trawler's owner had just moored her there and walked away from the boat and his business, who knew. For the past thirty minutes there'd been no movement within or around the vessel, although Ross had thought he'd seen someone near a window of the navigation bridge, but a second look proved him wrong.

According to Maziq's intel, Tamer, the CIA man they needed to 'neutralize,' had set up shop on the boat because it offered an unobstructed view of the Fadakno warehouses.

'Pepper, I like your plan,' said Ross. 'The only problem is this – if I'm Tamer, I don't go anywhere without my computer, and if we're going to compromise the information he's receiving from Langley, then we sure as hell need access to that computer.'

Pepper squinted into the distance. 'I've been thinking about that. It's complicated, but there's a way to make that happen. We just need Maziq to call in a few favors.'

'What did you have in mind?'

30K used one hand to hold the blanket tightly at his chin as he shifted quickly behind two natural-gas-powered forklifts parked beside stacks of wooden shipping pallets. Beside them lay rows of small boxes printed with the Fadakno logo. The mechanics were on the other side of the plane, standing atop their ladder, with the fuselage blocking 30K from their view.

Kozak, who was observing the entire hangar via the Dragonfly, spoke softly to 30K as he moved: 'Okay, bro. You're still clear.'

30K took a deep breath, left the wall, and began to cross the open area between the pallets and the plane – just five meters between himself and the forward landing gear.

'Dude, wait!' Kozak whispered loudly.

One of the mechanics came trudging down the ladder, wiping his hands on a greasy rag and shouting back to his buddy about what an incompetent asshole he was and how he had a good mind to just walk out on him.

The man crossed to a small workbench, fished around in a box of tools, then turned back toward the plane with several socket wrenches in his hands. He took about three steps –

Then froze, staring in 30K's direction.

'Oh, shit,' said Kozak. 'Do *not* move.'

Twenty-Six

While Ross, Pepper and Maziq were observing the fishing trawler, two late-model sedans that Ross assumed were rentals pulled up outside the Fadakno office. Out stepped a group of four well-dressed men, who, unbeknownst to them, were being observed by many eyes, including an electro-optical one flying in an elliptical orbit approximately 175 miles over their heads.

Each man was photographed as accurately as possible, the images instantaneously run through facial recognition databases for biometric tagging, part of what the military called TTL – Tagging, Tracking and Locating, which was further qualified by the designations 'Hostile Forces' (HF) or 'Clandestine or Continuous' (C) tracking.

Three of the faces came up empty for any criminal records, all of them Colombian nationals, but the fourth was positively IDed as Alfonso Valencia, a man well known and highly sought after by Colombian law enforcement.

Valencia was a graduate of the National University of Colombia in Medicine. Not long after receiving his degree, he left the country to continue his studies in Cuba and Mexico, and he remained abroad for more than eight years. He eventually returned to Colombia, where he was recruited by the FARC through his brother-in-law and rose up quickly through their ranks because of his professional experience. He was selected for the higher command, joining more than thirty top guerilla leaders, including the seven members of the secretariat, which included the group's commander in chief. Valencia established and helped organize the FARC's mobile medical facilities throughout the jungle regions. His presence in Tobruk struck Ross as unusual, unless he'd recently assumed new duties that involved drug smuggling.

'Captain,' Pepper called from behind his binoculars. 'Check out the trawler.'

Ross did, and through an open porthole hung a man eclipsed by his own binoculars, a man Maziq confirmed was Tamer. He, too, was watching the arrival of the FARC representatives.

Ross's pulse rose as he contacted Mitchell. They had confirmation that the FARC were in Libya and connected to Fadakno. Boom.

'If you go in heavy now, the rabbit hole caves in,' Mitchell warned him. 'Keep gathering intel. We're getting closer. Obviously, we'll need to tag a shipment and see where it goes. I want all the key players IDed before we drop the hammer.'

'Roger that, sir.' Ross then shared their 'dilemma' with the other three-letter agency in the area.

'I agree you need to eliminate that leak, but we don't

want a situation. You cannot break the law – as much as we'd both like to do that right now.'

'Before I overthink this, sir, I have to ask: Do you think we can just get Tamer recalled? Have him re-assigned to Tripoli or Cairo? That would save me at least one headache.'

'Sure thing,' Mitchell said, his sarcasm unmistakable. 'I'll call over to the Special Activities Division and say we got 'em covered. Send their boy home and save tax dollars.'

'All right, sir, I understand. I thought it wouldn't hurt to ask. You always check under the mat before you pick the lock, right?'

Mitchell's lips curled in a slight grin. 'That truck that left the airport should arrive soon. It's registered to Fadakno. If it parks at the warehouses, and it should, then we have at least one export route and vehicle established. Do we have a tracker on that plane?'

'Kozak and 30K are working on it.'

'Good. Keep me updated as usual. Guardian, out.'

'Captain, we got something else here that's kind of interesting,' called Pepper. 'It's a kid coming out of the main office.'

Ross watched the wiry teenager with shaggy hair climb aboard a bicycle he'd parked out of view behind the office. He rode away, past the FARC vehicles. 'Maziq, who's the kid?'

'Darhoub's men told me he's just a delivery boy. Brings lunch to the warehouse employees every day.'

'Oh, he's bringing them lunch,' said Pepper. 'But that's not his only job.'

'No, it's not,' Ross agreed.

Pepper pointed. 'Here's my take: that kid is a field agent recruited by Mr Tamer, our local spook.'

'I'd agree,' said Maziq. 'The boy is gathering intel for him.'

The kid reached the pier, and although he didn't turn out toward the marina where the fishing trawler was moored, he gave a look in that direction.

Ross stiffened. He loathed missions where kids were involved. When he was operating in Waziristan, he'd had little choice but to pay off many young boys to plant beacons inside the homes of known Taliban leaders so that those targets could be marked for drone strikes. Of the five or six he'd recruited, all of them had performed their missions expertly. All except one. Kid named Ali. He'd been caught in the act. They found what was left of him just outside the Forward Operating Base's gate. They'd left him there to send a message.

At the same time, the Taliban mullahs were forcibly recruiting nine-year-olds to become suicide bombers, and Ross had encountered several of them in his travels, innocent children brainwashed into throwing their lives away . . .

The memories turned his stomach. He closed his eyes and fought hard against a sudden flood of images.

His boy . . . his little boy . . .

Twenty-Seven

'All right,' said Kozak. 'Clear to move. Go . . .'

30K shifted over to the forward landing gear and paused once again.

'Still clear,' Kozak reported.

Rising so that the blanket fully obscured him, 30K placed the tracker up high in the undercarriage, where it would remain in place via trusty 3M tape and magnets. The tracker was about the size of an iPod Classic and weighed about the same.

30K wasn't through yet. He wanted to get a listening device in the cabin; however, the mechanics had not opened any doors nor had they lowered the rear cargo hatch. He considered planting the device within one of the stacks of cargo, which assumedly would be loaded on to the plane.

'What are you doing?' asked Kozak. 'You're done. Get out of there.'

30K took a deep breath.

'Just got a call from the boss,' Kozak added. 'He wants us back. Come on . . . get out of there.'

Half-assed wasn't the way he rolled, but if planting the listening the device meant creating a diversion and possibly blowing his cover, then his little brother was right. Gritting his teeth, he slipped back, out of the hangar, and met up with Kozak outside.

'This sucks. I only got the tracker on the plane.'

'That's good enough.'

'What's going on?'

'Stuff at the warehouse. I'll tell you on the way back.'

They jogged away from the hangar and were breathless by the time they reached their pickup truck. 30K seized the wheel and tore off, rumbling back on to the highway and toward the port.

He checked the rearview mirror, where dust clouds whipped behind the truck. For now, they were the only car on the desert highway.

But within five minutes they were passing several other shipping trucks heading back toward the airport, along with another motorcycle carrier.

Twenty-Eight

The truck driven by the C-212 pilot arrived at the Fadakno warehouses at sunset. Ross was frustrated because they'd failed to capture a distinct image of the man before he'd slipped into the main office, remained there for about ten minutes, then left in a car belonging to one of the employees.

Two of Darhoub's men, along with Pepper, followed the pilot to the posh and updated Hotel al-Massira, and Maziq went to work accessing the hotel's computer system, although Ross suspected that their pilot had fake credentials and had checked in under a false name.

One of Maziq's local operatives, a man who worked at the refinery, was sent out to keep tabs on the delivery boy, who turned out to be the son of a local restaurant owner, the place famous for its lamb and seafood, Maziq reported.

Their NLA observers, along with Maziq's men, had nothing to report from the trawler. CIA agent Tamer was either still there or had found a way to leave the boat without being seen.

Now, with everyone back at the church, Ross assembled the team in the basement and made an announcement: 'We're going in tonight. The warehouses are protected by motion trackers and surveillance cameras – nothing too difficult for a localized power outage to bring down. We'll use an EMP strike to fry the cameras and trackers. We go in light, just pistols with suppressors. I don't want a single shot fired. Not a single shot.'

Maziq lifted an index finger. 'I assume Tamer will be out of the equation by this time.'

'That's correct.'

'How?'

Ross smiled, then glanced over at Kozak. 'You ready?'

'Hell, yeah.'

Ross then faced Maziq. 'Okay, bro, here's how.'

Deploying the MUAV back at the airport hangar was, according to Ross, a stroke of genius, because it gave him an excellent idea of how to conduct reconnaissance inside the fishing trawler and pinpoint exactly where Tamer had set up his command post. Kozak was more than pleased with that assessment (most particularly the phrase 'stroke of genius'), and for his part he now was seated inside a car parked outside the marina and piloting the Dragonfly above the trawler and toward one of the open portholes on the ship's starboard side.

However, before he directed the drone inside the boat, something caught his attention, and he pulled up, steering the Dragonfly into a wide turn, then banking around to spot the restaurant delivery boy Ross had mentioned. Kozak was wearing his Cross-Com and issued his report.

'He's right on time. Good boy,' said Ross. 'See how close you can get, and patch me in to the signal.'

'Roger that.' Kozak then called out to his buddy: '30K, you're good to go.'

'Roger, bro, on my way.'

Kozak watched as the boy pedaled to the end of the pier, then got off and leaned his ride against one of the moorings. He removed a small box from his bike's rear basket and hiked it up the gangway.

Tamer, a bony man probably in his thirties with a bald pate, a closely cropped beard, and an unfortunate nose, came on to the gangway and accepted the package. He handed the boy a stack of blue, red and green dinar notes.

Kozak brought the Dragonfly down to the railing, just above and behind them, and with the waves lapping softly at the trawler's hull, the drone's buzzing wings went unnoticed.

'Thank you again for dinner. What else do you have for me today?' Tamer asked in Arabic.

'I heard them talking about the pilot, and a new shipment going out in the morning.'

'What about Delgado? Did you hear the name "Delgado"?'

'No, I did not.'

'This new shipment. Did they say what time it will go out?'

'No, just in the morning.'

'And where is it headed?'

'Sudan.'

'Anything else I should know?'

'Not that I can remember. That's all I heard.'

'Are you sure?'

'Yes. Your dinner is getting cold.'

'Bady, is there anything else you want to tell me?'

The kid shrugged.

'You're certain that no one else has tried to talk to you?'

'No.'

Tamer's voice grew menacing. 'Why are you lying to me, Bady?'

The kid took a step back.

'Come on, inside the boat,' said Tamer. 'We need to talk about this.'

'I can't,' Bady answered. 'I have to go.'

Ross and Pepper had met up with the boy at his father's restaurant, and they had explained to him and his father that he could no longer work for Tamer, that it was much too dangerous, and that they would offer him one final payment to deliver Tamer his dinner and then never come back.

The boy's father was ready to beat him because he

had known nothing of this, and Ross and Pepper defended him, saying that this was very common, that the boy was only trying to help his father with the extra money, and that they were here to help.

Bady, crying and scared, agreed to make the last delivery, and Ross figured this would be the break they needed. The kid would delay Tamer long enough for Kozak to get the Dragonfly inside and help guide 30K to his destination.

But now, as Ross crouched on the church's rooftop and watched Bady step back from Tamer, he knew the plan had suddenly and irrevocably gone south.

30K was floating soundlessly in the water at the trawler's stern. While Tamer was talking with the kid, 30K had tossed up a line and hook that had caught the gunwale with only the slightest thump since the hook was coated with heavy rubber.

Kozak had just given him the word, so he'd ascended the rope, come over the gunwale, and shifted across the deck to crouch down beside a ladder attached to the docking bridge.

He was waiting for Kozak to guide him directly to Tamer's computer while the man was distracted with the kid outside. To be even safer, 30K had changed into his Ghost fatigues with the Velcro patches removed so he'd have access to his optical camouflage and avoid the more cumbersome blanket. The camouflage was active, and he'd faded into the shadows. Clutched in his right hand was his familiar and reliable FN Five-seven with attached suppressor.

'Kozak, what's the delay, man? Come on, I'm ready.'

'Wait, dude, something's wrong.'

Kozak was losing his breath as Tamer took another step toward Bady.

'There's no reason to lie,' said Tamer. 'I know some other men came to you. They're my friends. Come with me now.'

'I told you I can't.'

'What did those men say?'

Bady was panting now. 'They . . . they told me I can't work for you anymore. They told me it's too dangerous.'

'Captain, are you hearing this?' Kozak asked.

'Yeah, stand by.'

'So, Bady,' Tamer said. 'Why didn't you just tell me about them?'

'I was afraid.'

Tamer glanced up, his gaze scanning the marina and surrounding buildings. 'Are they watching us now?'

'I don't know.'

Tamer seized Bady by the wrist and began to drag him up and on to the deck. 'You're coming with me.'

Kozak spoke quickly into his boom mike: 'Tamer must've had an informant at the restaurant. He knows we're on to him.'

*

Up on the church's rooftop, Ross glanced over at Maziq, who said, 'Send in Darhoub's troops.'

Ross gave the order, then switched to the team net: '30K? Get the boy! Now!'

'On my way,' the man answered.

'Oh my God!' cried Kozak.

Ross craned his head, and what he saw through his night-vision lens stole his breath.

Twenty-Nine

30K charged across the deck and toward the gangway.

Meanwhile, on the shoreline, the NLA troops burst from their observation positions and came rushing toward the trawler, rifles raised.

Kozak would later say that the blade in Tamer's hand seemed to come from nowhere. It flashed once in the dim light before the agent plunged it home in the boy's chest. The kid was falling back as Kozak screamed and Ross gave 30K the order to move in.

30K gritted his teeth. The rules of this game had suddenly changed. Tamer had committed a crime, and the Ghosts were now free to assist the NLA troops in capturing him.

'30K, we need Tamer alive,' Ross reminded him.

'Understood,' he spat, then swore under his breath.

Not two seconds after Tamer killed the boy – and seeing that the NLA troops were moving in – the little runt scurried back across the deck, through an open door, and disappeared into the navigation bridge.

30K was only a few heartbeats behind.

A dark passageway lay before him.

Then a sound from above, someone scaling a ladder just a few steps away.

He seized the rungs, rushed up –

Arriving breathlessly in the trawler's bridge, dimly lit by several battery-powered lights.

And there, near the main controls, was Tamer, initiating a rapid-fire sequence of keystrokes on his computer.

'Hold it,' 30K said in Arabic.

Tamer did not turn back.

Two more NLA troops rushed in behind 30K, along with Kozak.

'Get your hands off the keyboard!' screamed 30K.

Tamer kept banging away.

'I said stop!'

Tamer typed even faster now.

Well, the boss had said they needed Tamer *alive*. There had been no mention of *unharmed*.

30K shot him in the leg, and when the man whirled back to face 30K, he had a pistol in his hand.

But it wasn't pointed at 30K.

Tamer lifted the weapon to his own head, and 30K practically leaped toward the man, shouting, 'No, no, no!'

The gunshot was deafening inside the bridge, the windows sprayed with blood as though from a powerful hose. 30K caught the agent as he was collapsing to the floor, his limbs twisting at improbable angles.

Kozak rushed around 30K and went directly to the laptop. 'He's erased the entire drive, all the files, the whole nine.' Smoke began pouring from the keyboard.

'Holy shit, acid bomb, too,' said Kozak, beginning to cough.

30K checked Tamer for a pulse – a formality to be sure. At least the little bastard was proficient at suicide.

'This guy . . .' Kozak began, thinking aloud. 'He's gotta be dirty, killing the kid, man . . . He's in bed with Delgado probably. He didn't bolt because he wanted to question the kid, see how bad his own leak was. Shit . . .'

30K stood and backhanded something off his cheek. Blood. 'What a mess,' he grunted.

They stood there for a few seconds, just collecting themselves and staring down at Tamer until 30K took a deep breath, cleared his throat, then shared the grim news with Ross and Pepper.

'Clean it all up and get out of there ASAP. Do it now,' snapped Ross.

30K looked to Kozak. 'Get me something to wrap around this bastard's head so he doesn't bleed all over me.' Then 30K regarded the NLA troops and added in Arabic, 'Get outside and get the boy. Get him back to the church.'

The two troops nodded and rushed off.

'This was going to be so beautiful,' said Kozak. 'We'd hack into his computer, send him misinformation, order him out of here, and keep him in the dark the entire time. It was going to be sophisticated and high-tech, not a friggin' bloodbath.'

'Like you said, he had people watching that restaurant like a hawk. You can have all the toys in the world, but they don't beat a pair of eyes on a target – and there's no way to tell which set of eyes was watching. Could've been anybody in or around that restaurant. It was a calculated risk. They took it. And now look at what we got.'

'Well, our hands are clean. I got the boy's murder on video. Nobody can say shit,' said Kozak.

30K regarded Tamer's body. 'What about his suicide?'

'Cross-Com got that.'

'So then yeah, I guess you're right,' said 30K. 'We're clean. And our CIA leak has been plugged for now. But man, that poor kid . . .'

'Yeah,' said Kozak, his voice cracking now. 'I can't get him out of my head.'

'Me, too.'

Back in the church's basement office, Ross asked for a moment alone as he pulled back the blanket and stared down at the boy's face, now cast in a deepening pallor.

His first thought hadn't been how they'd cover up this mess; it'd been how they would tell the boy's father. Ross felt responsible and wanted to do that himself, but Mitchell would never allow that.

The boy, like many others during wartime, would simply vanish, and his father would mourn silently and avoid seeking help from the authorities because he'd fear retribution. When he'd learned for the first time what his son was doing, Ross had seen it in the old man's eyes: the impending danger, the thought that maybe my boy is already dead. A resignation.

And now, they couldn't even return the boy's body because of the security risks. It'd have to be 'taken care of' so that no evidence remained. The NLA troops would handle all of that. Meanwhile, Maziq would have the unenviable task of preparing Tamer's corpse for transport.

Ross put his hand on the boy's forehead, and he was wrenched back to Virginia Beach, to 14 August, a day he could not revisit now. Not now.

He slipped the blanket back over Bady's head, then left the office and returned to his men, who were waiting for him near the basement door.

'We're not sure if he called the Agency or not,' said Ross. 'But either way, our plans remain the same. We're going in tonight.'

'What about lunch?' asked 30K.

The question caught Ross off guard. 'Lunch? It's ten now. We'll hit the warehouses at 2 a.m. Why are you thinking about lunch?'

'I mean the kid. He delivered lunch every day to employees in the warehouse. He ain't gonna show up tomorrow.'

'Can't worry about it,' said Ross. 'Getting another kid or trying to put some other Band-Aid on that could be worse. They'll call the restaurant, the boy will be missing, and we'll leave it at that. It's a loose end that might be too risky to tie up.'

'How 'bout some good news?' Pepper asked wearily. 'I'm sure we could all use it. I heard back from the guys I left at the hotel. The pilot decided to have dinner, and we finally got some good pictures of him. I forwarded them back home, and we just received the ID.'

'Who is he?' asked Ross.

Pepper slipped a tablet computer from his armpit and read from the screen: 'Bakri Takana. He's a former Sudanese pilot who saw action in Darfur. Experienced combat jock overqualified for drug smuggling. He's probably a freelancer hired by our guys.'

Ross nodded and faced the group. 'All right. Let's see what Mr Takana plans to fly out of here in the morning.'

Thirty

A long raft of clouds obscured the waning moon and left the port in a deeper darkness.

A haunted darkness.

Few lights shone in the windows of the office and apartment buildings behind them as Ross, Pepper, Kozak, and 30K fanned out and moved down the shoreline road leading to the pier and warehouses. The Mediterranean was a sheet of smoked glass, and somewhere out there, a buoy flashed.

With the sea's dank scent now filling his nostrils, Ross reached the rear wall of the two-story building behind the warehouses, a nondescript facility with no security, signs, or other identifying markers of any kind, but one their intel had identified as a warehouse for medical supplies once supported and run by the old Gaddafi regime. Ross paused as the team reported in:

'Ghost Lead, this is Kozak. Sensor out, in position. Contacts marked.'

'Roger that.'

Pepper and 30K reported the same.

'Ghost Team, continue the sweep.'

'Maziq?' Ross called over the command net. 'Cut the power.'

'Roger that. Stand by.'

Maziq had recruited two engineers from the NLA to cut the power to several blocks along the pier. In the past, the power was often turned off at night anyway, and both brown- and blackouts were not unusual occurrences.

Ross shifted around the corner, and with his Cross-Com he zoomed in on the Fadakno office's security camera mounted over the front door. The red status light winked off. And three, two, one, it returned, operating on battery backup.

'Power's down,' said Maziq. 'Ghost Lead? Confirm.'

'Confirmed,' said Ross. 'Ghost Team? Everybody out of the zone?'

The men checked in. They were.

'Clear to drop EMP. Stand by.'

Ross withdrew the cylindrical EMP grenade from his web gear, pulled the pin, and hurled it toward the office's front door, just outside of the camera's view as it was panning toward the south corner.

The grenade, technically a flux compression generator bomb, was a metal cylinder surrounded by a coil of wire called a 'stator winding.' The cylinder was filled with high explosive surrounded by a jacket, and the stator winding and cylinder were separated by empty space. A bank of capacitors was attached to the stator, and a switch connected the capacitors to that stator, sending an electrical current through the wires to generate an intense magnetic field.

As the grenade hit the ground, a fuse ignited the explosive material, and the explosion traveled up through the middle of the cylinder, coming in contact with the stator winding and creating a short circuit that in turn cut off the stator from its power supply. This moving short circuit compressed the magnetic field to create an intense non-nuclear electromagnetic pulse that rendered useless all electronics within a prescribed target radius.

A faint thud came from near the door, followed by another sound, like static from a broken television.

The security camera's status light winked out once more; it remained black.

'Ghosts? Move out,' Ross ordered.

Each of the two Fadakno warehouses was approximately ten thousand square feet, with about a thousand square feet dedicated to secondary offices in addition to the main office building (no bigger than a double-wide trailer) situated between them. Each structure had fourteen-foot ceilings with several windows that had either been tinted or painted black from the inside. Two loading dock doors and a third door with a concrete ramp that allowed vehicles to drive straight inside were located at the far ends.

Based on his own experience trying to get into the minds of his enemies, 30K had voiced his concerns about the lack of security outside the buildings. He'd told Ross that despite the cameras, if those boys had something to hide and protect, they wouldn't leave it alone overnight, cameras and motion sensors notwith-standing. Sure, the place might appear to be minimally guarded (in an effort not to call attention to themselves), but they should, 30K had strongly argued, expect to find company inside. Heavily armed company.

He reached the front door and glanced back at the shimmer in the air behind him: Kozak under his cam-ouflage. While they entered the east warehouse, Pepper and Ross would take the west.

Standard door lock. Piece of cake. Most companies could not machine their parts to near flawless toler-ances and still make money; therefore, men like 30K with intentions of bypassing said locks exploited those manufacturing shortcomings with a few simple tools.

The lock opened. However, before opening, 30K fished out a tiny pump bottle of lube and drenched the door's hinges to be sure they wouldn't creak. That done, he glanced back to Kozak. 'You ready, bro?' he whispered.

'Let's do it.'

Wincing, 30K tugged open the door, and it opened effortlessly. He shifted inside, waited a moment, then shut the door, the darkness turning to liquid as Kozak passed him.

Rows of shelving stretched off into the shadows like monoliths lined up on a moonscape, and now voices echoed from somewhere on the other end, near the loading docks.

Were they speaking Arabic? He wasn't sure.

'We've got contact inside,' 30K whispered over the team net.

'Roger that, so do we,' said Ross. 'We confirm that the truck isn't here. Must be in your warehouse. Move in on it now.'

30K turned to Kozak and gave him a hand signal.

Time to earn their keep.

Thirty-One

To the casual eye, everything about the warehouse appeared legitimate, from the hundreds of various-size boxes stored on rows of steel industrial shelves to the orders packed on shipping pallets with attached invoices, the boxes stacked two meters high and bound together by clear stretch wrap.

At least twenty such pallets were lined up near the loading dock doors, and these commanded Ross's attention. He gave the signal for Pepper to lead them silently toward them, his Cross-Com displaying the current positions of the guards.

Ross had assumed that the three men inside were either ex-police or military, hired from the local population – but once they began speaking in Spanish, he concluded they were FARC troops, trucked in under cover each night to guard the shipments from the inside, thus drawing little attention from the locals. They were armed with compact Skorpion submachine guns procured from local stockpiles. They were probably aware of the clandestine shipping operation but weren't told much else, lest they be captured.

At the moment, the men were understandably confused, arguing over whether they should remain in place or venture out to see why the power had gone down. One remarked that his cell phone no longer worked and he was concerned that something very bad had taken place, perhaps at the capitol. Perhaps something nuclear. Ross smiled inwardly. Their imaginations were running wild. They began to fight over whether or not they should contact their buddies in the next warehouse, and one said he'd run over there to see what was happening.

Ross patched his own Cross-Com's signal into 30K's heads-up display so that the man could see the red outlined image of the guard hustling from the warehouse and moving toward him with a small flashlight in hand.

'Got 'em, boss. No worries.'

'Roger, stay sharp.'

There'd been some discussion of a plan to lure the guards out of the warehouses prior to the team entering, but once again, the fewer occurrences out of the norm, the better. The power outage and subsequent EMP burst were all Ross was willing to risk. Mitchell's intent was clear: They were to identify and tag a cargo shipment heading back to that plane and get out before these six men knew what was happening. The team needed to do that right under the guards' noses via technology and superior tactics, a mission perfectly suited for the GST.

However, just as Ross's confidence level was beginning to spike, Pepper, under camouflage but whose heat signature was visible in Ross's HUD, raised his hand, the signal to halt.

One of the guards was walking straight toward them, leaning over, frowning as though he'd seen something lying on the floor. His flashlight's batteries were weak, and the pale yellow beam barely lit his path.

Ross shifted slowly toward the shelves to his right, clearing a path down the aisle. Pepper did likewise.

Holding their breaths, they willed themselves into corpses, the camouflage steady now, reflecting the floor, the shelves, the ceiling. Pepper, who was right in front of Ross, was nearly impossible to discern.

Ross got a better look at the guard now, a man in his forties or fifties, graying beard, large eyes and slightly hunched back, as though the burdens of living in a war-torn jungle had weighed too heavily on him. Now they'd flown him around the world to do their dirty work. He'd traded in his jungle fatigues for a dark green uniform with the Fadakno logo on the breast and clutched the submachine gun in his right hand.

His quizzical look sharpening, he came to a dead stop beside Ross, who could reach out and grab his leg.

The guard swung around toward the docks and shouted to his comrade, 'I'm going outside! Be right back!'

Ross closed his eyes and repressed a sigh.

Pepper didn't move, not even a fraction.

No, that wasn't just 'close.' That was heart-attack close.

*

Kozak bit his lip and cursed.

The rear door on the cargo truck was rolled down and sealed with a combination lock. Burning the lock off with a laser torch would be easy. Camouflaging the light produced by the torch might be more difficult, but –

Opening the door without making a sound? Shit, that was *never* going to happen.

The major had never said that as a Ghost he'd be expected to defy the laws of physics. How the hell were they supposed to get in there now? There might be many techniques for quietly killing a man, but name one silent way of tugging open a heavy cargo door without calling every FARC guard to the party.

You're a fighter, he told himself. *You do not give up yet.* He was the new guy, always out to prove himself, so it was time to assess this problem and find a solution. That was what great SF operators did.

The truck's rear door was shut, yes, but he noted something curious: the hood had been left open, as though repairs or service were being made.

A thought took hold, one too obvious to be true, but he needed to follow his gut anyway. He held up his index finger to 30K: *Wait.* They huddled down behind a row of six pallets of boxes near the back of the truck.

There, Kozak removed the portable X-ray device (PXD) and accompanying wedge from his pack. Each two-man team was equipped with one. The X-ray itself was no larger than an old digital camcorder, the kind Kozak's mom had used to film his basketball games back in the day. The imaging wedge was about the size of a fifteen-inch notebook computer with a handle on the top. You held the wedge behind the object you wanted to X-ray, fired up the device, and zap, you got a digital image sent wirelessly to your Cross-Com. US Customs and Border Protection agents loved these little beauties.

30K seized the wedge, nodding to indicate that he understood what Kozak had in mind: X-ray the damned truck *first* before going through the hassle of breaking in.

The front door swung open, and in burst that guard from Ross's warehouse.

Time to play statue again. While the FARC troops were hardly geniuses, they were still formidable, if only because they each had a pulse and pair of eyes – and if any of those eyes were to catch a glimpse of them . . .

Nope. Kozak wouldn't let that happen. He was tense but not nervous as the guards lapsed once more into a rapid-fire debate. Two said they should go find another cell phone or gain computer access to see if anyone else had information. The others agreed, and during the commotion of their exit, 30K and Kozak slipped behind the pallets, reached the truck, and with excruciatingly slow movements, he stood on the driver's side of the truck, with 30K on the passenger's.

With a shudder of anticipation, Kozak aimed the X-ray at the truck, threw the switch, and doing his best to turn his back on the guards and have the PXD's status light concealed by his active camouflage, he began taking images of the cargo box's interior, with 30K holding up the imaging wedge. The distance between the PXD and the wedge was beyond normal parameters, but Kozak only needed to confirm the presence of cargo, and even the blurriest or most unclear images would suffice.

He almost snorted in disbelief. His hunch had paid off. The images glowing in his Cross-Com's HUD were clear enough: the damned truck was empty, hadn't been loaded yet – perhaps because the truck's engine hadn't been fully serviced?

Kozak craned his neck, eyes widening.

The intended cargo might be sitting right behind them.

With his breath quickening, he steered himself back toward the pallets, hunkering down behind the two rows, the boxes rising to just above his head.

That these shipments were rectangular shaped and much larger than any others in the warehouse had not struck him as odd, not at first anyway, but the reason for those oversize boxes became abundantly clear as he and 30K X-rayed the nearest one. He gasped and took a second X-ray to be sure.

There was no mistake.

Holy shit, he thought. *Mother lode.*

Footfalls now, along with a flickering light.

Kozak switched off the PXD, and both he and 30K lowered to their haunches as the remaining guards muttered to one another, their voices growing nearer.

Suddenly, 30K deactivated his camouflage, his face appearing from the darkness and glowing in Kozak's night-vision lens. He mouthed the words: *What did you see?* Then he pointed to the boxes.

Kozak opened his mouth, just as the guard with the flashlight strode alongside the truck.

'Did you hear something?' the guard asked his comrade.

'No.'

'I thought I heard something. I did. Right here.'

Kozak's hand went for the suppressed pistol in his holster, and in the next few seconds he saw it all fall apart in his mind's eye:

The guard's eyes widening in shock a second before he blew the man's head off, the other guard escaping, the whole clandestine operation going to holy hell as Ross and the major screamed at him, busted him out of the Ghosts, slapped him with a dishonorable discharge from the Army –

And now he was an alcoholic and flipping burgers back on Knickerbocker Avenue, not even making enough money to buy comic books, his mother crying herself to sleep every night because her son was a capital-L Loser who'd failed a mission and allowed terrorists to take over the world.

All because he twitched a fraction of an inch and was spotted.

Thirty-Two

Three weeks prior to the mission, Pepper had been told by one of the doctors at Womack Army Medical Center that he had high cholesterol and needed to change his diet. His LDL was 167, his HDL 138, but his charisma was off the charts. The doc had barely smiled over that personal assessment and had told him if he didn't change his ways and his numbers got worse, he'd wind up with a medical discharge and die of a heart attack.

'But what about all the PT I'm doing?'

'Won't matter if you keep eating Kentucky Fried Chicken, Pizza Hut and potato chips. And oh, yes, your triglycerides are very high as well. I take it you like your beer?'

'*Like* barely covers it. I'm married to beer.'

'Well, you're getting a divorce.'

'Aw, hell, you might as well kill me now!'

That meeting and those numbers occurred to Pepper while they were in the warehouse because, for just a moment, he felt palpitations, a heart flutter, something a little questionable in his chest, like he'd pressed on the gas pedal a little too hard and had flooded the engine.

He swore to himself, blew it off, and called it stress,

then glanced back to Ross as the guard who'd been standing next to them shut the warehouse door and left.

One guard remained at the far end, directly opposite that wall of plastic-wrapped shipments at the loading docks. Pepper led Ross around to the first pallet, got on his knees and fished out the PXD.

Ross took the wedge, and they got to work as a slight ache began to splinter across Pepper's chest.

30K was literally salivating with the desire to knife the guard who was shifting alongside the pallets, toward where he and Kozak where crouched down, waiting and listening.

There were times when being a Ghost, being swift and silent, no footprint as the major tirelessly argued, was infuriating. Sometimes, well, okay, most times, he simply wanted to sever a carotid artery and send his foes stumbling and gurgling to their deaths –

Instead of hiding from them like cowards.

Okay, so their tactics weren't supposed to be cowardly; they were audacious, cunning, and in the end, far deadlier than going in like barbarians swinging hammers high above their heads.

But sometimes being a dumb-ass barbarian was a hell of a lot more fun.

He took a deep breath. *Go with the flow. You're a Ghost. Just vanish . . .*

The guard walked past them, then suddenly swung

around and hurried off, passing down one of the far aisles. 'Hey, I've just thought of something,' he cried to his friends. 'The backup systems for the cameras and sensors aren't working. Did you notice that? Are the batteries all dead? That can't be . . .'

Using a small razor knife he'd retrieved from his pack, Kozak cut a thin seam in the plastic wrap that went right through one of the boxes. Through that seam he inserted another of their GPS tracking beacons.

And then he tapped a few commands on his smart-phone, linking it to his Cross-Com while also sending the X-ray's images to 30K's HUD.

30K took one look at those X-rays, faced Kozak, and mouthed the word *Damn!*

Kozak shook a fist, having a Christmas morning moment himself.

With the guard a few aisles down now, 30K gestured toward the door: Let's get the hell out of here!

The boxes that Ross and Pepper X-rayed contained a combination of parts for the refinery and bricks of cocaine, perhaps one hundred or more distributed throughout the shipment. He and Pepper were able to tag two pallets before slipping back out of the ware-house. Ross ordered Maziq to turn the power back on, then he and Pepper met up with 30K and Kozak behind the old medical supply building.

'What'd you get?' he asked Kozak.

'We should go back to the church,' Kozak began. 'That way you can sit down before I tell you.'

'Spit it out, son,' Pepper said impatiently.

'SA-24 Igla-S MANPADS.'

Those numbers and words might be gibberish to the average civilian, but to Ross and his Ghosts, they represented an alarming and deadly find.

'Aw, hell,' Ross said. 'How many?'

Kozak grimaced. 'By my count: one hundred and twenty-six.'

Ross began to shake his head; that was way more than he'd expected. 'You're right then. We need to get back to the church.'

'You know what this means, don't you, sir?' asked Kozak.

'I'll tell you what it means,' Pepper began.

'Not here, guys,' said Ross. 'Saddle up. Let's go.'

Ross led them back up the shoreline road and toward the church. His thoughts raced ahead as he considered the length and breadth of this alliance between the FARC and Hamid's group, the *Bedayat jadeda*.

Thirty-Three

The weapons report, schematics, world inventories and accompanying videos Ross showed the team were dark reminders of what they were dealing with:

The SA-24 Igla-S MANPADS (man-portable air defense system) was a shoulder-fired surface-to-air missile (SAM) fielded by the Russian Army since 2004. Dubbed the SA-24 Grinch by NATO, the 1.57-meter-long launcher unit fired a missile with a 1.17-kilogram warhead at a speed of Mach 2.3 via the solid fuel rocket motor. The Grinch had an operational range of nearly six kilometers and could kill its targets with a direct hit or by proximity fuse. The system was the equivalent of the US Stinger missile and currently regarded as one of the most lethal air defense systems ever made because of its sophisticated high jamming immunity provided by a dual-channel optical homing head with logic unit for true target selection against clutter.

If you were an Islamic terrorist, a Colombian rebel, or perhaps a Mexican cartel leader seeking portable firepower against air threats or a powerful weapon to carry out Allah's will against infidels, then the Grinch was, in Ross's humble opinion, the most bad-ass launcher of them all.

He took a seat at his desk as the team gathered around.

'So as I was saying,' Kozak began after the weapons briefing. 'Do you know what this means?'

'It means we ain't going home,' Pepper said. 'Not anytime soon . . .'

'Right,' Kozak agreed. 'But check this out.' He began reading from his own tablet computer. 'The Russians have been selling these Grinch launchers to Venezuela, and the State Department has been worried for a long time that those launchers could find their way into the hands of the FARC. They, in turn, might sell them to the Mexicans. You know how that goes: Here's a few bricks of cocaine, and with every order over five hundred grand, you get a free rocket launcher. Worse thing is, terrorists trying to get into the US through Mexico could get their hands on one of those puppies.'

'So why are these FARC guys shipping the launchers overseas?' 30K asked. 'Are they selling them?'

'These launchers don't come from Venezuela,' said Kozak.

'Okay, now I'm confused,' said 30K.

'He's right,' Ross interjected. 'During the civil war here in Libya, the warehouses in Tripoli were raided, and thousands of these Grinch launchers, along with the older SA-7s, went missing. Both sides stole them for their own use. I remember seeing pictures of civilian cars loaded with cases.'

'So are these babies going back to Colombia then?'

asked Pepper. 'Meaning the FARC have found another source for their weapons?'

'That's possible,' said Ross. 'If they're not headed back there, then maybe Hamid's new terrorist group is taking possession. Maybe he made a deal with the Libyans who stole them.'

'Or better yet, maybe they're splitting them up,' said 30K. 'Send some from Libya to Colombia, then send the rest to Mr Hamid's house. Weapons, money, drugs all flowing in multiple directions.'

Ross slapped his palms on his knees, about to stand. 'Well, this, gentlemen, is why they pay us the big bucks.' He turned to Pepper. 'Make sure your motorcycle's got a full tank.'

'Roger that.'

Ross glanced to the others. 'We've got observers on the hotel and the warehouses. We'll rotate out on watch. Everyone, try to grab a few z's. We have a big day tomorrow.'

Ross had his arm draped over his eyes and was lying on his back, the support poles of the bed digging into his spine. He'd been fading in and out of sleep for the past hour, his thoughts rising in explosive clouds then dissipating before he could fully grapple with them:

His first date with Wendy at the Abbey Road Pub in Virginia Beach, how the ketchup bottle exploded . . .

Taking her to the beach that night and proposing, on

178

his knees in the sand, the half-carat diamond small but the best he could afford . . .

Her calling him in Afghanistan to say they were going to have a baby, her voice cracking and making him cry . . .

The birth announcement card welcoming Jonathan Taylor Ross into the world, 10 pounds, 3 ounces . . .

Him telling Wendy at Jonathan's first birthday party: *'I can't wait. I'm going to teach him how to be a man.'*

And then, 14 August, the sunburn on Jonathan's nose, his swimming trunks hanging loosely from his bony waist . . .

'Dad? It's so hot outside. Can you shoot us with the hose?'

Ross didn't realize he'd been shaken awake and fallen on to the concrete floor until 30K was grabbing his arm and saying, 'Captain? Are you okay?'

He glanced around, disoriented for a few seconds then realizing what had happened. 'Oh, man, yeah. Thought I was back home in my own bed.'

'You were yelling something.'

'No, I wasn't.'

'Yeah, you were.'

Ross sat up and stared hard into 30K's eyes. 'No, I wasn't . . .'

30K just looked at him, shook his head and headed back across the basement to his own bed.

And there, in the dim glow of his tablet computer, was Pepper, just staring at him.

'Sorry, guys, I'm cool. Back to sleep.'

*

Kozak was up on the church's roof, watching as the guards at the Fadakno warehouse were checking the backup power status of the cameras and motion detectors. They had, he assumed, replaced the backup batteries and checked the fuse boxes, only to discover that all of the cameras and sensors were still not functioning. They might attribute the problem to a power surge, and that would put Kozak's mind at ease.

About ten minutes later, 30K arrived on the roof to relieve him. 'Thanks, buddy,' Kozak said.

'Hey, Sinbad had a nightmare. He fell right off his bed.'

'Are you talking about Captain Ross?' Kozak asked darkly.

'Yeah.' 30K began shaking his head.

'Don't go there,' warned Kozak. 'It's just stress.'

30K smirked. 'Whatever you say.'

Thirty-Four

At exactly 7:41 a.m. local time, a certain pilot of interest named Bakri Takana left the Hotel al-Massira in a rental car and drove directly to the Fadakno warehouses.

Sixteen minutes later a motorcycle courier arrived, parked his bike outside the main office for about three minutes, then climbed back on board and motored off, turning out on to the highway, assumedly bound for the airport.

Though only speculation at this point, Ross believed that the courier had delivered Takana's payment, then as usual had gone to the airport to both deliver mail and act as a forward scout to verify that the route was clear.

Pepper and 30K would confirm that. 'Okay, guys, he's on the way. Stand by.'

A single, suppressed, and expertly placed shot to the motorcycle courier's front tyre sent the man skidding off the road and into the dirt, where he spun out and nearly crashed, the smell of burning rubber and freshly dug-up sand filling the air around them.

30K couldn't believe that Pepper had made that damned shot as he hauled himself out of the ditch where'd they'd been lying and went charging over to the courier before the guy could reach for his cell phone.

'Hold it,' 30K hollered in Arabic.

He was just a kid really, barely twenty, with a narrow face and a very Western hipster knitted cap pulled over his shaggy hair. His face screwed up into a knot as he looked down the barrel of 30K's rifle.

'I won't hurt you,' 30K added, his eyes hidden behind sunglasses, his voice muffled behind the desert camouflage team scarf covering his nose and mouth.

The scarves were a Ghost tradition, beginning with your graduation and acceptance into the GST. 30K's scarf was modified with a skull's grin; Kozak's was painted like a cyborg with battle damage; Pepper's resembled the face of a Texas bull; and Ross's looked like a scuba diving regulator in his mouth.

At the moment, 30K had forgotten about how frightening he looked wearing his grim reaper, and the kid's sudden tears reminded him of that.

'I'm just a mail courier. I don't have any money.'

30K almost laughed. 'We're not here to rob you. What's your name?'

'Youssef.'

'Well, Youssef, today's your lucky day.'

Pepper walked over, wearing his bull face scarf and holding a wad of cash. 'You want to make some money?' he asked the kid.

'How?'

30K lifted the boy's chin with his rifle's barrel. 'All

you have to do is talk. We have enough money to buy
you a new bike and a new life.'

'Okay, okay. I will talk to you.'

Without thinking, 30K released an onslaught, his
mouth operating on full auto. 'What happened back at
the warehouse? Where did you come from? Did you
deliver money? Who hired you? Are you going to the
airport now?'

The kid visibly trembled.

'One question at a time,' Pepper told 30K.

A pickup truck came roaring up the highway, pulled
over, and out hopped Maziq and two of the NLA troops.

'Get the motorcycle in the truck right now,' Maziq
ordered his men. Then he faced Pepper. 'You need to
get on your bike and get going.'

'Roger that.'

Maziq came over to 30K. 'You get what we need?'

30K glanced to the courier. 'Okay, Youssef. This is
another one of my friends. You can tell him everything.'

'You won't kill me?'

'Hey, we don't have time. Start talking. NOW.'

Ross studied his Cross-Com's HUD, now displaying
the signal from the tracker Kozak had planted on the
missile launchers. They'd been loaded on to the truck,
and their boy Takana was now behind the wheel and
heading out of the warehouse.

'Ghost Team, listen up. The shipment's en route.
Maziq, how's the second team making out?'

'They're already in place and set to disrupt airport security if we need 'em. Keeping quiet for now. We intercepted the courier. Just finished interrogating him. Pepper's on his way to the hangar.'

'Excellent work. 30K, we get anything out of that kid?'

'Not much, boss. He makes the money run. Picks up the package in Tripoli at another Fadakno warehouse.'

'Names?'

'No, sorry. He doesn't know the names of the people who give him the money. He says he has no idea where the shipments go or what's in them, but he checks the route and gives the airplane mechanics the heads-up when the shipment is coming. That's all he does.'

'You trust him?'

'Yeah, he's too young and stupid to be given any more responsibility. He's just a runner like we thought.'

'Okay, but don't release him till we're done.'

'You got it – but technically speaking, is that kidnapping, sir?'

Ross snickered. 'Hell, no. We're just giving him time to count his tax-free donation in a safe and comfortable environment.'

30K laughed. 'Gotcha.'

Pepper rolled on to the access road running parallel to the hangars, the motorcycle's grumble announcing his approach. Oh, yeah, he was bad to the bone.

He throttled up, dust swirling in his wake as he sped

directly past the first few hangars, turning sharply past the open doors of the last one and roaring inside –

Where the two mechanics swung around, took one look at him, got pissed off, then began yelling at him from their perch atop their maintenance ladder.

As Pepper turned off the engine, lowered the kickstand, and began to dismount, the taller of the two men came rushing down and confronted him. 'Where's Youssef?'

Pepper had removed his bull scarf but still wore his dark sunglasses. He backhanded sweat from his forehead and just looked at the man.

'I said, Who are you?'

'Youssef called in sick,' Pepper finally answered. 'I'm the new guy.'

'They said they'd call me if there was any change. Why didn't they call? Is the truck on its way?'

'Yes. Those filthy bastards should've called you.'

The mechanic's gaze narrowed. 'You're a foreigner.'

Pepper smiled. 'Of course.'

The man muttered something, then said, 'The plane will be ready.' The guy turned back toward the ladder.

Pepper stood there, still wearing his stupid grin.

'What do you want?'

Pepper had the X3 Taser pistol in his fist before the mechanic could react. The safety was off, and a pair of laser dots had lined up vertically on the mechanic's chest, with the top dot flashing to mark the target.

At the same time, a second pair of laser dots appeared

on the shorter mechanic's chest, these also emitted from Pepper's weapon. A total of three cartridges could be inserted into the X3's box-shaped barrel, each containing a pair of probes, and now two of those cartridges were about to be emptied –

Simultaneously.

Pepper thumbed a side button to 'arc' the charge, the weapon crackling with electricity.

There was no need to do this, other than to scare the shit out of the guys. Pepper couldn't help himself.

The mechanics backed away, and the first looked to the workbench, about to make his move.

And then, with the crackling growing louder – like something out of Frankenstein's lab – the shorter mechanic cried, 'Don't shoot!' He was about to swing himself off the ladder like a gymnast when –

Pepper squeezed the trigger, firing both sets of probes, the attached wires zigzagging away from the barrel like folded fishing line, the mechanics now screaming like medieval torture chamber victims as they fell toward the deck, writhing. A weird metallic smell made Pepper grimace.

'Oh, come on, guys, man up,' he told them in Arabic. 'Take the pain. It won't last long.'

An airport security truck carrying 30K, along with four NLA troops, rolled up outside, squeaking to a halt. 30K hopped from the passenger's side and came jogging into the hangar.

'Hey, what do we got?' he cried, his voice echoing.

'Get him,' Pepper ordered, pointing to the shorter guy lying across part of the ladder.

While 30K hustled past him to comply, Pepper removed the Taser probes on the taller one, then dug his arms beneath the mechanic and dragged him up and toward the truck, handing him off to the NLA troops.

30K delivered his man to the truck, then told the driver to get out of there. The mechanics, along with the courier, would be taken back to the church and detained until Ross gave the order for their release. The truck squealed off with a rush of dust and gravel.

Pepper waved over 30K toward the wall of pallets to their left. 'When's the last time you drove a forklift?'

30K shrugged. 'How hard can it be?'

Thirty-Five

The shipment containing the bricks of cocaine that Ross and Pepper had tagged was still inside the warehouse and would probably be moved out sometime during the day. If the FARC-*Bedayat* network was smuggling cocaine into Europe, then they might utilize yet another Fadakno warehouse located in Croatia. Ross shared that hunch with Mitchell, who said he'd deploy another Ghost team to follow the shipment.

Kozak, who was at the wheel of the Tacoma, kept them about a kilometer behind the weapons truck. Even better, they were hidden behind several other vehicles also headed to the airport. They'd sent up the drone to keep a visual on the truck, even as the NSA supplied them with Keyhole satellite imagery of the road and airport. A sensor deployed outside the warehouse just as the truck was leaving revealed that four of the six FARC guards were in the back, rubbing shoulders with the pallets of SA-24s.

Because Kozak was driving, Ross operated the drone, and the young sergeant repeatedly told him to be careful. 'Don't worry, buddy, I won't let it crash.'

'They're not cheap,' Kozak warned. 'And, sir, I appreciate us going a little more on the offensive here.'

'These guys can expect to lose a few couriers,' said Ross. 'Those kids always get cold feet after a while. I lost a few myself back in the 'Stan. You win over a kid's loyalty, but he's only good for a few weeks till he realizes just how dangerous it is, then he bails. Anyway, Maziq will help us cover up the rest.'

'Cool.'

'30K say anything to you about last night?'

'What do you mean?'

'Oh, you know what I mean. I'm sure he said something.'

Kozak shifted uncomfortably in his seat. 'Uh, you fell off your bed.'

'Yeah, one of those rollovers, and oops, I'm not in my own bed things.'

'I've done that.'

'I'll tell you what,' said Ross, lifting his tone. 'I feel good today. Mission tempo is high. And in a few minutes, it'll be showtime!'

'Hell, yeah, sir!'

Ross banged fists with Kozak, then glanced through the open window, letting the hot wind whip over his face.

30K marveled over the expression on the guy's face:

Their not-so-friendly neighborhood pilot, Bakri Takana, had an extremely dark complexion and brilliant eyes, which shone all the more as he watched a miracle happen not two feet from his face.

He'd just parked the truck inside the hangar, had climbed out, and was now staring at 30K and Pepper with pistols pointed at his head.

From Takana's point of view, these men had materialized from thin air.

And 30K found it difficult to repress his shit-eating grin over absolutely shocking the guy with their optical camouflage.

'Hands on your head,' ordered 30K in Arabic.

'What the hell? How did you . . . where did you –'

'HANDS ON YOUR HEAD!'

Takana winced and obeyed.

'You're Bakri Takana,' said Pepper.

'How do you know me?'

Pepper's tone softened. 'We're not here to hurt you. We just need to talk.'

30K shifted behind Takana and patted him down, discovering a pistol tucked into the small of his back, another in a calf holster. He then grabbed one of Takana's wrists, slapped on a pair of zipper cuffs, then lowered the other wrist to finish the job. While clutching the man's bound wrists with one hand, 30K leaned in close and growled, 'Okay, Sundown, what's the combination on that lock?'

'Who are you?'

'Let's just say we're the good guys,' said Pepper. 'Give us that combination.'

'Why should I? You'll kill me anyway.'

'There's no need for that. Just cooperate.'

Takana thought a moment, then seemed to smile, as if over some private joke. He blurted out the numbers.

With that, 30K went jogging around to the other side of the truck. He understood why Takana had, for just a few seconds, looked so pleased with himself. He figured that Pepper and 30K were unaware of the guards inside the truck. He'd assumed that his 'friends' would ambush these 'good guys' who'd taken him prisoner.

What Mr Takana had not realized, though, was that he was dealing with four of the most highly trained and well-equipped Special Forces operators in the world. Flyboy was about to crash and burn.

30K worked the lock, removed it, then set it down.

He leaned past the truck, smiled, and waved at Takana while speaking through his teeth, 'Watch this, you mother.' He slipped on his gas mask and dug into his pocket –

To produce a gas grenade containing a newly formulated incapacitating agent known as Kolokol-7. It was based on the old Kolokol-1 synthetic opioid, and in part a derivative of fentanyl but in a much more stable and safer form that had been rigorously field tested by the Ghosts for several years. The idea was to put your adversaries to sleep, not accidentally poison them, which had happened much more often than not when deploying these types of gasses. Tear gas was okay, but your foes could still fire wildly while blinded. You wanted them on the ground, immobile, done.

Behind the rolling door, 30K imagined all four guards, submachine guns drawn, waiting for him to open the hatch.

He did –

Opened it about six inches, pulled the pin on the grenade, and threw it inside.

Then he slammed shut the rolling door, threw the latch, and leaped sideways –

Just as automatic fire ripped through the door and began shredding the area around that latch, rounds chewing into the concrete and ricocheting away, the sounds of the hissing grenade and screaming guards inside coming through the fresh bullet holes in the door. The men began kicking the door, trying in vain to pry it open, the gas now leaking from the bullet holes while 30K craned his head toward the hangar door –

Where Kozak and Ross skidded to a stop in their pickup. They donned gas masks, then came running over as 30K checked his watch. The truck grew very still as Kozak and the boss trained their rifles on the truck's back door, while 30K threw the latch.

With a slight shiver, he used both hands to shove the door upward as hard as he could, the rollers rattling as thick clouds came pouring out and finally thinned to expose the pallets and the four guards lying slumped on the floor or against the wall.

'Nice work,' Ross said from behind his mask. He slapped a palm on 30K's back. 'Let's do this!'

30K nodded and ran off, around the truck and toward the gas-powered forklift waiting for him.

A hundred things could have gone wrong, and they usually did, but for now, 30K would keep his head low so that fate would not spot him. He would get those pallets transferred to the plane pronto.

Ross told Pepper to bring Takana over to the office area while the gas was still clearing out. There, they shoved the pilot into a chair and Ross spoke evenly. 'We'll be turning you over to your own government. At best, you'll get life imprisonment for aiding and abetting an international terrorist organization. At worst, they'll execute you.'

'I'm just a pilot.'

'Yeah, a pilot who flies stolen rocket launchers.'

'I fly boxes of pipes and flanges.'

Ross hunkered down to level his gaze on the man. 'Bakri, listen to me. If you help us, I can guarantee you immunity. I'm talking no jail time at all.'

'I don't believe you. Who are you?'

'Excuse me, can I have a word?'

The question had come from Maziq, who'd returned to the warehouse. Ross shifted away toward the entrance, and they lowered their voices. 'I still don't like this. We shouldn't have intercepted them here. We should've let him take off and tracked the shipment electronically.'

'Sorry, bro, but like I told you, I wasn't taking that risk. Not with those weapons.'

'Yeah, well, now if his shipment doesn't show up on time –'

'I understand that. So are you here to criticize or help?'

'I can get him to cooperate, but you might not like it.'

'We're Ghosts. And we do *not* torture our prisoners. Right now, I just need him to fly the plane. He needs to make it look like business as usual.'

Maziq nodded. 'I'm not talking about physical torture.' Maziq pulled an envelope from his cargo pants and shoved it into Ross's hands. 'We found Takana's wife and two girls back in Sudan, in Khartoum.'

Ross closed his eyes for a moment and swore. 'Do we have to go there?'

'Hey, man, my team just gathers the intel. It's always your call.' Maziq sighed and stepped away, speaking into a radio he'd been holding, checking in on the NLA troops monitoring airport security.

Ross opened the envelope and examined the photographs of the woman and her two daughters, surveillance photos taken of them while they'd been shopping along a busy city street.

He looked up at Takana, then back at the photos. Then he checked his watch. Well, they didn't have time for long and sensible arguments that might win over the man.

With a surge of adrenaline, Ross marched back to the pilot, shoved the photos in the man's face, and said, 'I don't think I need to say anything else, except . . . will you *please* help us.'

Takana glanced at the photos, a sheen coming into his eyes. He looked up and said, 'I fly the cargo to Port Sudan. I don't ask questions. Sometimes I fly drugs, money shipments, sometimes weapons. I land, I hand off the cargo, and I fly back. For this they pay me very well.'

'Who are they?'

'I don't know their names. They tell me nothing. I'm paid at the warehouse, usually by a courier. If there's a boss there, I don't know who he is.'

'Will you fly us to Sudan?' asked Ross.

'If that's what you want.'

'Do the guards always go with the shipment?'

'Yes.'

'And do they fly back with you?'

'Yes. Now I want immunity like you said. I want my family kept safe. Will you keep your word?'

'I will.'

'I'm not a bad man,' said Takana.

Ross raised his brows. 'Not as bad as the people you work for.' Ross put his hand on the pilot's shoulder. 'You're doing the right thing.'

Takana pursed his lips. 'I hope so.'

A thunderous crash came from the hangar, sending Ross and Pepper rushing out toward the truck –

Where they found 30K still at the controls of the forklift. However he, the lift, and the pallet he'd been trying to remove from the truck were now lying sideways, the boxes of launchers now breaking through their shrinkwrap and splaying like dominoes across the floor.

Thirty-Six

'It could've happened to anyone,' Kozak told 30K as they rushed to repack the weapons pallet and get the forklift back in operation.

Pepper had already jumped behind the controls of the second forklift and was removing a pallet, noting, too, how terrible the traction was while bringing the lift down the truck's aluminum loading ramp, which buckled under the load.

30K's lift had started sliding halfway down the ramp, and he'd tried to correct it, but one wrong turn had sent him toppling over the side. His forklift's tires were bald – perhaps an indication that these guys were doing some serious shipping.

They finished with the pallet, and 30K got back to work, his cheeks still flush with embarrassment.

Once they were finished loading the plane, Pepper squeezed the back of 30K's neck and said, 'Driving a forklift. How hard can it be?'

30K wrenched himself free. 'Yeah, yeah, old man. I'll keep my day job. Pays better anyway.'

They relieved the FARC guards of their Fadakno uniforms and distributed them based on the nearest sizing. Kozak's pants were pretty baggy, but he didn't complain and overtightened the belt. The black ball caps helped conceal their faces.

They shook hands with and thanked Maziq for all his help.

'Oh, I'm not done with you yet,' he said with a smile. 'The ISA never sleeps. So yeah, be safe, guys, and even though none of us exist and everything we did never happened, it was good to work with the old team.'

'You miss it now, huh?' Ross asked.

Maziq smiled and raised an index finger. 'I wouldn't go that far.'

Kozak climbed into the C-212 with the rest of the team. Four seats attached to the bulkheads were positioned up front, just behind the cockpit, while the rest of the cabin had been stripped for cargo loading. They buckled in, and Ross sat in the copilot's seat, mentioning how he'd maintained a private pilot's license for the last ten years. The C-212 was usually operated with a copilot, but Takana said that his employers had preferred he work alone. For now, though, he seemed to welcome the assistance.

They took off without incident, Takana getting clearance from an air traffic controller who was on the group's payroll. The overbearing hum of the turboprop engines made it impossible to converse without headgear and microphones, so they just mouthed words and gestured to each other. The only electronic communications allowed now would be made by Takana.

Kozak leaned back in his seat and studied some

maps of Sudan and the surrounding terrain, part of a map system stored on his tablet computer's flash drive. Takana had already suggested that Port Sudan was not the weapons' final destination, and this had Kozak scanning the map and wondering where they were headed and what means of transport would be used.

Once he'd exhausted six or seven proposed routes and his eyes had grown weary of staring at the screen, he glanced over at 30K, eyes slammed shut, mouth open, his snoring almost as loud as the turboprops. Pepper was listening to his iPod, and Ross was monitoring the instruments.

Soon they were flying over Cairo, with the undulating expanse of the Nile River scrolling into view. Pepper saw it, too, and he motioned for Kozak to have a better look. Funny how the tourist in them never died. They traveled the world over on covert missions but never stopped appreciating the sights, sounds and cultures they encountered, along with the food – especially the food. Kozak swore as he realized they'd forgotten to get some of those magrood cookies 30K had promised. Maybe some other time.

Yes, all this world travel was definitely a bonus when the locals weren't pointing guns in your face.

Near the end of their flight, and with nothing else to do, Kozak had done the math.

The trip from Tobruk to Port Sudan New International Airport was a grand total of 1,036 nautical miles and utilized all but a few gallons of the C-212's fuel. They were, according to his calculations, flying on fumes by the time they hit the tarmac. When questioned about how close they were cutting it, Takana was nonchalant.

They taxied off the main runway (in truth it was the *only* runway in yet another small, third-world airport still referred to as 'international'), and Takana pointed to a group of single-story office buildings with a dozen or so cars parked outside. At the far end of the lot was a nondescript warehouse about twice the size of the ones back in Tobruk, and beside it, parked adjacent to the loading docks, was a tractor-trailer with the images of a plane, boat and truck superimposed over a blue globe painted across its sides. Written beneath the logo in both Arabic and English were the words 'GSIC – Global Shipping International Company.'

From the back of the trailer emerged a group of men dressed in dark coveralls with the GSIC emblem on their breasts. They were unarmed and got to work extending the truck's loading ramp.

Kozak was damned happy to be getting out of his seat. He felt like a Russian mafia victim, wearing the four-hour flight like a pair of concrete pants with matching boots.

'Okay, gentlemen, welcome to the Port of Sudan,' Ross said, sounding like a commercial flight captain. 'We hope you enjoyed the flight.'

'It sucked,' said 30K. 'No whiskey? No peanuts? What the hell?'

'And no hot flight attendants?' Pepper asked, feigning his outrage. 'I'm never booking again.'

Kozak shook his head. The lame humor kept them calm against thoughts of a firefight right here, right now.

Ross turned to Takana. 'You do all the talking.'

'Okay,' said the pilot. 'They usually unload. We just stand back and watch. There is not much to say.'

'Where does the shipment go from here?'

'You asked me that back in Tobruk. I told you I don't know. The port is about ten miles north. Maybe they go up there. I usually just refuel. Sometimes I fly right back to Tobruk. Sometimes I go home for a week or two. They will tell me what to do.'

'I bet you've thought about quitting, but you were just too scared,' said Ross. 'You thought if you quit, they'd wind up killing you because you know too much.'

'I have thought about that.'

Ross's tone grew more serious. 'Then just remember, buddy, we're holding your ticket. You'll have immunity. Your family kept safe. If you try anything here, you'll be throwing that all away. And for nothing.'

'I am a man of my word,' Takana said slowly, forcefully. 'I hope you are the same.'

Ross gazed unflinchingly at the pilot. 'My word is my bond. And you have it.'

Takana nodded.

Thirty-Seven

The plane rolled to a stop, and while Takana shut down the engines, Kozak counted eight GSIC loaders who looked a lot like FARC troops. Even here, in Sudan.

'If anything happens,' 30K said quietly, 'I got your back. Stay close.'

Kozak took a deep breath. 'Me, too, bro.'

Pepper shot them a warning glance. 'Calm down.'

30K returned an ugly smile. Kozak just nodded.

Despite Pepper's admonishment, Kozak's heart still hammered against his ribs as he hopped on to the pavement, the asphalt seeming to bubble beneath his shoes, the heat haze stifling. The stench of diesel fuel and natural gas came up strong on the wind.

He kept his head down and moved off, swinging his weapon around, acting as though he were securing the area. The tension had already found its way into his hands, and he gripped the rifle a bit too tightly. He knew this feeling all too well, and if he didn't keep it in check, he'd get off a round before he knew it, as though his hands had a mind of their own.

The others mirrored his movements while Takana strode over to the truck and spoke with one of the men, assumedly the leader, definitely an Arab.

From the rear of the truck came three more forklifts similar to the ones they'd used at the hangar. As some of the men began to unload the plane, one of them keeping watch walked over and said in Spanish: 'I don't see Carlos or Juan or any of them. You guys are all new, huh?'

Kozak just nodded and stared over the man's shoulder.

'So what happened?'

With a snort, Kozak lifted his rifle and blew the bastard's brains out.

Or at least he did so in his mind's eye.

In reality he took a deep breath and answered, 'I don't know what happened.'

'What do you mean, you don't know?'

'We got orders from Valencia,' Kozak snapped.

The man drew back his head. 'Oh, okay. Sorry I asked.' He turned and marched back toward the trailer, hollering for his buddies to load faster.

Interesting. The mere mention of Valencia, the FARC leader they'd identified back at the Tobruk warehouse, had stuck fear in this guy.

And that was good because only seconds prior –

Kozak had felt his heart stop, his veins ice up, and his head begin to spin. Now he breathed a sigh of relief so powerful that his knees buckled.

'What did he say to you?' Ross asked quietly.

'Just wondering where the other guys were.'

'We cool?'

'Hell, yeah, we going hard in the paint.'

Ross frowned, obviously unfamiliar with basketball slang terms, then he grinned awkwardly and moved away.

Within two minutes the GSIC guys had transferred the pallets to their trailer. Sans any formal good-byes, the men climbed quickly into their truck and were on their way. Takana returned to the plane and said, 'They told me I have another week off. I'm supposed to refuel the plane now, then I can go home to my family.'

Ross extended his hand. 'Yes, you can.'

A yellow airport taxi barreled around one of the buildings and turned toward them, trailing a chute of smoke.

Kozak and 30K took up positions on either side of the pilot, while Pepper started toward the car, making a face over all the burning oil.

'What is this?' asked Takana, shifting back from Ross and finding himself blocked.

'You'll have your immunity. But we need to ask you some more questions.'

Behind the taxi came another vehicle, a late-model sedan with tinted windows.

'You lied to me?' screamed Takana.

'No. They're here to keep you and your family safe,' Ross said. 'That's no lie.'

'I don't believe you!'

Standing there, watching the pilot's face knot in anger, was for Kozak a powerful moment of déjà vu:

He thought of his cousin Sergei, of how the FBI had come to him while he was still in high school, of how they'd coerced him into eavesdropping on his cousin. Kozak had been forced to go through with it, to send Sergei to jail for running drugs with the Russian mafia in Brooklyn. It was the only way to save his mother's business, which the Feds had threatened to close. *How can you do something like that to your own blood?* he'd asked himself. It made him feel dirty, as though he were as bad as his cousin – only he didn't have that killer instinct. He'd been a coward hiding behind wires and a weak will.

'It was you!' Sergei had cried. *'I know it! It was you!'*

Kozak had wanted to say, *'Yeah, it was me – because I'm saving you from yourself.'*

But he had just stood there in the kitchen of his mother's restaurant, watching as the agents dragged Sergei through the back door while his mother wailed. A pot on the stove boiled over, the water hissing loudly, the pierogies getting overcooked. Kozak had turned and couldn't take his eyes off all that steam.

With a heavy heart, Kozak leaned in toward Takana. 'Hey, bro. Don't worry about a thing. It'll be okay.'

Takana turned, eyes narrowed in anger. 'No, it won't.'

'Don't waste your time,' said 30K. 'He made his bed.'

Kozak tightened his lips and sighed. It was just sad. They didn't know what had driven Takana to this moment. No opportunities at home? The burdens of trying to provide for a family? Maybe he was being blackmailed or threatened by Hamid himself? 30K would say he was just a greedy bastard like the rest of them, but Kozak sensed there was something deeper here, something more painful. But no matter the motive, Takana was a proud man who would never admit his weaknesses.

'Come on, bro, let's go,' said 30K. 'Don't blow another second thinking about this scumbag.'

Kozak wished it were that easy, that he could be that cold. Other times he'd look at 30K and hate what he saw: a dark vacuum in the man's eyes that allowed him to operate without feeling, passion, or judgment.

Thirty-Eight

Prior to becoming a Ghost, Alicia Diaz had won the Service Rifle category of the National Long Range Rifle Championship at Camp Perry, Ohio, for two years running. Her record on the Ghost's shooting range for longest bull's-eye still held, and her reputation and exploits on missions in China and elsewhere with then Captain Scott Mitchell had been analysed and discussed for years after by men like Pepper, 30K and Kozak. Why Ross hadn't told the team that she, a legendary Ghost now retired, would be getting out of that sedan was a mystery. Maybe the captain didn't know? Or maybe he didn't consider that information important?

Pepper sure did.

He couldn't wait to shake Diaz's hand, hoping some of her marksmanship would rub off and that she'd offer a tip or two. Share a secret. Let him buy her a drink.

A man must have his dreams.

After leaving the Army, Diaz had taken a position as a paramilitary operations officer with the CIA's Special Activities Division. She engaged in covert intelligence gathering with people like herself, former Special Forces operators from all branches of the service. Given the team's most recent 'encounters' with her agency, Diaz's presence was long overdue. Pepper hoped she could shed some light on Delgado's position, motives and whereabouts, and restore their faith in an agency whose unwillingness to cooperate seemed to be undermining national security (in Pepper's humble opinion).

Admittedly a little starstruck, Pepper shifted past Ross and was the first to greet the former Ghost. 'Hello, ma'am. I'm Master Sergeant Robert Bonifacio, but they call me Pepper. I don't want to sound cheesy, but this is a real honor.'

Diaz had remained fit, only a streak of gray near one temple betraying her age, the rest of her jet-black hair pulled into a ponytail. She could star in a Nike commercial. She looked part embarrassed, part flattered by his comment. 'Nice to meet you, Pepper.'

'Let me introduce you to the team. This is Kozak, 30K, and that's our Ghost lead, Captain Andrew Ross, who used to be a command master chief SEAL. How do you like that?'

Kozak and 30K gave Diaz awkward nods while, behind her, two men dressed business casual and easily mistaken for locals came forward to stand near Takana.

Ross shook Diaz's hand and said, 'Ms Diaz, your reputation obviously precedes you.'

'Thank you, Captain. I've had a chance to work with a few of your colleagues, real first-class operators.'

'I'm sure they are. Now would you mind telling me what the hell is going on?'

Diaz's grin evaporated, and Pepper, too, was taken aback by Ross's tone. Pepper wanted to say something, but he'd catch hell for it later.

'Captain, I understand your frustration.'

'No, ma'am, you don't. If I'm going to put my people in harm's way, I want to know why. If we're here to clean up your mess, then at least have the decency to admit it.'

'I promise you, we'll talk. Right now we'll take Takana off your hands. Your team rides in the taxi. We'll begin tracking the arms.'

'I'm sorry, ma'am, but you didn't answer my question.'

Diaz moved up to Ross and lowered her voice. 'Look, as one old Ghost to another, don't ask that question.'

'The major told me you'd be an ally.'

'Langley doesn't even know I'm here. I owe your boss a few favors. Now, if you and your team will get in my car, we can talk and monitor the shipment at the same time, instead of standing here, choking our chains.' Diaz whirled and headed back toward her car.

Diaz's men escorted Takana over to the taxi cab.

Ross jogged over to the taxi to intercept them, and Pepper couldn't hear that exchange. He headed over to Diaz, who turned back and said, 'I used to envy your job. Then I had it. Now I'm glad I'm out.'

'Why's that?'

'Long story.'

'Over beers tonight?'

She sighed then looked away. 'If you're still here.'

Pepper felt his cheeks warm.

Ross returned and said, 'Everybody? Let's roll.' He faced Pepper. 'What?' Then he looked to Diaz. 'We good?'

'Yes, Captain. We're fine.'

Just before they got in the car, Kozak leaned in to Pepper and whispered, 'I think you got a shot with her. Pun intended, ha-ha.'

'Shut up, asshole.'

Diaz promised that Takana would be transferred to one of the Agency's private jets and flown down to Mogadishu's Aden Adde International Airport. At a facility near there, the CIA ran a counter-terrorism training program for Somali intelligence agents and operatives. The program was aimed at building an indigenous strike force capable of snatch operations and targeted 'combat' operations against Islamic militant groups like *Bedayat jadeda*. When she wasn't out in the field, Diaz taught classes there.

She had guaranteed that Takana and his family would be protected but said that relocating them would pose some challenges. She'd asked Ross why he was so concerned about helping a drug and weapons smuggler, and he'd just shrugged and said, 'Good people in bad situations . . . sometimes they just do bad things. You change the situation, and sometimes you fix the problem.'

'Be nice if it were that simple,' she said. 'I think your faith in Mr Takana might be a little misplaced.'

'I can't tell you how many people I've met just like him, people caught up in the shit with no way to escape. They don't even remember how they got there. I haven't given up hope yet.'

'Wow, and I thought being cynical and pissed off came with the territory.'

'Don't get me wrong,' Ross warned her. 'I still feel that way about you . . . and your people . . .'

She rolled her eyes.

He glanced out the window. They were headed north toward the port, following a strip of paved road running through rolling desert hills as mottled as tanned leather. 30K drove, with Kozak running shotgun. Ross, Pepper and Diaz were crammed into the backseat. Pepper had made sure to sit next to Diaz, his 'fascination' with her schoolboy-obvious and stronger than his resentment for her employers.

'Looks like they're still heading toward the port,' Ross said, studying a map of Sudan with the tracking beacon's location superimposed with a flashing red dot and data box displaying latitude and longitude. In another window flashed satellite photos of the tractor-trailer as it moved up the highway, passing beneath a broad stone archway.

'I have another car at the port that'll pick them up, so no worries, Captain, we have backup,' said Diaz.

'Must've been something big,' Ross said.

'What?'

'The favor you owe Mitchell.'

'Why do you say that?'

'Because you've got, what, two teams already helping?'

'Three, actually. All local informants employed by me, all unknown to Langley.'

'So what do *you* know?'

'That's the thing. Not much more than you. This one's completely compartmentalized. And to be honest, that scares the shit out of me.'

'Why?'

'Because it means they're trying to plug a leak.'

'A mole? Rogue? Double agent?'

She took a deep breath, clearly disgusted. 'Delgado is a wild card. They put Tamer on him, even though I warned against it. I worked with Tamer once before, and I told them he couldn't be trusted.'

Ross stiffened. 'You know the whole story?'

'If you're talking about the boy in Tobruk that he recruited and killed, then yes. Wouldn't be the first time he's terminated his own informant.'

'Son of a bitch.'

She shifted in her seat to face him. 'Ross, let me tell you something. It's a lot different on my side of the fence. They tell you to gather the intel. They tell you not to break the law. But they don't ask questions.'

'And you're okay with that?'

'No, I'm not. But sometimes I have to be . . . if I want to stay alive.'

Ross swore under his breath. They were both caught between duty and politics, between doing what was morally correct and what would best keep the country safe. If making those decisions had been easy, neither of them would have been there . . .

'All right, you've been around this block a few times and so have I,' he said. 'So what do we got? SAMs smuggled out of Libya, flown down to Sudan, and off to where? Afghanistan?'

'Maybe. Or the missiles could stay right here in Africa. You know, I could rattle off twenty other places they could go – Basilan, Chechnya, Syria . . .'

Ross felt her frustration. 'Here's something else bothering me. Why are the FARC being used overseas? Why doesn't Hamid use his own people?'

'Our intel on the *Bedayat* is still fragmentary and evolving. His al Qaeda allies are dead or in prison, so he's developing a new network. He's still recruiting the bulk of his force now. Maybe he's just brought over the FARC to bolster his numbers.'

'Either that or he's not wasting his people on these security missions because he needs them someplace else.'

'And where's that?'

Ross glanced at his tablet computer. 'I'm just a guy following a truckload of SAMs. You're the intelligence agent.'

She snickered. 'I'm sorry I couldn't be more . . . *intelligent*.'

'I was going to say *enlightening*.'

'Look, once we get to the port, we'll figure out what these bastards plan to do with the SAMs, then I can tap a few more resources if I need them.'

'I'm willing to bet our boy Delgado has all the answers. You guys need to find him.'

'Oh, trust me. We will.'

Thirty-Nine

Soon Port Sudan and its environs rose out of the ancient sands of the coastline desert, and Ross had never seen so many cargo ships gathered in one place, with forty-foot-long intermodal containers stacked like colorful pieces of Lego across their decks. The deep, coral-free harbor allowed those vessels to arrive with imports of machinery, cars, fuel oil and construction materials, while cotton, gum arabic, oilseeds, hides and skins and senna were shipped out. Behind the port lay the oil refinery receiving petroleum from onshore wells and piping more oil down to Khartoum.

They followed the GSIC tractor-trailer to the south side of the harbor, where the truck vanished down a road leading through a vast shipyard of cargo containers stacked in a labyrinth of rows and avenues. Diaz suggested they hold back there.

Within minutes the truck passed under a network of blue scaffolding as large as any major bridge Ross had seen, but that framework was actually part of the elaborate container crane system that traversed the quay and was equipped with a moving platform or spreader. The spreader lowered down on the container, fitting into the container's four corner castings, then twist-locked into place.

Ross watched as the spreader descended now toward a container positioned at the edge of the yard. He tugged out a pair of binoculars, rolled down his window, and turned his attention toward the cargo container ship being loaded. She belonged to the Maersk Line out of Liberia, the word 'MAERSK' prominently displayed on her hull. Diaz was pulling up data on the ship since the tractor-trailer was now parked, the pallets being offloaded into a container whose number – 11132001 – Ross forwarded back to Fort Bragg.

'Okay, I've got it,' Diaz said. 'That ship's the *Ocean Cavalier*, Liberian registry.'

'Bound for –' Ross began.

'Bound for a number of ports, any one of which could be our transfer point. Her first stop is Massawa in Eritrea, followed by the Port of Aden in Yemen.'

The latter struck a nerve with Ross.

The very first attack ever carried out by al Qaeda occurred in Aden back in late December '92. A bomb had been detonated at the Gold Mohur Hotel, where US troops were staying while en route to Somalia. Thankfully, the troops had already left before the explosion, but years later other American servicemen were not so lucky:

On 12 October 2000, the USS *Cole*, an Arleigh Burke–class destroyer, was moored and refueling at the port when she was attacked. The bastards came up alongside the destroyer in a small craft carrying four hundred to seven hundred pounds of explosives molded into a shaped charge. At 11:18 a.m. the bomb went off, blowing a gaping, forty-by-forty-foot hole in the *Cole*'s port side. Seventeen crew members were killed with another thirty-nine injured. The current rules of engagement at the time had prevented the *Cole*'s guards from firing upon the small boat as it approached, and even after the explosion, as a second boat neared, guards had been ordered to stand down.

Never again, Ross thought, gritting his teeth in anger. 'So Aden's on their list,' he said. 'But what if the SAMs never get there? What if they're transferred at sea?'

'No way,' said Diaz. 'Certainly not without us knowing about it.'

'Can we get on that ship?' Ross asked.

'I'd advise against it. I'll see if we can put up a long-range drone to shadow her.'

'The beacon's still good,' said Ross. 'But for how long? And good luck getting a drone up in this airspace.'

'Sir, may I interrupt?' asked Kozak from the front seat. 'The tracker's signal is clean, and for now the ship's not out on the ocean, so it's pretty doubtful we'll lose contact. Maziq and the ISA are still tracking as well. Let's just fly ahead of her. Get down to Massawa and wait. No chance of being spotted in a boat while trying to tail her. We know where she's going, so we should have the advantage.'

'I can get you a flight down there,' said Diaz.

'Let me clear it with Mitchell,' said Ross, trying to ward off his skepticism.

Diaz booked them passage to Massawa via one of the Agency's Gulf Stream jets. She told them not to bitch, as they were flying first class, and the jet was, in a word, sweet. There in Massawa, holed up in a hotel near the airport, they continued to track the *Ocean Cavalier*, and when she came into port the next day, they waited with bated breath while she unloaded.

The missile container was not moved.

With impatience clinging to them like napalm and igniting their tempers, the team got back on another jet, this one a Yakovlev Yak-40 three-engine airliner provided by Mitchell's contacts with the Yemeni Air Force. They flew to the Port of Aden, landing approximately eighteen hours before the ship was due to arrive.

On the tarmac they got a better look at the ancient city that lay in the caldera of an extinct volcano. Behind them rose the Shamsan Mountains, and farther off towered the lattice-work of cranes at the Aden Container Terminal on the north shore of the Inner Harbor.

They were met at their jet by a man pushing seventy who looked more like a sorcerer than a van operator. He ambled up to Ross and grunted in Arabic, 'Are you trying to find your luggage?' He stroked his wispy beard as though it helped him to think, and when he smiled, his picket fence of broken teeth made it difficult for Ross to return the same.

'Are you trying to find your luggage?'

That was the challenge question the major had given to Ross, and this old man knew it.

'Yes, we're looking for our luggage,' Ross told him.

The driver nodded and said, 'Then come with me, lads.' He spoke perfect English with a British accent.

They climbed into the van – a Mercedes whose seats were worn to the springs and whose engine gurgled as though it were running on mouthwash. The driver handed out small branches with dark green leaves.

Pepper and 30K had tentative looks on their faces, and Ross gave them a nod of reassurance. Kozak leaned over and whispered, 'Some kind of gift?'

'They call it *khat*,' Ross explained. 'You pluck off the leaves and chew them. Numbs your mouth a little. Tastes good.'

Kozak was about to pluck a leaf when Ross stopped him. 'Gets you high, too.'

'Okay, boss,' Kozak said, then tucked the branch into his pocket. He winked. 'I'll save it for later.'

'You'll throw it away, thanks,' snapped Ross.

'Uh, okay. No getting high while on the clock. I see how it is now . . .'

Ross grinned and thumbed on his tablet computer. He checked the map, along with their current GPS coordinates and accompanying landmark photographs.

Aden was shaped like a ladle whose handle was an isthmus connecting it to the mainland. The region was divided into a number of subcenters, with the original port city appropriately called Crater and comprised of tiny homes and apartments jammed along narrow streets leading to a central marketplace. The area had once been part of the British Commonwealth, clearly evidenced by the clock tower known as the 'Big Ben of the Arabs.' The tower, whose bell rang every hour, had been constructed of black brick and stood some twenty-two meters, with a brilliant redbrick roof that dominated the harbor's skyline.

The driver navigated through the warren of both dirt and asphalt roads, taking them into the heart of the city, to a six-story apartment building abutting the steep walls of the caldera. The building's perfectly square balconies formed a patchwork of chipped plaster railings festooned with multicolored laundry lines and dotted by portable air conditioners dripping with sweat. More residences had been built within the caves of the craterside above, and Ross imagined that if the volcano ever became active, Aden would become a modern-day Pompeii, leveled by a lake of lava.

The van pulled up outside the apartments, and standing in the shadows of an alcove before a pair of warped wooden doors was a bony man with a square jaw and narrow mustache. If this weren't Yemen, Ross might mistake this man for a carny working the Ferris wheel at Saint Matthew's annual picnic back in Virginia Beach.

He raked a hand through greasy hair and wiped sweat from his brow. He was probably Ross's age, his temples as gray as hot briquettes. Although he was dressed in civilian clothes, Ross recognized him from the intel photo Mitchell had provided. This was Naseem, a colonel with the Yemeni Republican Guard and a paid informant working for the CIA. His gaze lifted to the street beyond them, checking with an almost mechanical precision for observers before he left the alcove and hustled down to the van, opening the sliding door.

Ross greeted him while the others went to fetch the rectangular, heavy canvas load out bags containing their tactical gear.

'They didn't tell me your names,' said Naseem, his voice thin and barely rising above the van's sputtering engine.

'Operational security,' Ross said. 'You can just call me Captain.' He proffered his hand, and Naseem was about to accept it when a police car rolled up beside another car parked about twenty meters down the street.

They both turned in that direction.

Just as one of the cops was getting out –

And the parked car exploded in a deafening thunderclap that shattered windows and sent a fireball swelling into the sky.

Forty

'Get inside,' shouted Naseem, waving frantically to the team, then rushing forward to wrench open a door.

One by one the Ghosts stormed by Ross, who waited with Naseem, and once they were all inside the building's entrance foyer, the van driver screeched off as car alarms triggered by the explosion continued to wail.

Ross returned to the door and stole another look down the street, where pieces of the police officer, now lumps of pink viscera, lay strewn in the road and splattered against the opposite building. The police car had been catapulted on to its roof, the windows shattered, the passenger's side blackened and torn apart. A yellow mailbox that better resembled a fire hydrant had been blown out of the ground and had impaled the car's trunk. Several dogs were charging the flames, barking, then running back to charge again. Dozens of people were on their balconies now, staring down not so much in horror but with a deep sense of dread, Ross could tell, as this was something painfully familiar. And there it was, that smell – the burning rubber, fuel, and the sickly sweet stench of human flesh.

The war zone.

He thought of going outside to see if anyone else

was injured, but Naseem shoved himself in front of Ross and slammed shut the door. 'Follow me,' he ordered.

Shuddering off the adrenaline rush, Ross signaled the team, and they fell in behind the colonel, heading into the stairwell and double-timing their way up the stairs.

'They've just started the bombing again,' Naseem said as Ross got tight on the man's heels.

'Who are they?'

'I'll tell you in a moment.'

They climbed all six flights of stairs and came into a hallway of cracked plaster lit by dangling bulbs. Two armed men stood outside a door at the end of the hall. Naseem shouted for them to stand down as the team hurried behind. He unlocked the apartment door, holding it open as they filed inside.

The furnishings were meager, the rooms tiny, the entire place no more than 1,200 square feet by Ross's estimate yet large by Aden standards. A hole had been cut in the ceiling near the doors leading out to the balcony, and an aluminum ladder led up to the roof, where at the moment a man wearing a pistol holstered at his waist was descending, his long scarf trailing behind him. Naseem muttered a few words to him before he hopped down and rushed toward the front door.

Then Naseem regarded the entire group, with Ross staring hard at the man, demanding answers.

'The men you saw outside were not police officers.

They were my men, protecting me,' said Naseem. 'But they must've figured that out.'

'Who?'

'We call them the Harak, but you may know them as the South Yemen Movement. They've been organized since 2007, and they refer to us in the north as *dahbashi*, basically savages. They want the south to secede from the government, and their numbers and support are growing. Up in the mountains of Yafa, there's no longer any government control. They call it the "Free South," and now they've begun flying their flags here, just outside of Aden.'

'This like an Arab Spring thing?' asked Kozak.

'No, we had an uprising in 2011 to oust the president, which I'm sure you heard of, but this movement has been around for much longer,' said Naseem. 'Back in 1994 during our civil war, the north created several *fatwas* that advocated the killing of women and children and religious sheikhs in the south, branding them all Communists. That for me marked the beginning. Since then, the north has been trying to eradicate any southern identity and eliminate the desire for independence. But the harder they try, the deeper these people dig in. They see themselves as far more modern than us, abandoning the old ways, the tribes, and they view our military presence as an occupation.'

'Sounds a lot like the American Civil War,' said Pepper. 'And if you're heading in that direction, there's gonna be a lot of blood.'

'That's why my guard troops are here,' Naseem said. 'The rumors of war are growing.'

'I know a little about the Harak,' Ross chipped in. 'And I know it's pretty rare for them to resort to violence. There have been a few incidents over the years, but nothing wide scale.'

'That's all changed,' said Naseem. 'One of their more famous leaders, Zion Haza, was recently executed in the north. He's become a martyr, and his death we believe has sparked a new wave of violence. We've brought in two companies of Republican Guard and dressed them like local police to hide our numbers, but now . . .' He drifted off into a thought, then suddenly faced them. 'All of this is really none of your concern. You'll remain here until your ship nears the port, and then I'll take you to another safe house in Al-Ma'ala. From there you'll be able to observe the ship and cargo operations.'

'Excellent,' said Ross. 'And we appreciate your assessment of the situation here, but can we have a word in private?'

Naseem nodded and steered Ross into an adjoining bedroom, where on a small nightstand sat a pistol and a copy of the Quran, the image surreal and reminding Ross of any number of old Westerns he'd watched or read as a kid. 'What is it?' asked Naseem.

'Back in 2011 during the uprising, more than seven thousand of your colleagues in the Republican Guard defected to the anti-government movement. Let's just say the people in my community were watching that incident very closely.'

'That's true. I was in Nahm at the time, at our barracks. I fought against some of the traitors.'

'You were there, all right. But you let them take over the barracks.'

Naseem shifted back a few steps, his hand drifting down toward the pistol holstered at his waist, right beside the short, curved dagger known as a *jambiya*. 'Who are you?'

Ross shrugged. 'I'm just a guy, and I'm asking – why are you lying to us?'

Forty-One

Pepper was crouched near the window, watching as Aden's ill-equipped fire services attempted to put out the burning police car with portable extinguishers instead of high-pressure water from a hydrant. Behind them lay a funnel-shaped scorch mark that extended from the asphalt near the mangled car's chassis all the way to the opposite curb, where other first responders were gathering pieces of debris and shoving them in plastic garbage bags.

At the same time, Pepper was listening intently to the voices coming from the bedroom. The conversation had taken a turn for the worse, he feared, and as he was about to rise and head over toward the door, another explosion thundered from somewhere north, followed by a few shouts from men up on the roof. The small group of firefighters down below shoved radios into their back pockets, and a trio fled in a pickup truck toward the sound of the detonation.

'Somebody's having fun with firecrackers,' grunted 30K, coming up beside Pepper.

'Nothing ever gets to you, huh?'

'Actually this apartment does. Know why? Because

we can't defend it. The escape routes suck. Next building's too far to jump. Gotta run a line of paracord. I'd rather be on the first floor.'

'Me, too. This is shit. We're bailing.'

The bedroom door opened and out stepped Ross and Naseem, the latter looking a little pale. 'Stay away from the window,' he said.

'We get that,' said 30K with a roll of his eyes.

Ross waved over Kozak and they huddled up, staring at Naseem, whose eyes had taken on a sheen that suggested he had something grave to tell them.

However, it was Ross who spoke first:

'I had the major do a little extra digging for us when I heard our contact here was a CIA informant.' Ross lifted his chin toward the colonel. 'Naseem, it's hard for me to accept that you betrayed your own forces during the uprising, only to tell me you're working for them again.'

'The situation is very complicated, and you don't understand the politics of my country. You don't understand how your loyalty must sometimes shift – if only temporarily – to get the job done. What I did was meant to save lives.'

'I'm sorry, Colonel, but I don't understand that at all,' said Ross. 'See these guys here? We'd die for each other. That won't ever change. So let me ask you, point-blank, are you working for the Harak now? You plan on stabbing your own guys in the back?'

'Of course not. What I did back then was necessary. But as I said, this is none of your business. They asked me to get you to a safe house near the port, and I will do that.'

'Wow, shocking,' said 30K. 'Yet another local yokel we can't trust. I say we dump this guy. We go down to the goddamned port, and when the ship arrives, we board her –'

'And blow the whole operation,' said Kozak. 'Dude, that's your gun talking.'

30K made a pistol with his thumb and forefinger. 'Shoot first, apologize later.'

'Captain?' called Pepper. 'We can't stay here tonight. Not up here anyway.'

'That's correct, you won't be staying here,' said Naseem. 'I have an apartment on the first floor as well, with a back door exit and van waiting outside at all times. This place is for our observers on the roof. I took you here in case there were more car bombs.'

'All right, then,' said 30K. 'Let's get down there, check it out, and order up some pizza.'

'Pizza?' asked Kozak in disbelief.

Naseem answered for 30K. 'As a matter of fact, there *is* a Pizza Hut at the port, and they will deliver.'

'I know,' said 30K. 'I saw it on Google Earth.' He glanced at Pepper. 'Double pepperoni?'

Pepper sighed. 'Nah, pork's illegal here anyway. Probably just a salad.'

Another explosion close enough to shake the building sent Naseem darting for the ladder.

The *Ocean Cavalier* was running ahead of schedule and would dock at the Port of Aden at exactly 3:41 a.m. local time. Current time was 9:04 p.m., and Ross was satisfied that, for the time being, the team was safe. Kozak had deployed the drone, which was now in a fixed position on a rocky escarpment overlooking their position. They had marked all the friendly forces within an eight-hundred-meter perimeter and were closely monitoring the comings and goings of any pedestrians brave enough to hit the streets. There had only been a few, mostly police or fire personnel. No hostile contacts identified thus far. The bombing had stopped, and Naseem maintained his argument that Harak forces were responsible. This wouldn't be the first time they had targeted police and military checkpoints along the main highways.

That four men could devour a half dozen extra-large pizzas within fifteen minutes was a testament to the superior appetites of America's Special Forces operators. Go big or go home. Even Pepper had succumbed to temptation and ripped into his pie like a honey badger who'd been starved for a week. They'd ordered two veggie lovers, two cheese lovers, one gunfire lovers, and one called the supreme leader or something like that, Ross had mused.

Now they were lying back, rubbing their swollen bellies like pregnant women and burping up toppings, when Kozak gaped at the drone's remote monitor, leaned forward, and said quite evenly, 'Holy shit.'

30K and Pepper were up on the apartment building's roof within thirty seconds of Kozak's report. They were joined by three of Naseem's Republican Guard snipers, who were dressed in black fatigues and fielding Dragunov SVD rifles with attached night-vision scopes. The night was warm, the city lights shimmering out to the calm waters of the Arabian Sea unfurling like a black carpet in the distance. There was something strangely calm in the air as the drone of distant traffic faded and the barking mutts once scavenging through the endless alleys settled down for the night. A chill rippled across 30K's shoulders.

He made another sweep, surveying the rooftops through his rifle's scope, his chest tightening as he did so. 'Ghost Lead, this is 30K.'

'Talk to me, 30K,' said Ross over the team net. They'd donned their Cross-Coms, plates, helmets and web gear, and the boss had made a point of avoiding optical camouflage, at least around these guys. Better they thought of the Ghosts as another Special Forces team and nothing more.

'Boss, I'm patching you into my rifle's scope,' said 30K. 'You see we got snipers on the buildings there, there, and over there, to the north. See these two guys up there? And check this out. Look at these bastards over here. And that guy way up there, on the clock tower.'

'They're wearing desert fatigues. Are they Naseem's guys?' asked Ross.

30K asked one of the snipers, who shook his head, then he confirmed that with Ross.

The bottom line was that Harak forces had posted snipers all over the rooftops in Crater. That, in 30K's opinion, could mean only one thing.

He lowered his rifle and told Ross that they should get the drone out near Queen Arwa Road, the one leading through the mountain pass and over to the container port in Al Ma'ala – the only good route to reach the port without hiking across the mountain.

Or more precisely, their best escape route.

'I know what you're thinking, bro,' said Ross. 'Good call. I'll see if we have a Keyhole in position.'

'Drone's heading out now,' said Kozak.

30K shifted along the rooftop and came up alongside Pepper, who turned to him and said, 'The sons of Noah called this place the land of milk and honey. Did you know that?'

'What?'

'Gilgamesh came here to search for the secret to eternal life.'

'Did that pizza fry your brain?'

'Wise men gathered frankincense and myrrh from the mountains here.'

'Pepper, what the hell?'

'Dude, this is sacred ground, and these guys here, they're just turning it to shit.'

'You mean because they built a Pizza Hut here?'

'No, you idiot. I mean they keep fighting. You heard the man. The north and the south. It's never gonna end. I can almost feel God here – and he ain't happy.'

'Maybe they should have a pizza party. Everybody loves pizza.'

Pepper almost smiled. 'You should trade in your rifle for a briefcase and become a diplomat.'

'Yeah, that'd work. I'd start a war everywhere I went. Funny thing is –'

30K broke off as Kozak's voice crackled over the radio, his tone urgent:

'Ghost Team, this is Kozak. I put the drone up on the highway – and we need to get the hell out of here! Right now!'

30K cursed, lifted his rifle, then trained his scope on the highway, panning northwest until his heart sank. He shot to his feet and rapped a fist on Pepper's shoulder. 'Come on!'

Forty-Two

Ross had deployed the second drone himself, taking the UAV to one thousand feet in a broad sweep of Crater's south side. Superimposed over the streaming video was a city map identifying the roads and landmarks so that when the drone reached Al-Aydarus Street along which ran the mosque of Abu Bakr al-Aydarus and adjoining cemetery, he quickly designated the potential targets near the chipped stone wall below.

Men were rushing from a line of pickup trucks, carrying launch tubes, bipod support assemblies with heavy, round base plates, and optics and elevation/ traverse controls through a pair of wrought iron gates and on to the cemetery grounds. The grave markers extended in somewhat haphazard rows for five hundred meters eastward, but these men kept close to the entrance, taking up positions along the perimeter wall, where there were no trees or tall buildings to get in their way.

'Oh, are these clowns serious?' Ross muttered as he zoomed in with the drone's camera.

One group had already assembled their weapon, and a data box opened in Ross's Cross-Com to display an ID and specifications:

L16 81mm mortar, standard used by British armed forces. US version known as the M252. Capable of firing smoke, High Explosive (HE), and illuminating rounds.

A good crew could launch fifteen rounds per minute, and it appeared these men were setting up as many as ten mortars within the confines of the cemetery. A second group was already transferring metal ammo cases the size of foot lockers across the cemetery, each one containing four to six rounds, Ross assumed. The cases were being piled up beside each firing position. Some teams had thrown open latches and were removing the projectiles, arranging them on the ground, their small fins and broad nose cones making them resemble atomic bombs from the 1950s.

'Naseem! Get in here!' Ross shouted.

The man rushed into the small kitchen, where Ross had been sitting with the drone's remote. 'I've got ten mortar teams out near the mosque and cemetery.'

Naseem glanced away, as though he needed a minute for his brain to catch up with this news. He drew his pistol and chambered a round. 'I didn't think it would happen this soon. I thought you'd be gone before this.'

'Before what?'

'The Harak are launching a major offensive.'

Ross got to his feet. 'That's it, then. We're going to the safe house by the port – and you're taking us.'

'Captain, you don't understand –'

30K's voice broke over the team net:

'Ghost Lead, I got a SITREP you ain't gonna like. The guards at the checkpoint on Queen Arwa Road are dead. Those Harak guys have brought in some Panhards with ninety-millimeter guns. Count four blocking the whole road with two, maybe three, squads taking up defensive positions, over.'

The Panhard AMLs were light armored four-by-fours that resembled SUVs with tank-like main guns mounted on their roofs and pairs of 7.62mm machine guns as secondary weapons.

Ross began to reply when those 81mm rockets began to rain down over the city, popping and booming, reverberating and echoing, as secondary explosions rumbled through the first ones, the cacophony growing near, the building shaking once more, a few rounds sledgehammering into a building just down the street.

The Port of Aden was under siege.

'Ghost Team! Meet me out back. We're out of here!' Ross grabbed his load out bag and started for the door.

'Where are you going?' asked Naseem. 'We can't get to the port. Not now anyway.'

'The hell we can't. What's the address of the safe house?'

Naseem looked confused. 'I'm coming with you.'

'Fine, but give it to me anyway, in case something happens.'

Naseem tore free a page from a tablet lying near a landline phone and scribbled down the information. He proffered it to Ross, saying, 'Not sure this will matter. There may not be a safe place here. Not tonight.'

Ross took the paper, stole a look, then shoved it into his breast pocket.

Kozak had gone out on to the apartment's balcony, where he was now marking the positions of several more roadblocks manned by Harak troops, who were, at first glance, indistinguishable from Yemen's regular army. The three major highways running through Crater and intersecting with Queen Arwa Road were being cut off by more Panhards, while six M113 Armored Personnel Carriers had pulled up outside the Bank of Aden's modern office building, with ten troops dismounting from each. These men, Kozak believed, were the regular Army, moving up in timed intervals to confront the rebels.

'Kozak, where the hell are you?' shouted Ross.

'On my way,' he answered, then bolted off the balcony, through the apartment, and went slamming out the back door, where he found 30K holding open the side door of a van similar to the one driven by their airport driver.

He threw in his load out bag, then collapsed into one of the backseats beside 30K, who'd already rolled down the window and had his AK-47 in hand.

Meanwhile, Pepper smashed open the rear window with the butt of his own AK and was now covering their six o'clock. Naseem was at the wheel, and Ross was up front with him, still working the controls of the second drone, his gaze widening.

With both drones out, they were getting good intel of the oncoming battle, working with the analysts back home to identify both rebel and government forces on their maps. The GST was monitoring communications between Army forces and the Republican Guard, and Naseem had provided Mitchell with intel sent to him by his commanders.

Kozak began to designate the blue forces (friendlies) and began observing how those troops were being engaged by Harak forces operating in squads on hit-and-run missions. The rebels seemed to appear from nowhere.

Not nowhere, actually. They'd been in the city all along, cleaning their weapons, eating a big dinner, kissing their children good night, and waiting for the balloon to go up, which in this case had been represented by that series of car bombs. Those acts had signaled the rebels to move up into their attack positions, and the mortars were the final signal to strike.

'If I can get you to the safe house, I will. But then I'll need to return to my troops,' said Naseem. 'I don't want them to believe I'm a deserter.'

'I find that ironic,' Ross said. 'But okay.'

Just as they reached the end of the alley behind the row of apartment buildings, a mortar round struck with a blinding flash, as though Thor himself had come down and decided that this building had to go.

The explosion shaved off the whole side of the structure, with jagged chunks of stone the size of washing machines tumbling end over end to shatter on to the road just meters ahead while, above, laundry ripped from the lines began floating down like tiny, surreal parachutes swinging on a blast wave backlit by tongues of fire.

A portable air conditioner slammed into the windshield on the passenger's side, shattering the glass and dropping away with a metallic thud. More muffled thumps came from the rear, and Kozak craned his head and grimaced as shredded bodies struck in mangled, twisted heaps.

Naseem shouted something lost in the booming, but it was enough to draw Kozak's attention back to the front.

'Whoa, whoa, whoa!' hollered 30K.

'You gotta turn, dude!' added Pepper.

'Don't go in there!' Kozak cried.

Before Naseem could shift the wheel to navigate around the growing debris field, a dust cloud swept over them, the van's headlights unable to penetrate the blinding wave, the tires crunching across newly laid carpets of glass.

'Brake!' screamed Ross in Arabic. 'Brake!'

Kozak gasped as a boulder shaped like a jagged tooth materialized ahead and came cartwheeling toward them.

Naseem slammed his foot on the brake pedal, and Kozak felt his neck snap as the van's tires locked up — even as Naseem cut the wheel, banking hard around the boulder, which collapsed on to its side just behind them.

Without missing a beat, Naseem hit the gas again, tossing Kozak back into his seat as dust poured in through the open windows, choking the air and sending him into a fit of coughing.

And just as quickly, the dust cleared and Pepper shouted, 'Hey, I think I got something back here!'

Forty-Three

They emerged from the walls of dust like Celtic warriors on an early-morning battlefield –

Six men pairing off, one pair on each flank, with another dropping to cover behind a sedan whose windows had been blown apart by the mortar shell.

'You know what they're doing, don't you?' cried Naseem, pounding his foot once more on the brake pedal. 'They're shelling the city so they can blame it on the Republican Guard!'

After Pepper and the others were thrown forward, he shifted his aim back out the rear window and shouted again, 'Contacts to the rear! Two on each flank. Two more behind the car!'

With that, he opened fire, pinning down the two troops behind the car while their comrades on the flanks began to move up, shouldering the walls between alcoves and then dropping to their haunches –

To open fire.

Pepper could not scream any louder for Naseem to roll the wheel and get them around the debris as rounds popped and began punching into the van's tailgate.

At the same time, 30K braced his legs between the seat and hung out the open window, resting on his stomach so he could roll sideways and open fire, striking both troops to their right while Kozak had set down his remote and was delivering volleys of suppressing fire to the men on their left, his AK spitting out three-round bursts that sewed a jagged line in the wall above their heads, rounds ricocheting to strike a few more of the parked cars.

The van jerked hard to the right, hitting what felt like back-to-back speed bumps before the road leveled off and they cleared the debris, the piles of stone now shielding them from more incoming fire.

Pepper watched as Kozak gaped at the drone's remote, now piping in a wide view of the city. The rapid-fire thunder of mortars was increasing. 'Hey, boss, mortars have hit the bank, police station, even the clock tower, which is now blown to shit,' he reported. 'They're starting shift fires to the north, while the troops down near the bank are engaging rebels at the roadblocks. If they keep shelling Queen Arwa Road, they'll tear it up so much that nothing will get through. We'll be hiking over the mountain, and we'll never reach the port in time. Not on foot anyway.'

'Naseem?' called Ross. 'Slight detour. We need to take out those mortars. Get us down to the cemetery.'

Between the dust caked on the driver's side window and the shattered passenger's side, Ross wondered how Naseem could see anything at all. Ross shoved himself forward, balancing his elbow on the dashboard, and reached out through the hole in the glass to begin wiping it off with his sleeve, but then Naseem cut the wheel hard left, throwing Ross back and taking them down another alley. Naseem cursed and bit his lip.

Two more buildings up the road had been shelled, the rubble blocking their path, the air filled with the scent of leaking natural gas and shattered concrete while women and children were evacuating the buildings, screaming and crying, running along the sidewalk.

Naseem threw the truck in reverse –

Just as another explosion erupted from the ground ahead and Ross didn't need an engineering degree to know that the leaking gas had ignited.

His ears rang as Naseem swung around, rolling the wheel like a stunt driver, the van listing badly, tires squealing and burning as he hung a right at the next corner.

Allowing the man to drive had been a calculated risk – and a test. Naseem knew the city better than any of them, and if he wanted to prove his loyalty, he could do it right now, and the rebels provided plenty of opportunities to do that.

Ross shifted his attention to his Cross-Com, where the drone's feed had been updated to show a wider overhead image of the cemetery, the mortar teams hard at work, dropping shells into the launch tubes and rolling back, the tubes flashing brilliantly like a formation of lightning bugs as the rounds arced skyward. It was an indirect fire operation as deadly as they came, turning corners of the city into piles of debris and half-buried corpses. Typical fire missions included forwarded observers who made calls for and adjusted fire on the enemy, and Ross realized now that all those 'snipers' they'd seen on the rooftops were actually serving double duty as FOs. There was usually a fire direction center that computed range, trajectory, and shell use info to the gunners, but Ross suspected that the teams were speaking directly to their FOs and putting fires on grid coordinates northeast, directly north, and northwest of their positions.

'I want to come in behind them, so take us west of the mosque, get around it, then get us as close to the wall as possible. After that, we'll move in on foot,' Ross told Naseem.

Naseem shook his head in disbelief. 'How will you take out ten mortar positions with just four men?'

'What do you mean four?' asked Ross. 'I'm going to do it with just one.' Ross glanced to the back seat. '30K? You in?'

30K grinned like a werewolf.

Forty-Four

Kozak imagined the gravestones as pillars carved with hieroglyphics that told stories of how space travelers arrived on Earth millions of years ago to seed the human race. All right, his nerves had, admittedly, allowed his imagination to run wild. Time to buckle down and get to work. He ran his fingers along the headstone behind which he hid, then held his breath and peered out.

About fifteen meters ahead was the line of two-man mortar teams, positioned about twenty or thirty meters apart, standing before cases of ordnance and working like well-oiled machines, rounds dropped and fired, the chaotic explosions so loud that Kozak had shoved a plug in his exposed ear, the other filled with the Cross-Com's receiver.

The cemetery's perimeter wall was about two meters high, and the teams all stood within a few meters of it, utilizing the heavy barrier to shield them from any interference – gunfire or otherwise – from the road outside.

'Kozak, how we looking?' called Ross, his voice barely discernible above the din.

'Stand by, boss,' he answered, then consulted the

drone's remote. He thumbed a button, and his HUD lit with a data box showing the drone's overhead point of view, a wireframe grid superimposed over the cemetery and marking the positions of each mortar team, along with a ruler overlay showing the length and width of the wall.

'Okay, Ghost Lead, good to go from here,' Kozak said. 'I've got positions and the overlay.'

'Pepper, SITREP?' ordered Ross.

The chest pains were just indigestion, Pepper thought. *Famous last words of all heart attack victims, right?*

His love affair with food had to end. He couldn't ride the roller coaster anymore. He was kicking out that bitch, and no, he didn't care to know her name. Just leave – and take all your calories and bad health with you.

He swallowed hard and balanced his elbows on the edge of the balcony. He'd traded out the AK for his trusted M24A2 Remington and now clutched the sniper rifle, hoping the wood and smooth metal would help calm him. He'd found the mosque empty, the locks easy to hammer off, the staircase leading up to the minaret and balcony a bit too steep for his liking. Now the damned pizza was waging war with his gut, his breath shortening, his ribs feeling as though they were caving in.

'Pepper, are you there? SITREP?'

'Ghost Lead, Pepper here. I'm in position.'

As vantage points/sniper positions went, this little nest was first class, giving him a clean shot of any member of any mortar team. He was overlooking the entire graveyard, and if he blurred his vision, the stones resembled the spirits of infantrymen forming up for battle. If his colleagues did their jobs correctly, Pepper would not need to fire a single shot. He was just the All-State man. The team was in good hands.

A flash from just outside the cemetery caught his attention, and there, at the far end of the road, where Al-Aydarus intersected with another barely pronounceable street to the east, came a BTR-40, a Soviet-made wheeled armored personnel carrier – two operators up front, six troops in the back ready to dismount. The light Pepper had spotted had come from the BTR's roof-mounted 7.62mm machine gun, winking fire as it had crossed the intersection.

And then, a squad of troops came running up behind the BTR, attacking the vehicle from the rear, one man pausing in the middle of the road to shoulder and fire his rocket-propelled grenade, the back blast filling the intersection with smoke. A second explosion obscured by the buildings flickered like lightning a second before a mushroom cloud lit from below broke above the rooftops.

'Got some action down the street,' Pepper said. 'Better hold up for a minute.'

'We see it,' said Ross.

Pepper grimaced and clutched his chest. Now he was

just getting paranoid, the chest pains coming on because he was worried about chest pains coming on: stress begetting stress.

He should never have gone for that stupid physical. All that doc had done was make him paranoid.

'There is no fence to sit on between heaven and hell,' Johnny Cash had once said. 'Only a deep, wide gulf, a chasm that is no place for any man –'

Which was why Pepper knew that when their work was finished here, they needed to leave. This place literally was a crater, a chasm where they did not belong, where the loyalty of men waned and the fires of hatred had burned for thousands of years.

'Pepper, am I clear?' called 30K.

'Hang tight . . . and . . . yes, you are! Go now!'

The plastic explosives procured for the team's load out bags had come from the UK, so instead of being supplied with C-4, they were given bricks of PE4, an off-white colored solid whose explosive characteristics were nearly identical to C-4, although PE4 had a slightly greater velocity of detonation: 8,210 meters per second.

These technical attributes were largely unimportant to men like 30K, men with an affinity for blowing shit up. They didn't do the math because they *always* overestimated the amount of explosives required for the job.

'Kozak, you got me?' he asked as he skulked along the wall outside the cemetery, his active camouflage on, the pack strapped to his shoulders feeling as though it'd been stuffed with bowling balls.

'Roger, you're marked. Two meters.'

30K dragged his elbow across the wall, keeping tight to the shadows –

'Okay, okay, position one. Mark,' said Kozak.

Panting now, 30K reached into his pack and produced the first of ten blocks of PE4 fitted inside a shaped charge casing and rigged with a remote detonator. The casings were cone-shaped, and 30K carefully placed the first one at the foot of the wall, then he jogged off, listening for Kozak's next set of instructions:

'Five meters ... three ... one ... position two. Mark.'

30K continued placing each of the ten blocks where Kozak indicated so that when he was finished, the explosives all rested directly opposite the mortars, with only the wall standing between them.

Good old Sun Tzu, author of *The Art of War*, would've been proud. He'd said that subduing the enemy without fighting was the acme of skill. Sure, they could've gone into the cemetery as 30K had suggested, letting him do his Rambo/Conan/Gladiator thing, running and gunning like a fire-breathing serial killer inhabited by the spirits of ancient warriors and movie stars, but the chances were high that once he took out the second crew, the others would cease fire and turn their small arms on him, drawing the rest of the team into a firefight that would waste valuable time and even more valuable ammunition.

And oh, yeah, he could die.

Besides, the Ghosts were much more cunning than that. Consequently, they'd gone back to the drawing board, or more accurately, gone back to their packs, where they always carried explosives. They relied upon shaped charges for taking out armor or structures like bridges, and they were always looking for any excuse to lighten their packs and satisfy their inner pyros.

Of course, there were some men like 30K who just wanted to see the world *explode* . . .

Ross had come up with the plan after analysing the positions of the mortars, and while it was half as glamorous as 30K's run and governator maneuver, they needed to trade demigod status for deception.

However, if 30K was the designated pack mule, then he'd argued that he and only he got to push the button. Ross had been fine with that.

'Ghost Lead, 30K here. I'm at the end of the wall. Charges set.' The image displayed in 30K's HUD showed each of his charges as flashing red triangles nestled tightly against the wall. Just on the other side were the mortar teams, and 30K literally shivered with anticipation. 'On your mark,' he told Ross.

'Roger, on my mark. Pepper? What do you think?'

Silence.

'Pepper, this is Ghost Lead. SITREP!'

'Here, boss, sorry. We're clear. Ready to blow.'

'Okay, 30K. Mark.'

The remote detonators had all been set to the same frequency and would trigger the charges simultaneously. If for whatever reason a charge failed to go off, Pepper, 30K and Ross would take up the slack, moving in to finish off those crews.

30K had transferred detonation control to his Cross-Com, through which he could now issue a voice command. He took a long breath, braced himself, then opened his mouth to speak tersely into his boom mike.

'Wait, wait, wait!' cried Pepper. 'We got dismounts coming up the street, heading right toward you, 30K.'

He couldn't see them at first, but a squint and second look quickened his pulse. They were shifting between the parked cars – at least two squads in desert camouflage fatigues, either Harak or Yemeni Army, he just couldn't tell, and there were no IDs appearing in his Cross-Com.

'Pepper, I got 'em now. Ten, maybe twelve guys. Are they friendlies?' 30K asked.

'Dunno.'

'I'm checking,' said Kozak.

'We got no choice,' hollered Ross. '30K? Blow that wall right now!'

Forty-Five

While Sun Tzu might've been proud of their plan, he would've also told 30K to get his most deceptive and cunning hide out of there because by the time 30K opened his mouth and gave the command, 'Detonate charges,' those squads up the road were sprinting toward him –

And suddenly he was wrenched back to Army boot camp, listening to some instructor shout in a sarcastic lilt how no plan ever survives the first enemy contact, and that plans B and C usually go to shit within the next five minutes.

These were not glib statements devised by operators trying to scare new recruits; they were annoying facts often accompanied by gunfire at your feet and your buddies clutching their necks while blood oozed through their fingers.

And so here they were. They'd planned to ambush the mortar teams in one fell swoop. A one-man op. Bada bing, bada boom, as Kozak might say. They had not planned on dismounts making a sweep right into the zone.

And so with an almost reckless abandon, 30K turned tail and ran – just as the ensemble of explosives resounded with a tune so catastrophically glorious that he found himself smiling from ear to ear.

What a rush!

Unable to stop himself, 30K hazarded a look back, and dear God, it was a rapturous sight that would've brought any firecracker-addicted kid to his knees, his eyes welling up with tears as he experienced a glimpse of fiery nirvana while Beethoven's 9th Symphony played by a live five-hundred-piece orchestra floating in midair blared in the background:

Ten bricks of PE4 had lifted ten separate tornadoes of shrapnel and stone that blew through the cemetery toward the mortars. It was through one particular gaping hole in the wall that 30K watched as the explosions tore through men and launch tubes alike, silencing guns and mangling flesh, the blast waves sling-shotting bodies across the cemetery toward the first rows of gravestones, the men now like puppets, scarecrows, ragdolls with limbs torn off by sinister children, heads lolling to one side, helmets tumbling.

A data box from Kozak opened in 30K's HUD and showed him the overhead view from the drone, every mortar taken out, the teams splayed across the cemetery in a breath-robbing canvas of carnage, every man dead or dying.

But their victory celebration would have to come later. Sorry, Bubba, return the kegs, tell the strippers to go home, DVR the game and we'll catch it another day—

Because those dismounts were charging toward the cemetery like bees defending their nest, the swarm of red blips appearing in 30K's HUD and gaining on him.

'Ghosts, back to the van now!' ordered Ross. 'Do not engage those dismounts. Just get back to the van!'

At the moment the wall exploded at ten separate locations, the mortar team farthest away from Pepper had just loaded a round.

As the blast wave struck that mortar, knocking it sideways, the round burst from its launch tube, only it wasn't headed skyward on its intended trajectory.

Pepper had instinctively lowered his rifle and raised his hand.

Struck by a pang of utter helplessness that rendered him like a buck in the headlights, Pepper only had time to gasp and blink – the better part of two seconds –

As the round flashed across the cemetery and hit the minaret, just below the balcony.

He was in denial, he knew, telling himself that the shell had detonated much farther below than it really had, that he was going to be okay now, that the stone floor would not give way beneath his feet –

Until it did.

And he plunged some five meters down on to the crumbling staircase, along with hundreds of pieces of plaster and stone, his boots hitting hard, knees flexing a second before he fell on to his rump, looked up, saw another shower of stone superimposed against a field of stars plunging straight toward him. He rolled on to his side, covering his face with arms, as the rest of the wall began to collapse, shards of rock striking like roundhouses and right hooks into his arms, legs and chest, the minaret still shaking, the dust hissing, another section of wall breaking loose –

And burying him alive.

Ross had held back at the van with Naseem, while 30K had made the demo run, Kozak had engaged in some close quarters recon while providing drone intel, and Pepper had served as sniper and overwatch. They'd parked the van between the mosque and the cemetery, beneath a cluster of trees opposite the main parking lot –

So when that minaret had been struck by mortar fire, Ross knew instantly that Pepper was in trouble.

He screamed in vain over the radio, but Pepper did not reply. '30K? Kozak? Rally back on the mosque.'

Naseem threw the van in gear, whirled around, and raced through the parking lot, arriving just outside the minaret, where the dust was still rising from piles of stone that had fallen from the shattered tower and now blocked the main door.

Ross was out of the van before Naseem hit the brakes. He bounded up on to the shards of concrete and carefully picked his way across them, climbing down the other side to reach the wooden door whose knob and lock had been smashed off.

Seizing the door, Ross shoved hard, but it would only open a few inches, shit. It was blocked from the inside by more stone.

Ross cupped his hands around his mouth, pressed

his face into the gap between the wall and the door, and cried, 'Pepper, you hear me? Pepper?'

The voice was faint, distant . . . but there. 'I hear you, boss. I can't move.'

'Hang on, bro! We're coming to get you!' Ross stepped back then threw himself against the door. The son of a bitch still wouldn't budge.

'You got any more charges?' asked Naseem, reaching the top of the stone pile.

'No, but if I use a grenade, those dismounts will be here in a few seconds.'

Just then Kozak and 30K came charging up. Kozak immediately consulted the drone's remote while 30K struggled for breath and managed, 'Dismounts still coming. Don't think they saw us. Not sure. In the cemetery now.'

'Pepper's trapped inside,' said Ross. 'Can't get the door open.'

'Let me try,' said 30K, leaning over to pick his way across the mound of rock.

'It's blocked from the inside.'

'Sir?' called Kozak. 'Just got word. Those dismounts are Republican Guard.'

'Then let me talk to them,' said Naseem. 'I'll stall them while you try to free your man.'

'All right, do it,' said Ross as 30K hopped down beside him, then gave the door a tentative shove. Like Ross, he stepped back and drove his shoulder into the door, groaning loudly, the effort to no avail.

'Screw it, we gotta blow it,' he said.

'No,' said Ross. 'Too loud, and the explosion could shift the rubble and make it worse.'

30K stepped back and glanced up at the minaret, estimating that there were some ten meters to the jagged hole where the mortar had detonated. 'Maybe we can rig up a hook and some paracord – but if he's hurt, we gotta get him out through this door.'

'Gotta be another way in. Maybe through the mosque,' said Ross.

'How 'bout you search for that while I rig up a cord?' 30K suggested.

Ross turned to Kozak. 'Keep the drone close. Cover us. And I want to know what Naseem is doing.'

'You got it, Captain.'

Ross teetered across the pile of rubble, then jogged around the minaret toward the main mosque.

It might have been a selfish thought, and his hands trembled in frustration over it, but of the three men in his charge, Ross liked Pepper the best. Sure, that was almost like a father favoring one child over the rest, but he and Pepper had been on the same page from the get-go, and Pepper already had some admiration for Navy SEALs. They were about the same age, same generation, and Pepper was far more patient than the others. They just clicked.

Damn it, Ross would save this man. Or he would die trying.

They were up to their knees in the clear, warm water of Squaw Creek Reservoir, the Texas sun hanging low on the horizon, their shadows long across the riprap lining the shore.

They were exactly as he'd remembered them, dressed in full combat gear and wearing the fatal wounds that had ended their lives – Joe Joe, Tommy, Louis, Big Dan, Howie, Franklin and Radiator. Seven friends who'd all been there with him, bass fishing and beer tasting, brothers in arms enjoying some R & R before they had to leave the world and head back into the shit. And they were calling Pepper home now –

Or at least he was imagining they were, lying there, buried under the rock, feeling sorry for himself, half pissed off and half embarrassed, each breath a little harder than the last, his relationship with God suddenly a little keener, his guilt over being a half-assed Christian sending a shudder up his spine. This was definitely not the way to go, although being killed by a mortar blast sounded infinitely more heroic than being done in by a pizza-induced heart attack.

He'd purchased a small tract of land near the reservoir and had planned to build a retirement cabin there. He'd shown his buddies his dream lot, and they had agreed that this was the life. Or the death, in their case now. They'd taken over his little retirement getaway for some permanent R & R in the afterlife, and the bastards weren't even paying rent. Now they wanted Pepper to join them. Time for the landlord to come home.

He shifted his right ankle. He could move that. He fought against the pressure on his left arm, and it budged.

Well, shit, he was a long way from death, one hundred thousand miles at least, especially if he got the old ticker tuned up. Time to quit feeling sorry for himself.

'Pepper?' came 30K's distant, hollow-sounding voice. 'I'm coming up to get you, old man. Thirty seconds.'

Pepper closed his eyes and began muttering the lyrics from his favorite Hank Williams, Jr, song, 'Long Gone Lonesome Blues,' and by the time he reached the end, he heard two voices much closer now: Ross and 30K.

He was almost home free, and that was good because the pressure on his ribs was unbearable now, his breath growing shorter by the second.

'Roger that, Kozak,' said Ross. 'We're almost there – and yeah, I know we're out of time . . .'

'Pepper, can you hear me?' called Kozak.

'Yeah,' he said, barely recognizing his own voice. 'I'm here. Over here.'

'Captain, I see him,' called 30K. 'He's right down there.'

The whomping of the helicopter came on much too suddenly, and by the time Pepper sensed that 30K was near, the drumming of rotors made the rock vibrate, the wash seeping in through the cracks to blast dust into his eyes.

Forty-Six

Ross had found the secondary entrance to the minaret through the mosque, but the door there had also been blocked. He did manage to pry it inward enough to squeeze through, just as 30K had reached the hole in the tower and was staring down the stairwell.

But as 30K had dropped a second rope and was preparing to scale his way down toward the staircase – and Ross was about to climb his way up over the gauntlet of jagged stone – that helicopter had rumbled overhead, and Ross had activated his Cross-Com and HUD to see what the hell was going on. He patched into Kozak's drone and was cursing not two seconds after viewing the map floating in his HUD:

The dismounts had finished their sweep through the cemetery and were heading toward the mosque. Whether Naseem had spoken to them or not didn't matter anymore. They were coming, and Ross needed to get the team out of there.

Their second problem was the chopper, a MIL Mi-24D Hind known by Russian pilots as the *letayushchiy* tank, or the 'flying tank.' The Yemen Air Force had approximately fourteen of these attack helicopters in service, and this 'D' variant had two separate cockpits for the pilot and gunner.

A single 12.7mm four-barrel Yak-B machine gun jutted from under its nose turret, while four 57mm rocket pods were mounted beneath stubby wings. Ross didn't bother scanning the bird's additional weapons. The fact that CAS (Close Air Support) had arrived was bad news if you were running a clandestine operation and trying to make a swift and silent escape.

The gunship wheeled overhead as though its crew were going to lower a rescue line –

But then it suddenly pitched forward and raced off, its machine gun blazing.

Ross's HUD switched to drone video piped in by Kozak, who'd redirected the UAV to a higher position so they could see the gunner's target.

A convoy of four Panhards operated by the rebels had come racing up the street toward the cemetery, with more troops running alongside them, several carrying RPGs on their backs.

'You better hurry up, boss, because the fight's coming to us,' called Kozak.

'I hear you,' said Ross, then he started his way up the staircase, clutching chunks of stone and checking each new position for good purchase, his boots slipping over the dusty rock, his flashlight now Velcroed to the side of his helmet, the beam cutting through the dust motes like a light-saber. The sweat was burning his eyes, and he grimaced over the taste of plaster.

30K was coming down the inside wall with the speed and agility of a man who'd been bitten by a radioactive spider, and Ross couldn't help admiring the operator's youth and unwavering sense of purpose. He, too, was burning with the desire to rescue his buddy, and he reached Pepper a few seconds before Ross did.

Only Pepper's left boot was visible; otherwise, he was completely buried by chunks of rock, and one by one, Ross and 30K worked together to uncover him. They cleared away his face and legs, but the largest section of stone, about two meters square and a half meter thick, was lying across the sergeant's back, and it seemed the only thing that had saved him from not being crushed to death was that he'd been slammed and tucked into one of the stairs, with the staircase itself absorbing most of the kinetic energy.

'Explosion hit the mortar, and the damned thing went off right in my face,' Pepper explained. 'What are the odds? What kind of shitty bad luck is that?'

'I told you, Pepper,' 30K began, prying free another stone from the man's shoulder. 'You gotta start living on the straight and narrow like me. You need to stop tempting fate.'

'Oh, Jesus, you hear this, Captain? This from the monster of mayhem.'

'How you feeling?' asked Ross. 'I mean breathing.'

'It's rough,' said Pepper. 'I'm jammed in here really good. We need to find my Remington, too. We ain't leaving without it. I dropped it somewhere.'

'I see it up there,' said 30K. 'Don't worry, we'll get it.'

'You think anything's broken?' asked Ross.

Pepper snorted. 'Just my ego.'

Ross exchanged a mild grin with 30K, then shook his head at the piece of wall pinning their colleague. 'Any ideas?'

'I got a frag,' said 30K. 'Let's just blow it off of him.'

'Wait, hold on,' groaned Pepper.

'Relax, bro, I'm just kidding,' said 30K.

'Ghost Lead, it's Kozak. Are you done in there? The chopper's engaging the rebels, and Naseem's boys are moving up on them. We need to be out of here yesterday.'

'All right, Pepper, you think if we can lift this thing a little bit, you can try sliding out? There's no time to get a rope in here and try hauling up the rock. We gotta move, all right?'

'You lift it, boss, and I'll get my sorry ass out. What're you waiting for?'

Ross gave a nod to 30K, and they positioned themselves side by side, backs to the edge of the stone, hands locked under the edge, triceps ready to fire up and take some serious pain.

'On three,' said Ross.

'Aw, just pull on it,' said 30K –

And bang, they got to work, grimacing and groaning in agony as the stone began to lift, an inch, two inches, three, as Ross shouted:

'Can you move?'

Pepper gasped through his exertion. 'Not yet. Little more.'

30K exercised his right of free speech, drawing deeply into his vocabulary of four-letter words to create an R-rated mantra that would've had conservative blue-haired grandmothers clutching their hearts and fainting right in the middle of Father Thomas's homily.

Suddenly, sans any fanfare or even a word from Pepper, he drew himself out from beneath the stone, then finally cried, 'Clear!'

Ross took a slight step forward, then glanced at 30K and said, 'Let her drop.'

The hunk of stone came down with a heavy bass note, shaking the staircase and cracking in half.

Both Ross and 30K remembered their lessons on how to treat trauma victims and went over Pepper with a fine-tooth comb, checking each of his limbs for breaks, exposed bones, anything that might need immediate care. They examined his pupils, making sure they were equal and reactive to light. They looked for fluid coming out of his ears, which would indicate a head injury. They had him flex his arms and legs several times. His helmet had saved him from what could've been the very worst of it, but he did have a gash near his elbows, and probably a hundred other bruises that would only reveal themselves in the days to come. He was damned lucky to be alive.

'All right, big guy,' Ross began. 'I know it hurts, but we need to leave. I'll get your rifle.'

'Thanks,' said Pepper, being helped shakily to his feet. 'I'm banged up, but I can walk. Just don't ask me to dance.'

'Let me get down there first,' said 30K. 'Need to clear some rocks from that door so we can open it up all the way and get him through.'

'You saying I'm fat?' asked Pepper.

30K laughed. 'I wasn't the one who ate an entire pizza.'

Forty-Seven

Kozak kept close to the van, his rifle held high, his Cross-Com picking out a host of targets about fifty meters away, down the street. The gunship had just banked hard, coming around for another pass, laying down machine-gun fire that tore pockmarks in the road and struck the parked cars and the troops huddled behind them.

What happened next caused Kozak to blink. Hard.

Three of the rebels ran directly into the road, placing themselves in the gunners' sights.

At first, Kozak thought it was a suicide mission. Then he realized with a start that the Hind's pilot had been far too aggressive and had just made a fatal error.

Before the chopper's gunner could bring his machine gun around, each rebel shouldered an RPG, and nearly in unison all three fired, the rockets whooshing up from the ground as if attached to thin plumes of smoke, the chopper hovering there, too big and too slow to evade this expertly timed attack –

And again, in a moment torn from the screenplay of Kozak's imagination and brought to life against a pitch-black night rich with stars, three separate explosions resounded from the Hind, those rockets targeting the main and tail rotors, the smoke and roiling flames whipped by the heavy blades, the chopper beginning to list as the engines coughed and whined, and every rebel troop below screamed and turned their rifles skyward, showering the bird with small arms fire, the fuselage suddenly alive with a thousand sparking and ricocheting rounds. This poorly equipped band of warriors hooted and hollered, realizing they had just slain a dragon.

Trailing black smoke, the engines sputtering louder in their death throes, the chopper rolled to port on an erratic angle, then came around –

Plummeting straight toward Kozak.

He blinked again. *Really? Right toward me?*

With a stab of panic, he shot a look back, where 30K and Ross were helping Pepper hobble toward the van.

Off to the left came Naseem, running and waving his hands, screaming something, his voice completely muffled by the gunship.

'Oh my God,' 30K muttered as the light from the exploding chopper played over his face and the heat from the engines came at them like a million barbecues. He glanced at Ross and screamed, 'Let's get the –'

But he cut himself off, because the captain was already dragging Pepper toward the wall on their left – the nearest cover.

For his part, Kozak had already left the van and was sprinting toward the same rally point, his face contorted in an expression 30K had never seen before.

Naseem wasn't as lucky. Even though he'd turned around and started running in the opposite direction, the Hind pitched again, colliding with the van, crushing it like a can of Bud Light, then rolling on to its side, the five rotor blades slashing into the ground until they snapped off and boomeranged away, the fuselage continuing to roll several times, coming up behind Naseem – and then, with a twin thunderclap, the 500-liter external fuel tanks exploded.

30K could barely watch.

The colonel was swept into a pair of fireballs that blasted across the cemetery, leaving dense clouds of inky black smoke in their wake. The stench of all that burning fuel and rubber and flesh came with the concussion, and 30K took one breath and gagged.

'You see that shit?' cried Kozak, fighting for breath. 'Naseem's dead. He's dead, man. What now?'

'Time to call Guardian,' said 30K. 'See if he wants to send in backup.'

They all looked to Ross, whose eyes were narrowed in thought, his lips set. He'd just learned that their contact was killed, their ride destroyed . . . but the captain's expression was implacable.

'He's right, boss,' said Pepper. 'We ain't gonna make it to the port. Not through this attack.'

Ross took a long breath and finally opened his mouth. 'I know the address of the safe house. Kozak, get me the location of one of those APCs, the M113s used by the Army. We'll commandeer ourselves a little ride.'

Pepper made a face. Kozak was already seeing the impossibility of it all, but 30K began to nod and smile. 'I like it, sir.'

Ross snorted. 'I knew you would.'

'What about Pepper?' asked Kozak.

'What about me?' Pepper snapped. 'I won't slow you down. I'm good to go.'

'You don't look good to go.'

'I'm old. That's my normal look.'

'All right. Let's head back behind the mosque. Get the camouflage up.'

As the rebels and government troops began to clash in the cemetery behind them, gunfire and grenades booming with an almost rhythmic pulse, the chopper wreckage still burning, the renewed stench of gunpowder heavy on the wind, 30K kept close to Pepper, and in a couple of minutes they were back at the mosque. They'd found the place empty, the imams and other staff all evacuated once the mortar fire had commenced, but 30K wished they'd run into some civilian who'd take one look at their desperate faces and large-caliber weapons and hand over his keys without protest.

The M113 Armored Personnel Carrier, better known by grunts in the field as simply a 'track,' always reminded Kozak of the chariot from the old *Lost in Space* TV show, whose episodes he'd downloaded on to his iPod and had watched with an almost religious fervor. He was a science fiction fan from the age of seven, with a penchant for 1960s sci-fi films and TV series, a secret hobby that he'd never reveal to his fellow Ghosts, lest they have another reason to talk smack about him.

They'd found the APC parked on Queen Arwa Road near the bank building, one of the six they'd spotted earlier. After a few minutes of close-in reconnoitering to confirm that only the commander and .50-caliber gunner had been left on board, Kozak and 30K moved in.

The commander stood in his cupola and chatted quietly with the gunner, standing in his own hatch. They felt the vehicle shift and creak, and as they turned their heads back toward those vibrations, they saw a curtain of water part before their eyes –

And then, at once, they were staring down the barrels of two rifles. 30K aimed at the commander, and Kozak had the muzzle of his rifle just a few inches from the gunner's nose.

'Where did you come from?' gasped the commander.

'From Pizza Hut,' 30K said evenly.

'Ghost Lead,' Kozak began over the team net. 'We've got two for you.'

That was the signal for Ross. The captain mounted the APC from the front and shot both men with the Taser while they were preoccupied and stunned over the appearance of these aliens dressed like soldiers.

Pepper hustled up from behind and lowered the troop door from behind while 30K and Kozak dragged the stunned men from their hatches and with Ross's help got them down to the asphalt.

'Born to be wild,' grunted Ross as he dropped into the commander's cupola.

With that, he started the old diesel engine; she roared like a tyrannosaur and sprang forward, tracks clicking over asphalt.

Kozak manned the big gun, checked the ammo, and was already itching to fire.

Ross throttled up, and soon the wind was blasting in Kozak's face as they sped up the highway, explosions rising to the east and west, the sounds of more helicopters thrumming near the mountains, the lightning flashes of fragmentary grenades crackling from the alleys ahead.

Forty-Eight

It was nearly midnight, and Mitchell called to give Ross another update on the *Ocean Cavalier*'s ETA, now moved up to 2:41 a.m. local time.

Ross downplayed the exact nature of their situation, which was to say he did not lie but did not volunteer the full truth. He told Mitchell that Naseem had been killed and they were en route to the second safe house and would be there well before the ship's arrival. There was a rebel attack in progress, but local forces seemed to be getting the upper hand.

Mitchell was pleased, but some suspicion had leaked into his tone. 'Do you need help?'

'Negative.'

If Ross requested backup, he would, in his mind, be admitting defeat. At the same time, if he deliberately endangered his men to protect his ego and reputation with the GST, then he was a fool and didn't deserve the job. He was reminded of a quote from his favorite American president, Theodore Roosevelt, who had once said, 'Far better it is to dare mighty things, to win glorious triumphs, even though checkered by failure, than to take rank with those poor spirits who neither enjoy much nor suffer much, because they live in the gray twilight that knows neither victory nor defeat.'

Incoming fire forced Ross to cut short his update to Mitchell and put Kozak to work on some troops strung out along the highway and several snipers posted on the roof of a hotel. Ross ducked into his hatch as the rounds pinged and popped, and Kozak was going to town on the fifty, trying to silence the bastards, brass arcing over the APC's roof and tumbling over the sides. Ross couldn't pry any more speed out of the engine, barely doing 60 kilometers per hour, the steering yoke growing hot in his hands.

He hadn't forgotten about the roadblock ahead, lying just before the Gate of Aden, a stone bridge that spanned the soaring mountains on either side of the road.

'Pepper, what do you got?' Ross asked.

After leaving the mosque, they'd called in both drones, but just before commandeering the M113, Ross had ordered one UAV redeployed. Pepper, who'd sworn he was okay, was now monitoring that drone from the troop compartment, and his report was about as morale-lifting as warm beer and stale pretzels:

'Well, ladies, we still have four Panhards in the defile, which means we're staring down the barrels of four ninety-millimeter guns. Looks like three squads on the roadside now, with some RPGs and even a few mortars – although there might as well be a thousand dismounts because those guns will blow the shit out of us before we get within a hundred meters of the check-point. They'll need to call in some archeologists to dig us up and identify our remains.'

'I say we go in there and kill those bastards with our good looks,' 30K said. 'Sorry, Pepper, we don't need you.'

Pepper chuckled under his breath. 'Okay, bro, you're the scout. We'll send you up there and see what happens.'

'Glad you guys can joke around,' snapped Kozak. 'What the hell are we gonna do?'

'Relax, gentlemen,' Ross said. 'The fact is, Pepper's right. There's no way we'll breach that checkpoint. But we didn't borrow a tracked vehicle for nothing. There's a dirt road leading off into the mountains about a klick before the roadblock, just before a curve in the road so they shouldn't see us when we duck out. We'll ride this bitch into the mountains as far as we can, then if we have to, we'll dismount and hike the rest of the way. It's the best we can do, but I think we might reach the port in time. Are you in?'

'Hell, yeah, I'm in,' said Kozak.

'You Navy guys are all right,' 30K said.

'I'm not in the Navy anymore,' Ross reminded him. 'I'm a ground pounder, same as you.'

'Captain, that's a good plan,' said Pepper. 'But we're gonna burn a lot of fuel once we start climbing.'

'I know,' answered Ross. 'But like I said, we'll keep her going for as long as we can. So . . . hang on . . . it's time for a little off-roading.'

Ross took a deep breath and squinted at the highway ahead, the flickering streetlights, the section of the city now lying dark and without power, along with that turn he'd noted snaking off to their left, the dirt fanning across the road. He was slowly earning the team's trust. Now all he had to do was keep them alive.

Kozak was trembling.

As they turned off the highway and broke on to the dirt road, the M113 bouncing hard over some deep cuts in the path, he held up his hand and confirmed the fact.

What was the matter with him? He was better than this. Braver. But he kept hearing something Pepper had told him when they'd first met: *'If you spend enough time on patrol, you develop a sixth sense. You're out there just a few minutes, and you already know if it's going to be a good day or a bad day. You can't explain it. But you can feel it. People on the West Coast talk about earthquake weather, or how you can smell when a quake is coming. It's kinda like that.'*

Consequently, that powerful sense of foreboding had rested its heavy palms on Kozak's shoulders, and he knew he had to wrench free from it, like a boxer ripping himself off the ropes.

The one thing Ross had failed to mention was that traveling into the mountains would turn them into a lone heat source against the sheer rock faces, and any gunship pilot looking for a target of opportunity might decide to unload his rocket pods. The Yemeni Army was, to the best of Kozak's knowledge, not using any

Blue Force-like tracking system that would automatically tell that pilot they were friendlies, and even if he assumed the M113 belonged to government forces, he could mistake them for deserters or even make the correct assumption that the vehicle had been, ahem, *borrowed*. Kozak's shoulders slumped even more now. He began to shiver through his breath.

'Pepper, this is Kozak. Are you scanning for aircraft?' he asked.

'Yeah, they've got four gunships running CAS, spending most of their time taking out some APCs and small armor, but nothing coming this way, not yet anyway.'

'Cool.' Kozak glanced over at Ross, who gave him a quick nod, as if to say, *We'll be fine.*

They were kicking up one hell of a dust trail, the tracks grinding through the hard dirt and rock, Ross relying upon night vision to navigate around the larger rocks and keep them on the trail. But the farther they got from the road, the more vulnerable they became, Kozak knew, and his paranoia increased exponentially.

'Still clear?' he asked Pepper.

'I'll sound the alarm if the drone picks up anything, bro.'

'Okay, stay sharp, man.'

'What do you think I'm doing back here?'

'Sorry. I just . . . I kinda like flying the drone myself.'

'I noticed. Don't worry, I won't miss anything.'

'Thanks.'

The dirt road veered off to the left, and the grade increased dramatically to perhaps ten or twelve per cent. The engine's drone deepened for a moment then became much higher pitched as it strained against the slope.

Kozak stole another look at Ross. The captain's face was hard and unreadable. He'd had a plan and was working that plan like a machine. So this was the way to develop fierce loyalty, to get your men to follow you into hell. You were always thinking two steps ahead of them and kept your emotions in check. Your commitment and courage allowed them to believe in you, the mission, and themselves. Kozak still had a lot to learn.

He pricked up his ears. Was that the engine straining again? The tracks crushing more rocks?

Or was that a helicopter approaching?

Down below in the troop compartment, 30K was seated next to Pepper and staring over his shoulder at the UAV's remote. Pepper's breath was a little strained, and 30K suspected the man might have cracked a rib or two but wasn't saying.

'Hey, Pepper, before when I said you gotta lead the straight and narrow, I wasn't kidding.'

'What?'

'Seriously, you scared the shit out of me back there.'

'What're you talking about? I got banged up by some rocks.'

'Dude, listen to me, you're the most experienced guy we got. You're the best shot. We can't lose you.'

Pepper laughed under his breath. 'Okay, I'll try not to die.'

'Dude, I'm serious.'

'You're just overtired.'

'Look, every time we go out, I say the same thing: if Pepper buys it, I'm screwed.'

'Why's that?'

'Because like I said, if they can kill our best guy, then I don't stand a chance.'

'What about Ross? He's got more experience than me.'

'He don't count.'

'Why?'

'Because he just doesn't.'

Pepper frowned. 'Uh, you okay?'

'Look, I want you to stay close. No more risks, all right? I'll tell the captain we need to pair up from now on.'

'Where's this coming from? Maybe that pizza fried *your* brain. What's the matter with you?'

30K shook his head. 'I don't know. But I can't shake it. So just do me a favor? You stick with me.'

Pepper sighed, failing to hide his grimace. 'Jimmy, you're a good kid, but if I had a daughter, I still wouldn't let her date you.'

30K was about to smile when the drone's proximity alarm beeped, and Pepper's glance riveted on the remote. He lifted his voice into his boom mike: 'Kozak, you son of a bitch, you jinxed us.'

Forty-Nine

They were nearly at the summit of a mountain pass that would take them down toward the port, the lights of the cranes and container ships out at the terminal just coming into view, when Ross got Pepper's report:

Gunship inbound. ETA two minutes.

Unnerved by the news, Ross cut the steering yoke a little too sharply to the right – and the dreaded noise from the right track had him cursing. They'd just hit a large rock and thrown the track. With a screech of metal, the vehicle began pulling sharply to the left side and sliding sideways back down the hillside.

Even as Ross tried to brake, he realized with a start that throwing the track was only the first of their problems. The APC was losing ground quickly, and he screamed for Kozak to get down in his hatch. Ross did likewise, and not two heartbeats later –

The M113 rolled on to its side with a hundred groans of contorting metal, track shoes burrowing into rock, the side walls rumbling and making it sound as though they were trapped inside a snare drum during a rock concert.

And all at once, they came to a squealing, coughing, shimmying halt. Ross immediately turned off the engine and hit the master switch, trying to prevent a fire hazard. Knowing that spilled oil and gasoline could still catch fire – and with that incoming gunship still at the fore of his thoughts, Ross barked his orders, 'Everybody out! Out through my hatch right now!'

30K and Pepper looked shaken but were crawling forward across the side wall of the compartment, while Kozak flashed a thumbs-up and followed Ross outside.

Ross dragged himself down on to the dirt, then scrambled to his feet to turn back and help Kozak through the hatch. Next came Pepper, followed by 30K.

From the muffled booming of gunfire and explosions in the distance came the distinct and inevitable sound of beating rotors. Ross whirled in that direction and spotted the running lights – tiny and innocent – down there in the valley. He brought up his Cross-Com and zoomed in with night vision.

No, that wasn't the local news chopper come to report on fender benders down on the highway.

Pepper's gunship was less than sixty seconds away, wings spread, rocket pods full, fangs out.

'Let's go! Let's go!' he ordered. 'Pepper, call in the drone!'

Ahead lay a deep groove in the mountainside, and Ross was reminded that this entire place wasn't really a mountain at all but the inside of a volcano, and this groove might've been produced by flowing lava eons ago. They reached the entrance, and once Pepper had the drone back in its holster, they shifted deeper inside, tucking themselves in by some four meters and now completely shielded by the rock, their heat signatures difficult to spot by the gunship's cameras.

As the chopper neared, Ross got on his belly and crawled forward until he could see the M113. The chopper's pilot directed a searchlight across the disabled vehicle, probing it with slow, deliberate movements of the beam. He was probably noting the open hatch but forgetting that his rotor wash was now wiping clean the team's footprints.

He hovered for what seemed like five, ten minutes before finally breaking off. Ross sighed through a handful of curses, then returned to the others. 'Everyone all right?'

'Sir, it's nearly 2 a.m. now,' said Pepper. 'You think we can get down there in forty minutes?'

'I think we can defy the laws of physics, tell the universe to go to hell, and make this shit happen because we're the best there is. That's the way we roll. That's the way we put our money in the bank.'

'Hoo-ah, sir,' said 30K. 'Let's do this.'

Pepper shrugged. 'Still would've been nice to drive down there, but you take the good with the bad, and sometimes she ain't the prettiest girl but she's the only one in town.'

Kozak shrugged at Ross. 'What he said.'

They moved out into the darkness.

Exactly thirty-seven minutes later they reached the nearest road running parallel to the port, a main artery that no doubt by day was coursing with traffic. They kept low along the embankment, and Pepper confirmed that the *Ocean Cavalier* was already in the harbor. Ross spied the terminal through his binoculars. One other container ship was already moored there, and he spotted the second berth where he assumed the *Ocean Cavalier* would dock.

'I've got a clean signal from the tracker,' said Kozak. 'Missiles are still on board, and we're good to go so far.'

'I've got the safe house marked on our maps,' said 30K. 'It's about eight hundred meters. In your HUDs now.'

Ross examined the wireframe map and the suggested course they should take to reach the apartment building. 'All right, guys. Camouflage up. Here we go.'

Given the early-morning hour, the streets were mostly deserted, though any late-night pedestrian would've only seen a strange distortion in the air near several of the buildings. He would have attributed this to his lack of sleep or dust in his eyes, as alcohol was illegal in Yemen.

A familiar Mercedes van was parked outside the apartment, and Ross noted the licence plate and confirmed that the van belonged to their driver from the airport, one of Naseem's contacts. They reached the ninth-floor apartment, and before Ross had a chance to knock, the door swung open and the old man, who resembled Merlin, waved them soundlessly inside.

'You never told us your name,' Ross said.

'I'm Oliver,' he said with his crisp British accent.

'And I've lived in this city for a very long time. This is my home, so please don't get my rug dirty.'

'We'll do our best.'

Oliver waved them through a modestly appointed living room with a bookshelf that covered the entire wall and into a bedroom, where at the window stood an elaborate collection of tripods and telescopes, along with a computer station featuring three twenty-four-inch displays, a veritable cockpit for information gathering.

'How'd you know we were coming now?' Ross asked.

'Diaz told me. And if you don't mind my saying, you gentlemen are a sodding mess.'

'We could use a couple of minutes of downtime,' said Ross. 'Too bad we don't have it. You got an observation post on the roof?'

'I'll get you the key to get up there.'

'Kozak? You and 30K, up top. Get the drone ready. Fixed position near the ship. Obviously, I want eyes on those cargo containers as they come off.'

'What if this ain't it?' asked Pepper. 'What if this ain't even the port and the container just stays on board? Long-ass night all for nothing, huh?'

'If this ain't it, then we keep going,' said Ross.

Pepper sighed. 'I knew you were gonna say that.'

'You think we're getting too old for this shit?'

Pepper's eyes widened. 'Hell, no, sir. I think we're just developing a better appreciation for the irony of the situation.'

Ross smiled tightly. 'I agree.'

Fifty

While Kozak muttered to himself and worked the drone's remote, 30K scanned the well-lit terminal with his binoculars. The *Ocean Cavalier* had just slipped into her berth, and 30K's Cross-Com had just opened a new data window with specs on the terminal itself:

- Two berths of 350 meters each and alongside depth of 16 meters.
- Four 40-ton capacity post-Panamax gantry cranes available.
- Container yard covering 35 hectares and 2,500 ground slots to accommodate more than 10,000 TEUs (twenty-foot equivalent units – an acronym for the standard capacity of an intermodal container) and 252 reefer outlets.
- 4,700 square meter container freight station, consolidation shed, offices, independent power station, desalination plant, workshops, and water treatment plant.

All of that was well and good, he thought. But where the hell were they taking the missiles, if they were unloading them at all?

'Okay, guys, showtime,' said Kozak as the big cranes

got to work, and the cargo containers began to come off the ship.

30K and Kozak were joined on the roof by Ross, Pepper and the old man Oliver, and Kozak sent the drone's video out to their Cross-Coms.

'I guess I have to ask. There's a war going on, and port operations continue?' Ross said to Oliver.

The old man looked amused. 'Of course. Everyone still wants to get paid.'

After about twenty minutes of the most boring footage known to mankind, with 30K forcing himself to keep his eyes open, Kozak broke the silence with a sudden and urgent, 'There it is.'

Container 11132001 was lifted off the ship and transferred to the back of a tractor-trailer. The driver, a burly man at least six foot five, wearing a sleeveless T-shirt and heavily tattooed, spoke briefly with several workers on the dock, signed off on a few papers, then climbed in his cab and drove away.

Kozak made sure to capture some excellent close-up images of the man –

Who didn't drive very far. Just five hundred meters to the back of the container freight station, where he pulled directly into an unmarked warehouse.

'Who owns that warehouse?' Ross asked Oliver.

'I'll get that to you immediately.' The old man headed to the stairwell door.

'So maybe this is it,' said Kozak. 'The rockets are for the South Yemen Movement, and the trail ends here.'

Oliver stopped and turned back. 'No, the trail does not end here, sir. Hamid has nothing to do with what's happening in Yemen.'

'They've got you pretty dialed in, huh?' 30K asked.

The old man took a step toward them. 'Sir, I've been working for the CIA for over thirty years. Yes, I'm pretty dialed in, as you say.'

'I thought Naseem was our contact here, and you just worked for him,' said Ross.

'Naseem worked for me.'

'Why do you people have such a problem with the truth?' Pepper asked.

'Our business is finding the truth. We have no problem with that. We're actually rather good at it. Unfortunately, it's the people who make things rather complicated.'

Ross stepped between Pepper and the old man. 'All right. What do you think?'

'They're waiting to move the missiles again. Ground, ship, or air, who knows, but if they wait, we wait.'

'Agreed. Pepper, get the second drone on that warehouse. They won't make a move without us knowing about it.'

'And I'll you get you the information on that warehouse, though I suspect it won't matter much,' said Oliver.

Fifteen minutes later, Ross was down at Oliver's computer station and leaning over the old man's shoulder to scan the intel he'd gathered. The warehouse belonged to the Al-Monsoob Commercial Group and was part of their general shipping and storage operations that they provided to more than thirty client corporations. There was nothing obvious or immediate to indicate that the owners had ties to the FARC or *Bedayat jadeda*, and the link could simply involve a small collection of employees who had been bribed into looking the other way while they 'sat' on a very 'special' container until it was shipped out again.

Kozak flew the drone dangerously close to the warehouse to report only two doors, no windows and a few small vehicles parked outside, their tags run, registrations matched up to employees of Al-Monsoob, none of them fitting the description of the tractor-trailer driver who had picked up the container.

Oliver let them crash on his recliner and sofa, and they rotated in pairs on watch, with Kozak and 30K volunteering for the first shift since the 'old guys' needed their sleep. Ross took that jab without retort, and within ten minutes of his head hitting the sofa, he was sound asleep.

It was the old man who woke them, offering tea and biscuits for breakfast. Ross called up to Kozak and 30K, who said there'd been absolutely no movement around the warehouse and that the tracking beacon's signal was strong. The big guy with the tattoos who'd picked up the container must've had a bunk either in his cab or in the warehouse, as they were certain he had not left.

'The fighting in Crater has stopped for the time being,' said Oliver. 'But I suspect once night falls, the attacks will resume.'

Ross noticed a picture on one of the bookshelves. A much younger Oliver was standing on a white sand beach with a young woman of about twenty, a lithe blonde with a spectacular smile. 'Who's that in the picture with you?'

'My daughter, Evon. On her twenty-first birthday. A very special day.'

'Beautiful girl.'

'She was.'

Ross looked at Pepper, who averted his gaze.

Perhaps he was being too blunt, or prying, but Ross felt compelled to ask: 'How did you lose her?'

Oliver's gaze went distant. 'She was coming home from a friend's house. She got into a car accident with a drunk driver. They pronounced her dead at the scene. She was an only child when her mother passed away, so I'd raised her by myself. This was long before I joined the CIA.'

Ross closed his eyes. 'I'm very sorry for your loss.'

'Thank you. I miss her every day.'

Pepper had spent most of the night back inside that tower, reliving the moment when the floor collapsed and he had plunged toward the staircase. In addition to that looping nightmare, his body cried out with new pains that woke him at least a half dozen times. The bruises were beginning to form on his arms and legs, the once minor aches turning into shooting pains. He was pretty sure he'd broken a rib or two.

Now, as he hunkered down on the building's roof, quietly observing the warehouse through his binoculars, with Ross at his side, he imagined lying on a waterbed and being tenderly massaged by a team of supermodel nurses. He quickly shook off the thought. *Stay focused. Don't torture yourself.*

He and Ross spent the entire day on that rooftop, allowing 30K and Kozak to get some much-needed rest. Those two boys had looked pretty ragged when Ross and Pepper came up to relieve them. It'd been a long journey since Colombia.

'I don't like this,' Ross said, consulting his watch. 'Other ships have come and gone, trucks at the other warehouses, lots of activity and movement all around our target.'

'What do you mean?'

'I mean, if this is just a transfer point, wouldn't you want your cargo to be on its way as quickly as possible? The longer it remains in one location, the more vulnerable it is . . .'

'Not necessarily,' said Pepper. 'They could be waiting on another ship or truck. The delay could be a necessary evil.'

'So you think I'm just impatient?'

'I think by nightfall you'll send 30K and Kozak down there to pick the lock and get inside. Kozak will send off his little Dragonfly.'

'That's what you'd do?'

Pepper lowered his binoculars and regarded Ross with a faint smile. 'We ain't gettin' any younger.'

Fifty-One

30K's watch read 10:41 p.m. local time.

He had the warehouse door open in seven seconds and lost his bet with Kozak. He'd bragged to his team mate that he could do it in six. A second is a second, but at least the six-pack of Terrapin Hopsecutioner craft beer he now owed his buddy wouldn't set him back very much. Kozak had wanted to wager fifty bucks, but 30K was too damned cheap for a bet that large. So there it was: six seconds or a six-pack.

The warehouse was large enough to accommodate at least four tractor-trailers parked side by side, but they found only one with their cargo container still seated on the trailer. Assuming that at least the driver was still there, they shifted to the nearest wall and remained still, hidden beneath their optical camouflage while Kozak deployed the drone, wings buzzing as it flew toward the container.

Meanwhile, 30K surveyed the rest of the place. On shelves and stacked on at least fifty or more pallets were boxes with labels from the Abu Dhabi Tanker Company, Ethiopian Shipping Lines, Fuzhou Fishing Company, and Assaf Marine Services, among many others. Drums of fuel, lubricating oil, and marine chemicals filled nearly an entire wall near the loading dock at the rear. This was a busy warehouse, all right, which made the lack of activity for the past twenty-four hours all the more suspect.

'30K, this is Ghost Lead. SITREP?'

Ross was crouched down on the apartment building's roof, along with Pepper and Oliver. Pepper was staring through the sight of his Remington while Oliver had borrowed a pair of the team's binoculars.

'Ghost Lead, 30K. We're inside,' came 30K's whispered report.

A window opened in Ross's HUD. A night-vision-enhanced image of the warehouse's interior captured by 30K's helmet camera showed the tractor-trailer and container exactly as Ross had imagined them.

'Container's still locked up,' said Kozak. 'Cab is empty. Our driver's either sleeping in the back and I can't see him, or somehow he got out of here.'

'Go check that office in the back,' Ross ordered.

At the same time, Ross's cell phone vibrated: It was an incoming call from Diaz. *Not now* . . .

The call was immediately followed by a text: I need to talk to you! Urgent!

Another data window opened in Ross's HUD, and he now had access to the drone's video as the micro UAV swooped down and through an open door, wheeling over a desk —

To find their driver lying on the floor with a foam cup still clutched in his hands.

'Holy shit, Captain, you seeing this?' asked Kozak. 'He looks dead.'

Ross's cell phone vibrated again – another text message from Diaz:

We've questioned Takana all day. Accessed his e-mail account.
There's a chance the weapons exchange in Sudan was observed.
Security may have been compromised!

'30K, I need you inside that container,' Ross cried. 'Do it now!'

'Roger that.'

'Kozak, I want to know what happened to that driver. Get over there and check him out. See if he's got an ID.'

'On it.'

'What's up, boss?' Pepper asked.

'Remember how you said this might've been for nothing?'

Pepper's shoulders slumped. 'Can I take it back?'

Kozak charged through the warehouse, arrived at the tractor-trailer driver's feet, and began to examine him, searching his pockets and coming up empty. 'No ID on this guy. I don't see a cell phone around here. Maybe in the truck. No visible signs of trauma, no gunshot wounds, nothing,' he told Ross. 'Died with the cup in his hands. Maybe he was poisoned.' Kozak removed the cup and tucked it into his pack, then began snapping close-up photographs of the man. A coffeepot sat on the desk, the carafe half-full, and Kozak reminded himself to grab a sample.

He had just taken his third picture when 30K shouted from across the warehouse, 'Kozak! Get out right now! Run!'

30K had cut the combination lock with his portable laser torch, had removed his safety glasses, and had swung open the heavy container door, which squeaked loudly on its rusting hinges. He'd turned and directed his flashlight into the container –

Which was empty, save for two things:

Their tracking beacon . . . and a 9,600-pound Daewoo G25e forklift sitting askew in the container.

The SAMs were gone. Transferred to another container. And once the crew had finished, they'd left the forklift behind, but the dumb shits hadn't tied it down. The forklift had shifted on its own, coaxed by the ship's pitch and roll.

And he'd been wrong. There were three things inside the container . . .

Their tracking beacon was now taped on top of four or five blocks of C-4 rigged to a motion-activated detonator. The good news was that the forklift had blocked the path to the motion sensor receiver; however, 30K's flashlight had just energized a photovoltaic cell – probably a jerry-rigged nightlight from one of the ship's sea cabins – that had cranked up some kind of blinking backup timer.

30K didn't get an exact count of those blocks of explosives. He'd already gone into fight or flight mode, deciding in that millisecond that yes, holy shit, it was flight time. *Get out!*

Ross was hollering for a SITREP over the radio as 30K bounded for the side door, then slowed, whipped back, spotted Kozak. 'Come on, buddy! Come on!'

30K's eyes were literally tearing at that moment, and his voice was cracking. He could tell Kozak was already scared out of his mind, but that was okay. If they were going to survive – and that was already doubtful – they needed an inhuman effort.

By the time Kozak reached the door and 30K was about to turn back, toward the end of the pier and the water beyond, the explosion came like a thousand lightning strikes and a thousand crashes of thunder all at the same time, his hearing suddenly gone, the night sky turning white. Even though the mass of the five-ton forklift absorbed and deflected nearly half of the blast pressure, 30K's frame was struck by a tremendous force that launched him like a Wiffle ball into the air and across the pier, the wind whipping so hard that it blinded him.

That he remained conscious was either a blessing or a curse, he couldn't decide. It either meant he had a chance to live or a few more seconds to contemplate his death.

He thought he heard Kozak shout, but he wasn't sure. There was no life flashing before his mind's eye, just that resigned thought that, yes, he was about to die.

Yet as a warrior through and through, he'd taught himself to abandon that negativity and just go on.

So maybe he wouldn't die. Maybe he'd have one hell of a story to tell those apes back at Fort Bragg . . .

Ross gasped and watched the warehouse burst into a hundred thousand flaming pieces, the fire and smoke beginning to rise as he sprang away from his position and bounded for the stairwell.

Pepper was just behind, and they reached the street within another few seconds and were racing across the road and down on to the pier as heat from the blast struck like jet engine exhaust.

An alarm blared out near the end of the terminal, a second explosion booming from within the piles of debris, knocking down a small section of the warehouse's wall that had remained standing. Fires were raging now, the flames six meters tall, the place a powder keg of noxious chemicals.

Ross coughed and waved his hands in front of his face as he jogged along the road, leaping over sections of aluminum, shipping pallets splintered and burning, along with a tattooed arm that nearly sent him tripping to the asphalt.

They reached the back of the warehouse, saw how

the cars parked there had been blasted clear across the lot and into the water some eight meters below.

Ross ran along the pier at the water's edge, spotting a few of the cars in the darkness, a glimmer from a rear bumper, a sudden coruscation from a side mirror as the vehicles began to sink . . .

And then it began to settle in, like talons clutching his heart, the nails piercing valves, the blood beginning to spill and slowly kill him.

His men had not escaped. 30K and Kozak were dead.

Fifty-Two

What 30K saw at the moment might've been painted by an artist who'd swallowed some magic mushrooms, a long-haired recluse who preferred watercolors and whose pallet was limited to simply black. And white.

As for the rest of his senses, well, they seemed jerry-rigged back together with electrical cords, duct tape, and a dab of Gorilla Glue.

30K blinked. He blinked again.

A baritone hum rang in his ears.

The sky was a tarpaulin of black with thin gray scratch marks, as though from a cat, and the water, which he felt now on his neck, was like a warm and salty soup. He could finally taste the waves and began to wince and spit.

And then, slowly, his vision returned, the pier growing distinct, the men gaping at him from above in their fatigues and helmets, their mouths working, their words garbled against the hum.

He began to paddle forward, marveling over the fact that his arms and legs still worked. He craned his head and screamed, 'Kozak? Kozak?'

The problem with being a geek is that you know too precisely how explosives and other ordnance can kill you, which was why Kozak should not have stolen a look into that open shipping container to spot that C-4. He could have spared himself the misery.

But no, he had, and even as he'd vaulted forward, knowing that he might only have a few seconds to live, he'd been contemplating the math, calculating how much force the explosives would produce, how much air pressure the human body could survive versus the pressure produced by the explosion –

And he'd been doing that right until the explosion stole all of his senses.

It was the pier, the descent, and the water combined that had helped to save their lives, he concluded as he swam toward 30K, barely hearing the man's voice above that sound in his ears that reminded him of the Emergency Alert System.

His mind kept taking him back to the exact moment of detonation. They'd been launched like RPGs, carried by the blast wave, then had drifted out of it to plunge into the water before further damage could be done to their bodies. Had they not been adjacent to the pier, Kozak speculated that they would probably be dead – the pressure, debris turned to shrapnel, and the fires all vying with one another to kill them.

There might also be an easier explanation. The monks back at Saint Tikhon's would simply call it a miracle and stop there. No need to calculate God's will.

Kozak sighed as he thought about how they'd tell his mother of his death. The dreaded car, the men in uniforms getting out, she back in the kitchen of the restaurant, coming to the front door, dropping the spatula in her hand.

Ross and Pepper were hollering and pointing for them to swim toward an adjoining dock, where several ladders led down to the water, allowing smaller craft to berth. Kozak saw the ladders and came up alongside 30K, who was talking to him, but again, Kozak could barely hear a word.

They reached the ladders and shakily ascended. Not two breaths after they crawled on to the pier, Oliver was there with his van, and Ross and Pepper helped them inside. Despite the warm air, Kozak was shaking like the misfiring engine of his first car – a 1987 Mustang GT, and he realized that all this shuddering was not from the cold. He'd had some close calls as a Ghost, but never anything like this.

30K glanced at him, mouthed some curses, then held up his fist. Kozak banged fists, then threw back his head and began to chuckle, softly at first, then at the top of his lungs, laughing like a madman – all the stress coming out.

And 30K was right there, joining him.

Fifty-Three

'They arranged to have the weapons transferred to another container – either in Massawa or while en route to Aden,' Mitchell told Ross via a video call. 'They searched the boxes and found our beacon.'

'We think they poisoned their driver, too. Any ID on him?'

'Nothing so far. But I'm afraid the weapons could be anywhere now. I'm sorry, Captain. Time to come home.'

Every muscle tensed, the blood feeling as though it had ceased running through Ross's veins. He knew if he spoke now, argued in any way, he'd regret it. The major was right.

Or was he?

There was something gnawing at Ross, something about that driver that had been strangely familiar, but he'd been unable to make the connection.

And there was a connection. There had to be; otherwise the feeling wouldn't persist.

'I understand, sir. However, we've still got some skirmishes in the city. Once we think it's safe enough, we'll have Oliver get us back to the airport, if you could send us a ride back.'

'Roger that.'

'And, sir, what about the cocaine we tagged in Tobruk? Second team find anything?'

'Believe it or not, it's still sitting there in that warehouse. They know they're being watched, and they don't want to reveal more of their shipping route. They'll move it, but they'll send it someplace else – maybe even back to Colombia.'

'I wonder if Takana gave us up at the airport. I shouldn't have let him do all the talking.'

'Honestly, Ross, I would've made the same call, and I don't think he did – not with his family at stake. They had observers and something spooked them. Don't beat yourself up over it.'

'Roger that, sir.'

'I'll contact you once your evac is en route.'

'Thank you, sir.'

Ross slammed shut his notebook computer, shifted across Oliver's living room, and went to the window, where below the emergency crews scrambled to put out the warehouse fire.

The F-word escaped his lips three times as Pepper reached his side. 'It's okay, sir, we did our best. We can walk away feeling confident about that.'

Ross turned back toward the sofa, where 30K and Kozak were seated and sipping warm tea, their eyes bloodshot, faces ashen. They'd nearly shaken hands with the reaper – and so had Pepper.

And for what? To walk away after coming this far?

Balling his hands into fists, Ross faced Pepper and

said, 'Mitchell's cutting me some slack now, but they'll hang me when we get back.'

Pepper took a deep breath. 'You mind if I speak bluntly?'

Ross couldn't help the sarcasm in his tone. 'Permission granted.'

'I get what you're feeling. First big op. New guy. Not even from the Army. Trying to prove something. You want it all to go down by the numbers, but with us, it never does. It's sloppy work. That's why we get it. Always loose ends. We try to put out fires before they start, but while we're doing that, some asshole is playing with gasoline right behind us. But what am I saying? You were a SEAL. You know the drill. They won't hang you.'

A chill suddenly woke at the base of Ross's neck. 'What did you say?'

Pepper shrugged. 'You want me to repeat the whole thing?'

'No, no, you said I know the drill. That's it!'

'That's what?'

Ross stormed back to his computer, threw back the lid, and logged on with shaking fingers.

'Sir, what the hell?' Pepper asked.

'That guy with the tattoos. Those weren't just any tattoos. I've seen them before. I just couldn't remember till now. It was back in '05. We were doing some anti-terrorism drills in Jakarta, and we had a couple of local liaisons to work with. I remember one guy having all the same tattoos. He'd told us about them, but I still can't remember what the hell he said. It was Jakarta, though.'

Ross dug out his phone and called Diaz. 'The driver with the tattoos. They're Indonesian. See what you can get on them. Specifics. And I need it yesterday.'

'Shit, I'll have it for you last week.' Diaz winked and broke the link.

With a rising pulse, Ross called their old buddy Maziq from the ISA and put in a request for a list of every ship that had left Massawa and Aden, along with all their destinations. Maziq said he'd establish the search parameters and get back to him ASAP.

'Sir, you think we got a lead here?' asked Pepper.

'Hell, yeah, I do. The way you beat these guys is through their mistakes. The little things they overlook.'

Ross clicked on the pictures Kozak had taken of the driver. The guy had been wearing that sleeveless T-shirt so they could see how the tattoos came in black lines down the center of his neck, across his Adam's apple, then spanned his shoulders like an oversize necklace. More lines ran vertically down his arms and across the backs of his hands, while rings encompassed his wrists.

Oliver, who'd been listening to them from his own computer station, lifted his voice. 'I've heard back from one of my contacts down at the terminal. The driver's name was Shihab. He was a foreman there, but he'd only been working for about three months. He handled special deliveries and didn't talk with anyone. He might've stayed at a private residence while he was here since my contacts at the hotels don't show any registry under his name, nor have any of them seen him. With those tattoos, he'd be fairly memorable.'

'Thanks for that, Oliver,' said Ross. 'And I'm telling you, I think this guy's the key.'

'I don't know,' said 30K from the sofa. 'Yeah, you're right about beating these guys through their mistakes, but how did they screw up? I mean, the missiles are gone and we're sitting here . . .'

Ross held up an index finger. 'You just wait. And I'll show you.'

Fifty-Four

A piece of debris must've struck Kozak's shoulder blade during the explosion, because he had a welt the size of a grapefruit forming there. He stood in front of the bathroom mirror, strangely fascinated by the wound. After a moment, he rinsed his face and frowned over the commotion coming from the living room. He ventured outside to find everyone huddled around Ross's computer, with Diaz's face appearing in one window, Mitchell's in another. Diaz was glancing off-screen, scanning a report:

'Those tattoos are Mentawai from Sumatra, Indonesia,' she explained. 'They come in three phases. The first takes place during childhood, at eleven or twelve, with tattoos beginning on the upper arms. The second happens at eighteen or nineteen, when they get tattoos on their thighs. The third and final phase occurs when someone is fully grown. What interests me the most are the tattoos on your driver's wrists.'

Ross nodded. 'They look newer, don't they?'

'Yeah, they do. Maybe a few weeks, maybe just a month ago, suggesting that he's been there recently.'

'Suggesting that maybe they recruited him from that area,' said Ross. 'And he's been coming back and forth.'

'You could be right,' said Diaz.

Another window opened on Ross's laptop, and now Maziq had joined the call. 'Hello there, Captain. I have the information you requested – all the ships that left both Massawa and Aden after the *Ocean Cavalier* arrived. I used a six-hour window. But I have to tell you, the list is pretty long. I count seventeen vessels between both ports.'

'Are any of those ships headed for Sumatra, Singapore or Malaysia?' Ross asked.

'Checking.'

'Ross, I admire your tenacity, but this is a long shot,' said Mitchell.

'I know that, sir, but if you'll just give me a chance. I'm confident they recruited this guy out of Sumatra.'

'This is interesting,' Diaz said. 'About three months ago, Saif Hamid was spotted in Singapore before we lost him. The sighting has been confirmed, so he was definitely in the neighborhood.'

'I've got three ships all headed in that general vicinity,' said Maziq. 'Two out of Massawa, but this one looks like your best bet. She's a Panamanian-registered bulk carrier, *Duman*. She arrived in Aden at 0623 local time and pulled out at 1420. If the weapons were transferred to another container, they could've been off-loaded to the container yard in Aden and just sat there until *Duman* arrived.'

'That's exactly what happened,' Ross said.

'*Duman*'s not scheduled to arrive in Singapore for another eleven days.'

'Eleven days?' asked Pepper.

Maziq frowned. 'She weighs thirty-six thousand tons, and her max speed is only twelve knots.'

'What're you complaining about?' said 30K. 'That'll give you plenty of time to heal up.'

'Ms Diaz? Maziq? Thank you for the intel,' said Mitchell. 'We're in your debt. Now if you don't mind, I need to speak to Captain Ross.'

'No problem, sir,' said Diaz. 'Good to see you again.'

'You, too.'

'I'm here if you need me,' said Maziq before his comm window vanished.

Mitchell waited a moment, then cleared his throat. 'Captain, you might be on to something, but I have to say . . . I've still got a lot of reservations. Let me gather a little more intel, and I'll get back to you. In the meantime, your evac is still on the way.'

'Thank you, sir,' said Ross. 'We look forward to hearing from you soon.' He ended the link and glanced up at Kozak. 'We're not walking away.'

Kozak sighed with relief. 'Hell, no, sir.'

The next morning Ross and the others were driven to the airport by Oliver. Before they boarded the Gulf Stream jet that Mitchell had sent for them, they said their good-byes to the old man, who pulled Ross aside. 'You lost someone close to you, which is why you asked about my daughter. The pain is who you are . . .'

Ross would not allow the burning sensation behind his eyes to go any further. He nodded and hurried away.

By the time the jet left the ground, Ross had learned that Mitchell had put in a request with the Navy to have one of their littoral combat ships (LCS) intercept and shadow the *Duman* from just over the horizon.

'Are we still on mission?' he asked the major, who stared back at him from a window on Ross's laptop.

A smile nicked the corners of Mitchell's mouth. 'What do you think?'

Fifty-Five

Ten days later, on a moonlit night at 1930 hours, Ross and his men were shielding their eyes from the rotor wash of a CH-53 Sea Stallion heavy lift transport helicopter landing at Paya Lebar Air Base in eastern Singapore. The base was used by many flying units of the US Navy and Air Force as a refueling stopover and staging post/transit point, and it was also the permanent home of the 497th Combat Training Squadron, which provided operational and logistical support to US Air Force fighters currently training with the Republic of Singapore Air Force.

The Sea Stallion was operated by a crew of four: pilot, copilot, crew chief, and an aerial observer, but it was the crew chief who waved them inside while he and the observer supervised the loading of a crate the size of a Volkswagen Beetle up the chopper's rear ramp.

'What the hell you got in the box?' the chief asked Ross, once they were under way and wearing their headphones and mikes.

'That's classified,' Ross said. 'But I'll tell you one thing: It makes a lot of noise when it's angry.' Ross wiggled his eyebrows and smiled.

Once they'd learned that *Duman* was, indeed, heading toward Singapore, Ross had a sneaking suspicion that the weapons' final destination was close, and with that in mind, he'd requested from Mitchell a few of the team's more offensive tools, one of them particularly large, but that wouldn't be a problem since there'd be plenty of room to store it on the LCS.

After about a two-hour ride, they neared the USS *Independence* (LCS-2), a unique littoral combat trimaran warship. Her most recognizable physical feature was an elongated narrow bow with three parallel hulls that inspired the crew to call her a Klingon warship. Her silhouette was most definitely futuristic, with aft landing deck and container-size mission modules on her port sides, the containers capable of carrying all types of mission-specific hardware, vehicles and ordnance. 'Littoral' meant that she spent most of her time near the shoreline, and she was the perfect vessel to hunt a ship like *Duman* in these waters.

Independence's skipper, Commander Troy Ladd Wagner, Gold Team, was, Ross imagined, settling into his starboard bridge chair and sighting along the ship's bow, which reminded Ross of a cigar boat. Driving a 418-foot LCS at thirty knots in twenty feet of water was no easy task, Ross knew, but add to that the three dozen fishing boats directly in his path, and Ross figured that Wagner was not having a great night. The pilot had told Ross that the Malaccan Strait fishing fleet was an issue whenever air ops were carried out during east-west prevailing winds that required *Independence* to travel at right angles to the main shipping channel.

They were four minutes out now and on final approach. The pilot confessed that their landing would be close. If they didn't set down exactly on time, they would have to abort, be put in a holding pattern, then sent around for another pass, once Wagner repositioned the LCS to avoid the fishing fleet. If Ross were that skipper, he would be wondering why some Special Forces prima donnas from the Army had taken so long to get there. A SEAL operation would have transited aboard three minutes early and with half as much equipment.

Thankfully, the landing went off without a hitch, and within ten minutes Ross was standing in the LCS's narrow wardroom, speaking with the skipper himself: 'My apologies, sir. I know our timing wasn't the greatest. I saw all those fishing boats up ahead. It was getting dicier by the minute.'

'Nonsense, I welcomed the opportunity to live up to our motto, *Libertas Per Laborem Audentium* – Independence Through Bold Action.'

'I appreciate that, sir.'

Wagner was at least six feet tall, graying, and nearly bald. His faded blue eyes had telltale crow's feet from squinting directly into far too many sunrises and sunsets. He hadn't escaped from becoming a little chunky from a combination of good Navy chow and living a confined life aboard ship. 'Now my XO tells me that five or six years ago he transported a SEAL team run by a guy named Andrew Ross. Any relation?'

'That would be me, sir.'

'Really? I find that strange. What the hell did you do to get fed to the Army?'

Ross chuckled. 'Well, they told me the Group for Specialized Tactics is the wave of the future, so I figured I'd give it a try.'

'And how's that working out for you?'

'The hardest part was getting used to being called "captain." For the first few weeks I kept looking around to see who my guys were talking to.'

'Well, we'll forgive you for leaving us too soon.'

'Thank you again.'

'All right, let's get down to it then. We've put our Fire Scout over *Duman* for the past three nights. She's tracking right down the channel, and we haven't heard her request a pilot to enter any port. If her skipper is familiar with his destination, he might not even need the services of a local pilot.'

The 'C' version Fire Scout Unmanned Aerial Vehicle was equipped with a sensor ball turret that carried electro-optics, IR cameras, and a laser range finder. The robot chopper operated over a line of sight to a distance of 172 miles and had an endurance of fourteen hours at cruising speed of 110 knots. *Independence* could comfortably shadow the *Duman* from 100 miles away without fear of counterdetection.

'I'm alternating my two Seahawks on standby every

night. The crew will sleep on board,' said Wagner. 'In addition, we have a platoon of Fleet Anti-Terrorism Marines out of Manama, Bahrain, on board. The Chief of Naval Operations ordered the Third Fleet Anti-Terrorism Security Battalion to place them under your command. I'll introduce you to their CO.'

'That's excellent,' Ross replied. 'And if you've got the time, why don't we head down to the hangar deck, and you can meet the fifth member of my team.'

'I take it you keep him in that giant crate?'

Ross nodded. 'He seems to like it in there.'

Fifty-Six

Later in the evening, word reached Ross that *Duman* had left the shipping channel and was heading toward the northern entrance to the Rupat Strait, which detoured around the western side of Rupat Island before again merging with the Strait of Malacca. The following evening, a helo had lifted off from the island and was heading toward the container ship.

'That looks suspicious enough to me,' Wagner told Ross.

'Roger that. We need to reconnoiter that island.'

'We'll get you there. In the meantime, we'll have higher work things out with the Sumatran government so you boys don't get a ticket for trespassing.' Wagner grinned and winked.

Ross and the others quickly familiarized themselves with the area and worked out a hasty reconnaissance mission with Wagner and Mitchell, along with intel updates from Maziq.

Rupat was a circular island lying three miles off the eastern coast of Sumatra, in the Riau province of Indonesia. The island was swampy and sparsely populated, with only one primary settlement, Batupanjang, on the southwestern coast. A few primitive villages of thatched-roof huts, along with some rickety piers and a small fishing boat rental place, were up on the northern coast. Just up the beach from them stood the more modern Tanjung Medang Lighthouse, an impressive 171-foot-tall tower with lantern and gallery, along with keepers' huts on the small cape. Every ten seconds a brilliant white flash marked the narrower section of the strait. Most of the island's tropical wet interior was too difficult to explore and still belonged to the insects and wildlife. Seasonal floods made farming all but impossible, save for some rice paddies in the south. With a diameter of just thirty miles, Rupat was a mere blip on the map, and Ross had never heard of the island until now. The Malaysian government planned to build a bridge from Melaka to Rupat and on to Dumai, the 'Malacca Strait Bridge.'

Down in their quarters, Ross briefed the team, and they were champing at the bit to get off the ship and get back on dry land. Pepper was okay, but Kozak and 30K had suffered mild cases of seasickness, and that amused Ross no end.

'All right, this is a recon,' Ross said. 'And as you boys might say, we're going in light to get the ground truth, doing what we do best. See you up top.'

Fifty-Seven

At 0020 hours, Ross and the team were fast-roping down from one of the Seahawks, inserting into a clearing on the south side of the island. At one point all four were dangling from the same line, the rope running hotly through their gloved hands and between their boots as they maintained a three-meter gap from the next guy.

In addition to the team's reconnaissance load out, the chopper crew lowered an F470 Combat Rubber Raiding Craft (CRRC) with outboard engine. Within minutes, 30K and Kozak had the CRRC inflated via the CO_2 tank, and once they had the outboard attached, they dragged the rubber boat over to a river just twenty meters north of the drop zone. Technically, it wasn't a river, just part of a heavily flooded tropical jungle, with mangroves that reminded Ross of Colombia, along with that oppressive humidity.

They climbed into the CRRC, and Kozak served as coxswain, switching on the battery-powered outboard, the engine humming quietly like a bass boat's trolling motor. He clutched the tiller, steering them into the jungle, the course wide open for a few minutes until they were forced to groan and duck under a few low-hanging limbs and broad palm fronds.

Ross's night vision turned the swamp into a pale green maze glowing on its edges, an almost photo negative perspective that made spotting what Pepper called 'the creepy crawlies' a bit more difficult. That twisted root was actually a reticulated python coiled around a tree, and that silhouette that seemed like a collection of branches was really a hornbill bird with his head tipped to one side.

Occasionally, Ross would motion to Kozak to take this path or that one, checking their bearing and GPS coordinates against *Duman*'s current position. That they'd doused themselves in bug spray and wore camouflage face paint that also contained DEET was fortunate; the constant buzzing of mosquitoes in Ross's ears and the giant wood spiders that dropped down on to the boat, having been torn from their webs, were enough to make him and even a tough guy like 30K get the willies. 30K swatted away bugs with his rifle's muzzle, whispering obscenities at their unwelcome hitchhikers. Ross had trained quite extensively in the jungle, and he'd learned that addressing the bug problem was a true priority. Swatting a mosquito could compromise your position and literally get you killed.

After the first five miles, Ross mused that they really had found the heart of darkness. He'd never been in a swamp this tight or remote. If any one of them got hurt, bitten, stung, what have you, it'd be hours before they could get him out of there for proper medical treatment. There were no clearings within which a chopper could land, and hauling a man up through the canopy was well-nigh impossible, at least in this region. They'd crossed the River Styx, traversed the valley of the shadow of death, and had laughed at the signpost marking the point of no return. Now the doormat read: 'Welcome to the Underworld.'

They'd been heading due north, and at the first sound of the helicopter, Ross ordered Kozak to head northeast, toward the chopper and the distant flashes from the lighthouse.

Within an hour they had reached a muddy riverbank, which swallowed their boots up to their ankles as they hauled themselves out of the raft. Ross spat out the mosquito that had flown into his mouth and gave a hand signal to 30K, putting him on point. He whispered for Kozak to begin dropping markers so they could find their way back to the boat.

And with that, they trudged off, their boots squishing as they pushed farther northeast, the jungle beginning to thin a bit, the timpani roll of that helicopter much closer.

Some twenty minutes later, near a cluster of nipah palms whose fronds grew straight from the ground, making them appear like trunkless palm trees, 30K had his fist in the air, and they dropped to their haunches. His voice came softly over the team net: 'Tree line ends just ahead. I see a very narrow dirt road, then another

319

section of jungle, and then something, maybe another clearing, a little farther out.'

'Roger that,' said Ross. 'Keep moving. We'll cross the road together.'

A window opened in Ross's Cross-Com, and Mitchell appeared. 'No need to reply, Captain. Just an intel update from Maziq. Keyhole satellite got some good pictures of that chopper, an old Caracel transport/cargo bird deployed from the island. She's offloading pallets of what we believe are your Grinch launchers from the *Duman*, taking them to coordinates about two kilometers from your position.'

Another window showed a map of Rupat with a glowing red overlay that marked the team's current position, as well as the cargo ship's and the chopper's drop-off point.

Ross shared that map with the rest of the team, and Kozak said, 'Maybe it's some kind of weapons depot. They pick a remote island and hide the stuff here.'

'Maybe so,' Ross answered. 'But I have a feeling it's a lot more than that.'

After ensuring that the road was clear, 30K gave the signal, and they darted forward, Ross casting a look to the west, where the road stretched off in an almost perfectly straight line, all the way to the beach.

Just ahead, the second patch of jungle was noticeably thinner, the ground much firmer, and they made good time, weaving around the giant palms, ducking and turning, covering ground twice as fast as they had before – until 30K tripped and crashed on to his stomach.

'Holy shit, bro, you all right?' stage-whispered Kozak.

30K rolled over and sat up. 'What the hell was that?'

Ross came forward and got on his haunches, staring down in disbelief over the obstacle in 30K's path: railroad tracks.

They'd been constructed just within the tree line and wove out to the next clearing. As far as Ross could tell, they kept going, extending much farther north, and the beauty of their placement made them difficult if not impossible to see on a satellite photograph – if you didn't know what you were looking for. They curved while in the clearing, then vanished again, the pattern haphazard, irregular.

'Look at these ties and spikes,' said Kozak. 'They're new. These tracks were just put in here.'

'Why the hell do they need a train running along the coastline?' asked Pepper.

'30K, you all right?' Ross asked.

'Yeah, I guess I should've been looking out for F-ing railroad tracks in the middle of the jungle.'

Ross snorted. 'Yeah, and if they've got railroad tracks, then they've got an engine,' said Ross. 'Wonder why . . .'

Five minutes later they reached the next clearing, and from there, crouched down at the edge, Ross marked a line of four lean-tos heavily camouflaged with more fronds. Beneath each one, perfectly hidden from satellites and other prying eyes, was a boxy APC, which Ross photographed and uploaded for identification.

'This is Ghost Lead. Hold up,' he ordered the others.

Barely thirty seconds later, the photos and schematics flashed across Ross's HUD: Puma M26-15 Armored Personnel Carrier with mine and IED protection. Its main users were military, police, and security companies during peacekeeping operations. They were manufactured by OTT Technologies, a South African defense contractor.

'Contacts,' said 30K. 'Four just behind the lean-tos. Probably guards for the APCs.'

'Sir, check it out,' said Pepper, pointing to their left, where the railroad tracks broke free of the trees.

Ross zoomed in with his night-vision lens, and for a moment, he had to wipe his eyes, blink hard, then stare again, wanting to make sure that the image was real, that his lens wasn't out of focus, and that Hamid and his cronies had really gone this far.

Fifty-Eight

Ross took point now, forging a path about fifteen meters behind the railroad tracks until they came around the lean-tos and got a better look at the clearing –

Where the helicopter was lowering one of the pallets to a team of about ten men below. Ross called for a halt, and they watched as these soldiers removed the crates from the pallets, stacking them on hand trucks to be rolled into a thatched-roof hut identical to the ones present on the northern part of the island. Ross shifted his position to spy at least ten more huts lying beneath the denser canopy, and beyond them, just visible through the maze of trees, was another surprise: a network of bunkers constructed of rectangular walls that formed a semicircular perimeter between the outpost, the final patch of jungle and the white sand beach beyond.

'You believe this? They got Hescos,' said 30K. 'Weird thing is, even with the trenches they've dug, I don't see where they got enough dirt.'

A 'Hesco' was a 'concertainer' manufactured by the Hesco company, basically a cellular mesh framework with geotextile lining filled with dirt to create protective walls that were strong and structurally sound. They were used by the US Army to build Forward Operating

Bases (FOBs) and other outposts all over the world. How these bastards had gotten their hands on them was another story; then again, there was always a black market for everything.

APCs . . . Hescos . . . surface-to-air missiles . . .

And their deadliest weapon lying ahead, the one that Ross had just caught the barest glimpse of and still couldn't believe was there.

He signaled the team to move out once more, and they came within twenty meters of the terrible confirmation that the *Bedayat jadeda* were importing much more than just shoulder-fired weapons. The real reason for the railroad tracks was undeniably clear.

There, sitting at the edge of the clearing but still veiled from above by a natural awning of branches and broadleafed fronds, was a diesel engine attached to a flatbed railcar.

This would have been an unremarkable sight were it not for the Penguin MK3 missile launch system custom fitted to that car, along with its six-missile launch canister aimed skyward.

Ross didn't need the analysts back home to help identify the weapon. He'd seen these eight-finned rockets before, their launch assemblies mounted to ships, and he'd watched videos of their test firing.

The Penguin was, indeed, a Norwegian-built antiship missile, pulse-laser or passive IR guidance, with a range of 55km plus (34 miles), covering the entire distance across the Strait of Malacca. No ship was safe from them. And worse, the launchers were mobile. They could show up anywhere on the tracks. It seemed the *Bedayat jadeda* had taken a page from the Russians, who'd used their extensive rail system to hide their ICBMs from the West during the Cold War.

'Guardian, this is Delta Dragon. Are you seeing this?'

'Roger that. We traced the tracks, now that we know what to look for. Believe we've spotted a second diesel and railcar launcher a few miles south of your location.'

'Roger that, stand by.' Ross switched to the team net. 'Okay, guys, the SA-24s we've been chasing since Tobruk were just the tip of the iceberg. These crazy mothers are planning to terrorize one of the most important shipping lanes in the entire world, and they've got these missiles running right along the choke point.'

'Well, what're we going to do about that, sir?' asked 30K.

'You got a plan, 30K?'

'Hell, yeah, I do, sir.'

Ross beamed back at him. 'You'll get your chance.'

'Sir, suggest we continue our sweep north then head east to get a better look at that chopper operation,' said Kozak. 'Who knows what else they're bringing in here.'

'Roger that. Let's go.'

Pepper rotated to the front and took them along a natural fence line of nipah running around the outpost's perimeter. They reached the very edge of the forest, where out on the strait they spotted *Duman* lumbering dangerously close to the shoreline in an effort to make the chopper's off-loading operation as expeditious as possible. At the moment, the helicopter was carrying back the sixth and final pallet of missile launchers dangling from its cargo line. The pallet came down and was unloaded, even as the pilot turned and headed back, with hints of red and orange already on the horizon.

When the chopper was about halfway back to the ship, Kozak's voice broke over the radio, and he could barely contain himself:

'Sir, we got some people on the deck now, and no shit, sir, I think one of them is Hamid.'

Ross zoomed in with his helmet camera, then abandoned it for his high-powered binoculars. The images were still a little grainy, but there was one man among the deck crew who fitted that terrorist scumbag's description.

It wasn't until he took the cargo line in his hands, and was strapped into a harness, that Ross began to nod and say, 'Kozak, I think you're right. I think that's our man.' And once they had lifted him in the air and his face had turned toward Ross, he called Mitchell and said, 'Sir, I think we know how deep the rabbit hole goes.'

'Roger that. Fall back and continue your reconnaissance. Diaz, Maziq and I are piecing this all together now with some new intel. Stand by.'

'Guys, we need to get in close to that clearing where they dropped the missiles,' Ross told the team. 'I want a good look at our buddy.' With that, he gave the signal, and they vanished back into the jungle, retracing their perimeter advance, this time marking the positions of several guards at the clearing's edge, outside their bunkers.

Ross found another unobstructed view of the drop zone within a cluster of palms, and 30K edged up to him and said, 'You want to get in close? Like *real* close?'

'Let's do it. Pepper? Kozak? Hold here.'

30K activated his camouflage, and Ross fell in behind him, dematerializing himself. 30K took them right up to the lean-tos, not two meters away from a guard standing there, and Ross, concealed under his camouflage, stared up at the man's profile. This, he believed, was a FARC solider, recruited all the way from Colombia to work here.

The chopper and accompanying gale force wash showered the area with dirt and rattled the huts as it touched down, and the man they believed was Saif Hamid climbed out, ducking reflexively against the rotor blades. Indeed, it was him. He was tall and lanky, a younger version of bin Laden, with an equally long beard and neck. Radical jihadists weren't known for their spectacular personal hygiene, fashion sense, or anything else that made them stand out much from their fellow fanatics. Hamid was dressed in the same jungle pattern camouflage fatigues as his men and was quickly addressed by another bearded man, slightly older and grayer, as Ross zoomed in with his Cross-Com and began taking pictures, which were automatically sent to Mitchell.

Hamid and the second unidentified man headed back toward one of the huts, escorted by guards, while the chopper pilot switched off his engine. Ross wasn't close enough to hear their conversation, but he imagined a lot of self-congratulatory remarks were being made.

Hello, you son of a bitch. We're coming for you. And we're bringing the blood, sweat and tears of all those innocent people you killed . . .

'Delta Dragon, this is Guardian,' called Mitchell. 'We've marked your positions. Fall back. I have another update.'

Fifty-Nine

Once Ross and 30K returned to the others, he ordered the team another hundred meters away from the outpost, then he reestablished the link to Mitchell, who shared both the backstory and complex relationship Hamid had with his associates:

'The man talking with Hamid is a player we've been following for a long time now: Amir Bahar. He's the former spiritual leader of a Southeast Asian terrorist group known as *Jemaah Islamiyah*, and he used to buy pirated arms until his al Qaeda funding dried up. He's formed an alliance with a group called the *Jemaah Ansharut Tauhid*, or JAT, to front his operation. Our sources close to him say his intent is to control the strait because he who controls the strait has the power to topple existing governments and restore Sharia Law.'

'He who controls the strait has the power to affect the world's oil supply,' said Ross.

'Oh, I'm sure he understands that very well. Now Maziq tells me that shipments of arms and armaments between Norway and the South African Air Force have been pirated during transits around the Horn of Africa, which explains where these guys picked up some of their toys like those Penguins you found.'

'Okay, but what's in it for Bahar? Just more fighters? And how do the Colombians play into all this?'

'Well, if you think about it, there aren't many places to hide heavy armament and large weapons caches in that region. Up until Bahar made contact with Hamid and the *Bedayat jadeda*, he was forced to hide his contraband in the holds of ships sympathetic to JAT – and we know this because we've intercepted a few of those ships. Hamid's base of operations on Rupat has solved his and Bahar's problems. Bahar has a secure place for his weapons cache safely hidden from satellites and our Navy in Singapore, and Hamid has a strategically operational stronghold overlooking a narrow section of the strait. Plus he's got a propaganda tool to recruit new warriors. The FARC are employees of Hamid, trading partners, and a source of funding. However, if this plays out the way they want, South American oil would become much more valuable if the Middle East supply were disrupted, particularly Venezuelan oil, and it's a known fact that the FARC have had a relationship with that government.'

'So what's their next move? Take out an oil tanker?'

'We assume they'll begin by striking boats from the Malacca Strait Patrol, a security force staffed by personnel from Malaysia, Singapore, Indonesia, and Thailand. With the MSP weakened, they can go to town on the oil tankers.'

During his tenure as a SEAL, Ross had attended many presentations on how America had become the world's maritime police force, and he understood well how he and his team now fitted into the larger picture.

Mitchell continued: 'Increased risk in the strait will increase the price of oil, raise maritime insurance rates, and force some ships to find alternate – and expensive – routes to the Pacific. Under treaties with both Saudi Arabia and OPEC, securitizing oil is in our national interest.'

'I understand, sir.'

US Navy units operating in the Indian Ocean would, according to America's foreign policy, maintain the sea lines of communication (SLOC) for trade, logistics, and naval forces. Now, this policy also authorized the Group for Specialized Tactics to conduct as necessary reconnaissance and direct action operations that would secure that oil and keep those sea lines open.

In sum and in layman's terms, the Ghosts would have permission to blow the shit out of the entire outpost –

And as Mitchell uttered the words 'direct action mission,' Ross sprang to his feet.

Pepper snorted over the audacity of these sons of bitches. If they couldn't kill us on American soil like they had back on 9/11, they'd figured out the next best way to hurt us – by hitting us in the wallet. They wanted to convert all these small countries to their way of thinking and decide which oil tankers would be allowed through the choke point and which ones they'd destroy. They'd create some serious chaos before they all got martyred and sent to hell.

Well, they had another think coming.

Pepper was on one knee just behind a pair of huts constructed on stilts, his camouflage activated, a sensor grenade in his right hand. The major wanted an exact troop count, and the Ghosts would get that intel for him.

With just the slightest toss, Pepper deployed the sensor beneath the hut, then he waited as his Cross-Com rippled to life, the sensor picking up the hostile contacts and marking their exact number and locations inside those huts and those within a .25 kilometer hemisphere.

At the same time, Ross, Kozak and 30K were doing likewise, all their data instantly compiled to give Mitchell a three-dimensional map of the battle space as well as the size and composition of their enemy.

The images in Pepper's HUD showed the men inside the huts outlined in red and bowing in prayer. As Muslims, they prayed five times a day, a heck of a lot more than Pepper did, and if they had known how close the Ghosts were, they'd have a lot more to pray about.

Exploiting the moment, Pepper hauled ass across the clearing and reached the tangled web of palms. His ribs felt a lot better now, his breathing hardly as labored as it had been. He was back in the fight.

Near the denser jungle along the south side of the camp, Ross discovered a Quonset hut draped in fronds.

Stacked outside the rear door were empty boxes whose Spanish language labels indicated they were medical supplies. Ross shifted through the undergrowth, freezing beneath his camouflage as the hut's front door opened and out stepped a familiar man – a man he'd seen outside the warehouses in Tobruk:

Alfonso Valencia, the FARC leader with the medical background.

What's more, another man accompanied him.

And when Ross got a better glimpse of his face, he nearly fell back off his haunches.

It was Delgado, the paramilitary operations officer for the CIA, better known as the little runt bastard who had deceived the team back in Colombia. The prick was either under cover or simply a traitor working for the FARC and their terrorist connections. It almost didn't matter anymore. Despite being a law-abiding citizen and model soldier, Ross imagined himself strangling the man to death – a moment of weakness that still felt damned good.

Shuddering off that thought, he captured Valencia and Delgado on video and immediately sent that file back to Mitchell.

Then he shifted farther into the jungle, kneeling in the long shadows of some fronds dripping with dew. He trembled with excitement as he called the major. 'Sir, I just sent you a file, but I'll cut to the chase. Valencia's here, along with Delgado.'

'Say again?'

'That FARC doctor Valencia is here. Looks like he's setting up a field hospital for them. And our CIA buddy Delgado is with him.'

No response from Mitchell.

'Sir, are you there?'

'I'm here, Captain. I'll notify the NCS and get back to you.'

'Thank you, sir.'

'Ghost Lead, Kozak here. Best I can tell from the sensor reports is we got about seventy-five infantry armed with the basics: AKs, side arms, grenades, RPGs, and of course, the SA-24s. Got at least one fifty cal at every bunker. Looks like a mixed group of Arabs and FARC troops. Got some officer types in charge of the bunkers, another guy heading up security for the APCs, and squads for the vehicles. Biggest contingent is guarding the two trains – ten guys on each engine, with some nerdy types who look like launch operators, over.'

'Excellent work,' Ross said. 'Ghosts, fall back to the rally point.'

Ross was about to take off running when two *Bedayat jadeda* fighters came elbowing their way into the brush.

'Just out here,' said one of them in Arabic. 'I heard something out here.'

Swearing inwardly, Ross held his position as the men came toward him, rustling branches and leaves until they stopped, waited, rifles held at the ready.

One of them looked directly at Ross, then he took a

334

deep breath and said to his comrade, 'Maybe it was over there.' He pointed to the west. They turned and started away.

Sweat was dripping from Ross's chin by the time he stood and got out of there, passing between two bunkers positioned about ten meters apart, where a team of four men was setting up some claymores with trip wires. *Great. More obstacles.*

Sixty

30K reached the rally point at the CRRC first, switching off his active camouflage and sweeping the area to be sure he hadn't been followed. Then he dropped his pack and sat on it, keeping his Stoner at the ready.

He glanced up at the shafts of morning light filtering down through the canopy, gnats swarming in the beams, the humidity beginning to rise. The place was a sauna, all right, and by late afternoon he predicted heavy rains.

Sometimes, when he had too much time to think, he'd take a hard look at his surroundings and wonder: is this where I'm going to die? Does it meet all my expectations? Or is it just some disgusting hellhole and I'm going to become another statistic whose name can't even be revealed?

No, they weren't here for the glory, but he was, after all, a man, and a little recognition for laying down his life for his country wasn't such a bad thing, was it? He'd want his family to know that he'd fought and died for their freedom, and that his actions had been worth the sacrifice.

He decided right then and there that he would not die here on this island. Nope. This place sucked. And there was still too much work to do, too many people to piss off –

And one of them came hustling over, his green outline flickering like kryptonite in the HUD.

'Hey,' said Pepper, shifting around a tree and reaching the boat. He placed his palms on his hips, leaned over, and took in long, slow breaths.

'You okay, Grandpa?'

'I'll kick your ass, punk.'

'Any time, any place.'

'Hey, how much C-4 we got?'

'You know what we got. This was a recon. We came light, a block apiece.'

'That won't do shit.'

'We hitting them tonight?'

Pepper shrugged.

Kozak and Ross arrived, and the captain quickly gathered them around. 'We've got three High-Value Targets here, and one wild card,' he said. 'No warning or ops order yet, but I'm betting the major's already working on it.' Ross uploaded the intel photographs Mitchell had sent him of Bahar to the team's HUDs, and he gave them a capsule summary of the man's involvement.

'And the wild card?' asked Kozak once Ross was finished.

'Guess who?' Ross said.

'Delgado?' 30K said, lifting his brows.

'Yeah, he's here. Might be working for Valencia.'

'I don't get it,' said Kozak. 'His cover was blown, the FARC kidnapped him in Colombia, then he manages to trick us and escape. How can he be working for Valencia if they know who he is?'

'If he's still working for Valencia, then I'm sure it's complicated. Bottom line: We might be tasked with bringing him in alive,' said Ross. 'And to be honest, I'd like to kill him more than any of you, but we're professionals, and we'll do exactly what's asked of us. Understood?'

Pepper and Kozak grunted their ascent, but 30K remained silent.

'And you?' Ross asked him.

'All right,' 30K said resignedly. 'I'll cut his throat. But only a little.' He held up his thumb and index finger to indicate the exact size of the incision he planned to make.

'You're a team player, 30K,' Ross said with a wink.

'Yeah, yeah, that's me.'

'All right, we need to set up a little bivy,' said Ross. 'We'll be here for a while.'

The bivouac they chose was within the tightest cluster of nipah palms they could find, and Pepper helped Kozak quietly cut free more fronds, from which they constructed a crude roof that, even from a few feet away, was indistinguishable from the rest of the rain forest.

They had taken along some Meals Ready to Eat (MREs) from the ship, and they had a late lunch before Mitchell finally called back with the Operations Order (OPORD).

Ross went over the plan in exacting detail – covering all five parts of the order much more slowly than Pepper was used to. That was fine. The boss wanted to leave no stone unturned, no question unanswered. They pored over the (1) Situation, (2) Mission, (3) Execution, (4) Service & Support, and (5) Command & Signals aspects of the mission.

Pepper could already hear 30K translating the OPORD into 30K-speak:

Situation: Bad guys on island with missiles and shit.

Mission: Kill the bastards unmercifully.

Execution: Well, yeah, we're going to excute them with help from the Marines on board the LCS.

And the rest was just details.

Pepper smiled to himself, but then out of nowhere he was struck by the length and breadth of the operation, and by these men who were about to put themselves in harm's way.

A powerful chill fanned across his shoulders.

It was a moment to confront his own mortality – and theirs – and these feelings were happening more often and at the most inopportune times. Nearly getting buried to death inside that minaret hadn't helped matters. He closed his eyes and swore he would do everything he could to complete the mission and protect them, and when he opened his eyes, 30K was staring at him.

'You hear that?' he asked.

Pepper frowned. 'What?'

'Listen . . . I hear one of the trains . . .'

Sixty-One

The storm hit by 1830 hours, the sky gone to soot, the thunderheads finally upon them, and they huddled in their tiny bivouac, waiting it out, while Ross kept in close contact with Mitchell and with the LCS's skipper.

What wasn't wet already was about to get wet, and Ross wished they could just get on with it instead of waiting around, getting waterlogged. Story of your life in the military: Hurry up and wait. That it stopped raining forty minutes later offered only a brief respite. They still had to hold there for another four hours before Mitchell finally gave them the signal to move out, and Ross's ankles cracked as he got to his feet.

Pepper and Kozak headed off south along the railroad tracks, with Ross and 30K taking the northern route, each two-man team tasked with reconnoitering the outpost one more time as three Rigid Hull Inflatable Boats (RHIBs) carrying a Marine platoon of nearly forty were deployed from the LCS.

Ross noted immediately that the Penguin missile launcher they'd spotted earlier was no longer there and had been moved farther north, perhaps as far as ten or fifteen miles away, well out of their reach to conduct a demolition operation, and Mitchell called to confirm that the second diesel and launcher had been moved again as well. Hamid wasn't taking any chances with his most valuable weapons, keeping them rolling and well guarded, especially at night when he probably (and rightly) suspected he might be attacked.

Wagner on board the LCS reported that no boats had approached or left the island, and no aircraft had been spotted on the Sea GIRAFFE radar, just the routine shipping traffic passing through the strait. He'd assured everyone that the system could detect small targets like sea skimmers, anti-radiation missiles, mortars, and even RHIBs from his position approximately one hundred kilometers southeast of the island. The LCS was now speeding their way.

30K blazed a trail like a relentless cyborg, leading Ross to the outpost's perimeter bunkers on its northwest side. He found the first set of trip wires and placed a marker there, then pointed for Ross to step carefully over the wires, while the men in the bunkers saw nothing.

They advanced to the lean-tos where the APCs were parked, and once there, they glanced at each other and bit back their expletives. The trucks were gone. Ross reminded himself that two of those Pumas were the patrol variant, six-man crew, fitted with a protected cupola with 360-degree traverse that carried either a 12.7 or 14.5mm heavy machine gun.

The other two APCs were the basic armored variant,

carrying crews of ten and fitted with two exterior-mounted light machine guns and eleven shooting ports so the crew could fire their personal weapons from within the vehicle. Ross strained to hear their engines in the distance, assuming they were on patrol, rolling up and down the island along the beach or on that narrow dirt road they'd crossed.

Well, plan A was shot to shit. Ross and 30K were supposed to place their blocks of C-4 between the APCs and take them out the easy way. They moved inside the empty lean-tos, and Ross whispered into his boom mike: 'Guardian, Delta Dragon. APCs are out and on patrol. We'll need the Seahawks to take them out.'

'Roger that, Delta Dragon.'

The LCS's two Seahawk helicopters were each armed with eight AGM-114 Hellfire Missiles, single 7.62mm pintle-mounted machine guns, and equipped with an AN/AAS-44 Infrared Laser Detecting/Ranging/Tracking set.

Despite the choppers' offensive capabilities, the ship's skipper and the Seahawk pilots and crew would not be thrilled by this news because while they could stand off and fire beyond the range of enemy surface-to-air missiles, they were also needed to provide Close Air Support for Ross and his men. The Seahawks were tolerant to small arms fire and medium-caliber high-explosive projectiles, but Hamid and his troops did indeed possess those Grinch SA-24s, and any one of them could lift a launcher to his shoulder, get off a shot, and send one of the Seahawks exploding across the sky.

30K signaled to Ross: They would leave the lean-to now and head toward the forward bunkers past the tree line.

Ross understood what 30K wanted to do now, and he nodded.

If they couldn't blow up the APCs, they'd take out some bunkers for the Marines. That C-4 was, after all, burning a hole in their pockets.

The Eurocopter EC275 Caracel transport/cargo chopper sat in the dirt clearing where it had landed the morning before, after dropping off Hamid.

At the edge of the clearing, facing the beach, sat two bunkers about ten meters apart, each manned by two guards equipped with night-vision goggles (NVGs). There were no men posted near the chopper itself, so if Kozak and Pepper made it past the bunkers, they were home free to plant their charges and withdraw toward the jungle behind the bird.

Kozak reminded himself that this was a no-brainer – nothing to be worried about. Create a diversion. Cut off your enemy's lines of escape. Celebrate with beer and rock 'n' roll. All in a night's work. What could possibly go wrong?

Shit. He shouldn't have considered that question.

They each clutched a block of C-4 with remote

detonator, but damn, from their position they had no choice but to move in the wide open, right between the bunkers to reach the chopper. Active camouflage or not, this was pucker-up time.

Pepper signaled that he would go first. Hell, yeah, he would. No argument from Kozak. Taking long, deliberate strides, Pepper advanced several meters, then stopped and crouched down, allowing his camouflage to catch up with the surroundings. The NVGs worn by the guards would make it even more difficult to spot Pepper, but he remained vigilant, his footfalls light, his movements slow and practiced. By the time he reached the helicopter, Kozak gasped. He'd been holding his breath the entire time.

Pepper, whose outline stood in sharp juxtaposition in Kozak's HUD, waved him over.

Walk and stop. Walk and stop. Swift and silent. Once he was between both bunkers, Kozak stole a look to the left, a look to the right. The guards were just sitting there, one of them cleaning his .50-caliber machine gun, the other staring out across the strait. At the other bunker, practically the same thing. And then a shout in Spanish:

'Hey, you got one of those snacks?'

'Yes, come over and get it.'

One man climbed up a small ladder and on to the beach, marching a few meters behind Kozak to the opposite bunker. As he neared his comrade, Kozak took a deep breath and started off, reaching the chopper precisely two seconds before his heart exploded. Or at least it felt so.

They planted their charges fore and aft, then retreated to the shadows of the forest, where Kozak issued his report: 'Ghost Lead, we're set over here.'

'Roger that. The Marines are about twenty minutes out. Shift to your secondary and stand by.'

'On our way.'

Sixty-Two

'Delta Dragon, this is Cannonball,' came a familiar voice over the command net. Ross had met Captain Pat Rugg on the LCS. At six-five, 270 pounds, the Marine was an irradiated beast, lacking only the green skin and glowing eyes. His biceps were as thick as Ross's hips. He had this Genghis Khan/Conan the Barbarian rap about not being happy until his enemies were crushed, their cities reduced to ashes, their women lamenting. This, he explained, was what was best in life.

Well, it was time to make the platoon leader happy.

'Cannonball, this is Delta Dragon. Where are you guys?'

'Getting into position now.'

'Roger that. Wait for our charges, then cut loose.'

'Understood. Cannonball, out.'

The Marines had planted charges along the railroad tracks and would also take out the trip wire booby traps Ross and the team had marked for them.

A window popped up in Ross's HUD, and there was Mitchell, seated at a command terminal back home in Fort Bragg, his face illuminated by the bank of monitors around him. 'Ross, the Stallion and Seahawks are inbound, ETA two minutes.'

'Roger that, sir. We're set. I can already hear the choppers.'

'Good hunting, Captain.'

'Thank you, sir.'

30K, who was crouched down beside Ross in the trees behind the bunkers, lowered his binoculars and said, 'They're starting to freak out now.'

'Kozak? Pepper? You ready?'

They chimed in, one after the other.

'All right, guys. On three. One, two –'

Ross thumbed the button on his remote detonator, as did 30K. Two of the bunkers vanished in white-hot flashes followed by an echoing boom and blast wave that stretched as far back as their position. Even as the dirt was still flying, multiple explosions went off behind them, and that was Rugg and his people exercising their addiction to high explosives.

As those random thunderclaps rose, an even larger explosion resounded from the opposite side of the outpost, where Kozak and Pepper had planted their charges on Hamid's helicopter.

Not a gasp after those fires lifted into the air, the remaining men in the perimeter bunkers turned their machine gun fire skyward, tracer rounds gleaming like laser fire and reaching out toward the approaching Seahawks –

But that offensive lasted only a few seconds before Rugg's Marines, carefully concealed in the jungle, opened fire on those bunker positions, while he sent in another squad to flank them.

Ross and 30K sprinted off, weaving through the trees and toward the huts, just thirty meters away, where their own intel indicated that Valencia, Delgado, and Hamid were inside the center hut, where they'd established a command post. Bahar had not been spotted since his first appearance with Hamid near the chopper. They were about to find out if he was still there.

'Delta Dragon, if you're gonna move, move now,' cried Cannonball over the command net. 'I've got the bunkers tied up for you, but I don't know for how long.'

'Roger, we're on it!'

As Ross and 30K drew closer, 30K tossed out a sensor grenade that revealed six more men posted beside and on top of at least three of the huts.

'Kozak? How're you doing?' Ross asked.

'The big boy's still about a minute out. Stallion's just coming in now.'

'Get a move on!'

'Hell, yeah, sir!'

Sixty-Three

The fifth member of the Ghost Team, the Warhound, was sitting in the back of the Sea Stallion chopper, waiting to be dropped off on the beach. Kozak had already powered up the four-legged, heavily armored Unmanned Ground Vehicle (UGV). He guided the robot around the cargo compartment to be sure all systems were nominal. When he panned the Warhound's digital camera with stereo vision system to the right, he spotted the chopper's crew chief, whose jaw was still dropped.

'It's okay, Chief,' Kozak said via the Warhound's public address system. 'I'm in control from down here, and I promise not to blow up your helicopter.'

'Thanks!' hollered the chief, his tone turning heavily sarcastic. 'Thanks a lot!'

Kozak checked to be sure that the 60mm mortar and micro guided missile systems were online, then he turned the Warhound around, facing it out toward the ramp, the octagonal-shaped plates on its articulated legs shielding its hydraulics, its communications antenna sprouting from its back. With a few quick movements on the Warhound's touchscreen remote, Kozak could get the drone to crouch like a dog, then spring up and attack. More armor plating covered its body, which was shaped like a diamond whose pointy bottom had been chiseled off. The mortar and missile launchers sat piggyback. With the drone's legs fully extended, it was almost as tall as Pepper, who was positioned beside him, having just released the team's UCAV.

'Pepper, how're you doing?' Kozak asked.

The battle plan was rapidly evolving before Pepper's eyes, and if he had his choice, he'd rather be in a good old-fashioned gunfight instead of crouching in the jungle to remote pilot an Unmanned Combat Aerial Vehicle; however, his role was now more vital than ever.

The Seahawks and their Hellfires were supposed to take out the Penguin launchers on the train tracks, but they'd been temporarily diverted to put fire on the APCs. That meant that Pepper's task was to get the UCAV in position to launch both of its EMP missiles simultaneously in an effort to knock out power to the missile control system (MCS) of each launcher.

The UCAV was soaring over the treetops, gaining altitude, when something flashed from the corner of the drone's camera, and a moment later Pepper lost all contact with the drone. He cursed and bolted to his feet. 'Ghost Lead? RPG must've got the UCAV. Lost contact. Bird's down. Need another way to take out those Penguins.'

Just then, one of the Seahawks came slicing overhead with a tremendous roar while launching two of its missiles, which tore twin seams in the night, rocket motors burning like tiny orange suns as they sank over the treetops and, a breath later, exploded in successive bursts, the ground rumbling beneath Pepper's boots.

The sound of that diesel engine began to rise in the distance, the train traveling toward the area where the Marines had blown the tracks. As Pepper turned back toward it, he gasped in disbelief.

One of the eight-finned Penguins had been fired and now streaked away from its unseen launcher, arcing high in the sky and out toward the strait, where the LCS was now moving in at top speed.

Barely a second later, a second Penguin from about a quarter mile south punched the air, curving just behind the first, twin smoke trails filled with white-hot light.

'Ghost Lead, missiles in the air!' Pepper cried.

'I know,' replied Ross. 'You and Kozak, fall back to my position. Damn it, Kozak, get the Warhound over here!'

'He's coming!'

Big Pat Rugg called over the command net to tell Ross his Marines had moved up on the outpost but were now pinned down and heavily outnumbered. Hamid's fighters maintained cover behind their Hesco walls and continued to hammer Rugg's men with withering .50-caliber fire and an almost constant rotation of RPG fire, rockets with HEAT warheads coming every five or six seconds, the jungle around the outpost already coiled with smoke, palms shredded and set ablaze, tracers drawing fiery ribbons overhead like they'd been caught in a meteorite shower.

Meanwhile, the command hut Ross and 30K had been observing was now shielded by two of the patrol variant APCs whose drivers had positioned their rides close to the hut doors and whose crews had remained aboard to fire from their heavily armored positions. If Ross was reading it right, Hamid and the others were waiting for the right moment to flee from the hut and into one of those carriers. They would hightail it to the north side of the island, where they'd try to escape by a boat or second helicopter they'd already called in.

'Delta Dragon, this is Guardian,' called Mitchell. He'd opted for voice-only communication now that the battle had commenced so Ross could maintain better situational awareness.

'Go ahead, Guardian.'

'I just put the Seahawks back on those Penguin launchers. You saw they got off two missiles. *Independence* fired countermeasures, but one missile struck her bow near the 57mm gun. Wagner's contending with the damage now. She's taking on water, compartments closed. You'll need to take out the APCs yourself, over.'

'Roger that.'

Two more Penguin missiles thundered in the sky from behind them, and Ross craned his head in disbelief. Where the hell were those Seahawks?

Even as he finished the thought, both choppers wheeled around, each firing pairs of Hellfires, with one pair arrowing off to the south, the other to the north, the whooshing powerful enough to make him duck –

Just as both choppers pitched up, about to come around, as though they, like the diesel engine, were riding on rails. A flash of pale yellow light woke about twenty meters away at one of the bunkers, and Ross cursed over what he'd just seen: an SA-24 being fired into the air. The soldier who'd gotten off that shot was already on the ground, clutching the gaping chest wound inflicted upon him by the Marines as he watched his Grinch soar through the air.

The rocket struck one of the Seahawks on its port-side, the detonation lighting up half the outpost with flickering veins of igniting fuel as the chopper's engine sputtered, the black smoke already trailing, the pilot losing control, the bird breaking into a spin and losing altitude, revolving more swiftly and coming within five hundred feet, three hundred, the smell of fuel finally reaching Ross, and one hundred feet –

Ross bit his lip and cursed at the sound of impact, metal twisting, fuel tanks igniting in secondary explosions, the gunfire being traded by the Marines and the FARC-*Bedayat* soldiers in the bunker seeming to double, the downing of the helicopter now a battle cry for the enemy.

Ross stiffened. He felt responsible for that chopper crew who had just been killed. He and the Ghosts had allowed the SA-24s to get this far . . .

But now he swore to avenge them.

Sixty-Four

30K had the drone crawler in the air, and then, with the APC crews preoccupied with the Marines targeting them just off to the east, he set down the drone, quad-rotors turning into wheels. He began rolling it beneath the APCs and toward the huts, marking targets as he did so. He realized then that the farthest hut on the east side closest to the jungle was entirely unprotected, probably no one home. If he could scale it and assume a position on its roof, he'd have an excellent supporting fires perch. He shared this news with Ross, who gave him permission to head out there and get up top, but stay under active camouflage as much as possible.

This time he would be the insurance man instead of Pepper, and that was the whole idea, wasn't it? Keep the old man safe. He took off running only a few seconds before Pepper and Kozak reached Ross, with Pepper calling after him.

30K was halfway to the hut when the night sky blinked to white as that second pair of Penguins exploded before they ever reached the LCS. The ship's Phalanx CIWS (Close-In Weapons System) had put its 20mm M61 Vulcan Gatling autocannon on target and blasted apart both antiship missiles. Captain Wagner had given 30K and the others a tour of the entire vessel, including the high-tech bridge with its joystick controller and flat-screen monitors. Of course, he'd been sure to boast about the Phalanx's capabilities. That the ship was still above water and still able to defend herself was a damned good sign.

30K reached the hut and crouched behind it. He fished out the drone's remote from his pocket and got the UAV back in the air and on autopilot, in case Major Mitchell decided to take control of the drone himself for a bird's-eye view of the battle.

A crude ladder constructed of planks and twine leaned against the hut, and 30K quietly mounted it, coming up on to the slightly angled roof that was made of tin and covered with palm fronds. He propped himself up on his elbows and was there one second, gone the next as his camouflage caught back up with his movements. He set up the Stoner on its bipod, with this particular weapon being magazine-fed from the top and the sights set off to the left to accommodate the mag.

He craned his head and scanned the jungle behind him, panning slowly to be sure no other FARC or *Bedayat jadeda* soldiers had moved up there – because the moment he opened fire, he'd become vulnerable. His escape plan involved a little jump off the back of the hut, nothing too elaborate, just a drop and run maneuver – a seven-foot bailout to the sand.

But then his hasty recon of the jungle to the rear

gave him pause. What the hell was that, just behind that cluster of nipah palms? Was that a fifth APC? One they hadn't seen before? It was just sitting nearby, heavily draped in foliage.

30K glanced back to the command hut, some fifty meters away. He thought about the position of his hut and the twenty-meter distance behind him, out to that hidden APC.

And he thought about the Hescos and his first reaction to them. Hamid's men had dug trenches, but the dirt they'd collected was hardly enough to fill those broad Hesco walls, yet there was no sign of excavation anywhere else near or around the outpost.

He almost fell off the roof as he realized what they'd done . . . and what was about to happen.

Sixty-Five

The discord rising to a crescendo across the outpost was enough to nearly deafen Ross and his men. The cracking of automatic gunfire, the blasting of fragmentation grenades and .50-caliber machine guns, and the roaring and subsequent bursts from RPGs were backed by the sudden and shockingly close whomping of rotors.

Ross looked up and saw the bulky silhouette of the Sea Stallion pass overhead, one of its door gunners delivering a blistering hailstorm of fire on a position out past the huts, presumably on one of the Penguin missile launchers, the .50-caliber shell casings falling just a meter away, thumping like bugs on the sand until a louder sound drowned them out: two more Hellfire missiles charged off from the remaining Seahawk, and a heartbeat later, a one-two explosive punch rumbled in the distance, followed by strobing bursts of light across the bellies of clouds.

'Delta Dragon, this is Guardian,' called Mitchell. 'The Penguins are disabled. Now get me those men.'

'It'll be my pleasure, sir.'

Ross turned to Kozak, who'd just dropped on to his gut beside him. 'You and our buddy good to go?'

Kozak glanced down at his remote control. 'Just say the word.'

Ross looked past Kozak to Pepper. 'I need a sniper on those APCs.'

Pepper gave a curt nod. 'I'll show them some love.'

After a quick glance back at the APCs, whose surfaces were still glinting with ricocheting gunfire, Ross took a deep breath and gave the order.

The Warhound came lumbering around the huts to confront both vehicles —

But then 30K was hollering over the radio, and Ross's attention was divided — because he couldn't hear a damned thing.

Just after he tried to call Ross, 30K tugged free a fragmentation grenade, pulled the pin, and hurled it toward the ground between his hut and the others. He lowered his head as the ear-piercing ka-boom resounded and the hut rattled while the dirt began raining down —

And not two seconds after the dust was clearing, 30K was zooming in with his binoculars and probing the ground where he'd thrown that grenade . . . and there it was, a much deeper impression than normal, one too deep to be caused by just a single grenade . . .

Hamid's men had created a tunnel system leading out from beneath the command hut to 30K's hut, and from there, they could flee to the waiting APC in the jungle. That's where they'd found the dirt to fill all those Hescos, and if 30K was right, those bastards were right under him at this very moment.

He saw now why Ross hadn't replied: Kozak had brought around the Warhound, which was taking massive fire from the troops within the APCs – and Pepper was dishing out swift justice with his Remington, head shots routinely placed and delivered.

That sudden racket must've spooked the men inside the hut, and they must've heard 30K because gunfire came punching up through the tin roof, stitching a deadly line before 30K could shift to avoid it, the rounds ripping through his legs.

It was fortuitous that Pepper happened to be staring through his scope and had shifted his aim slightly to the right. There, out behind the huts, he saw them, at least three squads of troops, fifteen or twenty in all, racing back toward the command hut.

At the same time, Kozak put the Warhound between them and the APCs, the big boy glistening with gunfire, 60mm mortars bursting from its back to arc down on unseen bunkers beyond. A guided missile suddenly erupted from its launcher to streak toward one of the APCs and explode across its hood, sending the vehicle skittering sideways and the men falling out the back, some decapitated, some bloody and disoriented, others climbing over the bodies to whip around and fire from their hips.

This would've been a perfect moment for 30K to open up on them, his supporting fire finishing the Warhound's job.

So where was he?

Pepper shifted his aim toward that far hut, where the door was now opening. Out burst Hamid, Valencia and Delgado, all wearing vests and armed with AK-47s. They saw the jungle, the raging battle around them, and the choice was damned clear. Jungle . . .

For a second, Pepper was so overwhelmed by the moment and the image (the men they sought were right there!) that he could barely get the words out of his mouth. But then, finally, they came.

And just as he finished his report to Ross, he panned up to spy 30K – his active camouflage disabled – dragging himself across the hut's roof, trying to lift his machine gun in the direction of Hamid's party.

Only a second-rate operator would get on the radio and scream, 'I'm hit! I'm hit,' thought 30K as he struggled to bring his rifle around. You don't cry about your wounds. You suck it up and take revenge. But damn, his pack must've been hit as well, the active camouflage unit damaged, its status bar flickering in his HUD.

It was moments like this that made him appreciate all the training they did. The training made him harder, and hard men are tougher to kill –

Which was why getting shot in the legs and dragging his wounded ass into an upright position so he could kill the bastards trying to escape was not a problem . . .

Until one of them, Valencia, rolled back to face him, just as 30K was lifting his weapon.

Sixty-Six

Kozak was a multitasking maniac, a grand maestro of death, having divided his brain into four separate parts all working in concert with one another, his eyes flicking between –

The targets being hit by the Warhound's mortars, which appeared as throbbing red blips on a digital map in his HUD . . .

The video piped in from the guided missile camera as he launched a second rocket at the other APC . . .

The grenade sensor's readout marking the positions of the Marines along with the team, and the hostiles framed in red . . .

And, finally, what he saw with his own eyes: the profiles of Hamid, Valencia and Delgado out by the far hut, and above them, surrounded by a bed of palm fronds, 30K rising to his knees with his rifle in hand . . .

Screw the multitasking.

That was his friend out there.

30K, his big brother. The guy who always got him into trouble but the guy he wished he could be, with so much courage that he'd throw himself into a barrage of bullets and ask why the enemy was so cheap with ammo.

Valencia had his rifle raised —

Kozak was about to scream but a barrage of incoming fire ten times heavier than before came out of nowhere, as if every remaining troop at the outpost had suddenly converged on their position, and this tiny piece of swamp and sand on an island smaller than Brooklyn was about to become a slaughterhouse.

Before Kozak could take another breath, the second APC was struck by the Warhound's guided missile, Valencia's rifle flashed and popped, and Pepper swung around and fired a shot at the fleeing men.

The plates on 30K's chest took a few of the rounds, but one caught him in the arm, another grazing his neck, the multiple impacts making him lose his balance before he could return fire, damn it —

And two more gunshots later, he was falling back off the hut's roof and into the air . . .

He landed on his head and shoulder, a horrible crunch reverberating through his neck, the feeling of bones shattering, and then his breath gone, the Cross-Com torn from his face, the dirt in his mouth, his eyes flickering open, another burning pain in his side turning prickly and sharper, just after a rifle report. He'd been shot again.

His left arm was useless, the collarbone most certainly broken, the bone already popping in his shoulder. He reached back for his pistol, saw Valencia lying on the ground clutching a gunshot wound at his hip, saw

Hamid and Delgado darting off for the APC, as a fresh wave of gunfire began shredding the hut above him.

After stealing a quick breath, he pulled himself up on one elbow and tried to crawl forward. Nothing. He tried again with everything he had. Cursed. Tried again.

Damn it. He would not be killed by this hybrid half-assed army. They didn't deserve a prize like him, these amateur bastards. They'd hardly earned his respect. He drove his elbow deeper into the sand and groaned, just as a round pinged off his helmet.

It was a Sunday afternoon, and Ross was home in Virginia Beach for two weeks of R & R. Wendy had gone out to Target with her friends to buy something for a baby shower happening the following week, and she'd warned him twice to keep an eye on the boys, and he'd sworn he would.

'Dad? It's so hot outside. Can you shoot us with the hose?'

Jonathan and his little buddy Marcus were running around on the front lawn, playing catch with a Nerf football, but they were sweating bullets and needed to cool off.

Ross had argued against the pool, citing the initial expense, high maintenance costs, and trying to joke that he didn't want his wife fraternizing with the pool boy while he was on the other side the world.

The boys would've been in that pool on a day like that. On 14 August.

'Okay, guys, give me a minute. I'll go get the hose.'

Backhanding sweat from his brow, Ross padded across the lawn, opened the gate, then crossed the backyard patio to unscrew the hose from the spigot.

He was gone all of twenty seconds, and since then he'd counted and recounted every one of them, each seeming to strip a year off his life.

Although he never heard their conversation, Marcus conveyed it later on, how he'd thrown the ball too hard, how it'd gone over Jonathan's head and Jonathan had said he'd get it. He hadn't even looked as he'd run into the street.

The guy who hit him was thirty years old, the brother of a Navy SEAL who lived at the end of the block. That was no coincidence since many operators lived in that area. He was driving back up to Long Island after coming down to see his brother for the weekend. He was under the speed limit, completely sober, utterly devastated. He just couldn't stop his pickup in time.

Ross had heard the brakes squealing, the thump, Marcus yelling, and another voice: 'Oh my God! Oh my God!'

He dropped the hose and went sprinting around the side of the house –

To find his little boy lying facedown in the middle of the road.

And at that moment, Ross was struck with the hollowest, most painful feeling he had ever known, a piece of his soul dying as he staggered toward the scene, mouth falling open, breath suddenly gone, legs failing to work . . .

Now, as he squinted toward 30K lying facedown in the sand, struggling to pull himself up, he realized with gritted teeth that this time – *this fucking time* – it wasn't too late.

'Pepper, Kozak, take the Warhound and go after Hamid!' he ordered.

'What about 30K?' cried Kozak.

'I got him! You go now!'

Sixty-Seven

Pepper got choked up as he and Kozak broke from cover and sprinted toward the Warhound. Pepper just couldn't bear to abandon 30K and felt as though he needed to save 30K himself — but the mission required him elsewhere. Period.

When 30K had told Pepper not to take any more risks, that if Pepper bought it, the rest of the team would be doomed, Pepper secretly felt the same way about him. While Pepper might've been the most experienced, he knew in his heart of hearts that 30K was the bravest man they had; in fact, he was the bravest soldier Pepper had ever known. Seeing him there, shot to shit and groping for life, was incomprehensible because if their bravest guy was going to buy it, where did that leave them?

Utilizing the Warhound for cover, they passed through a fusillade of fire so dense that Pepper found himself flinching over every round that caromed off the UGV, its feet stomping like an elephant's for a few more meters, the air rank with the scent of gunpowder until —

The ground heaved and splintered, and then, with a creak and groan, some heavy wooden beams — the same ones used to contrast the railway — came popping through the dirt like broken bones through flesh, the Warhound's weight too much for them. Pepper realized that this was a reinforced tunnel, and he, Kozak and the Warhound were now plummeting some three meters toward the floor below, the dirt coming with a hiss, Kozak hollering, the Warhound whining as it slammed into a side wall then hit the dirt floor and toppled on to its side.

30K could barely see through all the sand in his eyes, but for a moment, the Warhound was there, breaching the gap between huts, and in the next second, it was gone – what the hell?

Through a rising cloud of dust came Ross, sprinting toward him and dragging a wave of gunfire as though it were a cape. He came within three meters –

But a frag exploded with an orange glare behind him, catapulting him into the air, his silhouette morphing into an eagle in 30K's imagination, a star-filled eagle with talons of gold that swooped down to collapse next to him.

'Boss? Boss? Shit, man, come on,' he cried.

Ross stirred and raised his head. 'I'm still alive. Good. I'm getting you out of here. Ready?'

'Forget it. My legs are gone. Took another round in my side. Internal bleeding, man, I can feel it. Don't waste your time.'

'Oh, I see how it is. You just can't handle the fact that it's *me* who's saving you. The Navy fucker with all the baggage. Well, I got news for you, Rambo, right now my baggage is *you*.'

'Then leave me!' 30K screamed.

'You giving up?'

'No!'

'Then let's go, motherfucker!' With that Ross got up on his hands and knees, pulled 30K around, then managed to position him so he could rise, lifting him into a fireman's carry.

With what felt like inhuman strength, Ross started out, knees wobbling at first, but he was up with 30K braced across his back and now crossing toward the first patch of fronds near the jungle, his gait shifting to the left and right as he fought against 30K's weight.

Without warning, an incredible sound from behind them had 30K lifting his head:

The Marines must have been watching their escape and wanted to provide cover, because at least ten came charging forward, breathing the fire of their war cries, throwing themselves right into the line of fire, lobbing grenades and scaring the living shit out of the FARC and *Bedayat* infantry who'd moved up. The entire outpost turned medieval, infantry killing one another point-blank, the sand turning dark with blood. Not since Afghanistan had 30K seen anything as grisly. But the gambit worked, and Ross was able to reach cover.

'Thank you,' 30K told those boys. 'Thank you.'

Pepper clambered to his feet, coughing and waving dust from his eyes. He craned his head left and right. 'Kozak? Kozak?'

'Here . . .' came a thin, almost unrecognizable voice from somewhere ahead.

Pepper rushed forward, and there, where he'd seen the Warhound topple on to its side, was Kozak –

Pinned beneath the half-ton monstrosity.

'Aw, dude, how the hell?' Pepper asked. 'Where's the remote? Let me see if I can get him off you.'

'No time, bro. I'm just stuck, not dying. You take off. They're getting away!'

Pepper shuddered with indecision, but deep down he knew Kozak was right. 'All right, buddy, hang on.'

'I'm not going anywhere,' said Kozak. 'Just go!'

Torn once more, Pepper finally nodded and took off sprinting, adjusting his night-vision lens as he came over the mound where the collapse had occurred and followed the remaining section of the tunnel toward a ladder at the far end. He ascended and emerged into a hut filled with ammo crates, burst out the front door, and realized where he was. He looked toward the jungle where Hamid and Delgado had run and saw an APC blasting through the brush.

He raised his rifle, took aim at one of the tires, fired. He wasn't sure if he'd struck the tire or not. The vehicle cut hard to the right, behind a thicker section of palms, now well out of his reach.

And they must've helped their injured colleague Valencia, because he, too, was gone.

Sixty-Eight

Ross's legs finally gave out before he could lower 30K to the ground. Instead, they both came down like boulders off a cliff. Boom. The shock waves of pain ripped through him.

He hadn't said anything to 30K, but shrapnel from that grenade had torn into his arms and legs, and there was even a small piece that had stung the back of his neck. He could still move all right, but the hot flashes of pain were increasing by the minute.

As he gasped for air, Pepper's report came over the radio, and he wanted to tear off his Cross-Com and smash it. But then he looked at 30K, rolling on to his back, coughing, blood leaking from his lips now. Saving this man was all that mattered now.

And Pepper had been so right about this. What they did was sloppy work. The heroes didn't always capture the bad guys.

Then again, this was an island, and all Hamid had was an APC . . .

Ross acknowledged Pepper, ordered him to go back for Kozak, then got on the horn to Mitchell. 'I need the Stallion or the Seahawk to track and interdict that APC,' he told the major.

'Roger that,' said Mitchell.

Next, Ross called Captain Rugg. 'Cannonball, corpsman up, my position, right now, over!'

'You got it. On his way!'

Ross slipped off his pack and wrenched out his first aid supplies, the gunfire still popping near the huts, the APCs on fire now. 30K had been shot in the arm, both legs, and there was blood at his waist and on his neck. He was a mess, but Ross fought against the tremors in his hands and decided that the wound on 30K's side needed the most attention. He got out some big four-by-four bandages and some scissors, beginning to cut away the man's shirt to expose his chest. 30K looked at him, licked his lips, and was about to say something when Ross shook his head and said, 'Don't talk, bro. Corpsman on the way.'

30K nodded, blinked hard, then stared up at the canopy, and for a moment, Ross thought he'd lost him, but then he blinked again and coughed.

Kozak must've dropped the remote during the cave-in, and he forced his head up and tried to peer through the darkness. His Cross-Com's monocle had been shoved near his ear, and he couldn't reach up to adjust it.

He'd lied to Pepper. He didn't want to be overly dramatic, but it felt like something very bad had crushed in his chest – ribs, spine, who knew? – and now it was painful to breathe and he could taste blood at the back of his throat.

Well, wasn't this ironic? Here he was, the team's technophile, the proponent of all things electronic, the gadget master who often tried to convince his teammates that it wasn't a competition between technology and instincts – it was the technology that enhanced your instincts –

Or crushed you to death.

Footfalls came hard and fast, and Kozak bit his lip and tensed. He tried reaching for a frag in his web gear, thinking maybe he could do himself in before they did. Nope. There wasn't anything he could do if the enemy found him, save for closing his eyes and resigning to the inevitable.

'Kozak? Buddy? I'm back,' cried Pepper, allowing him to breathe once again. 'Now where's the remote? Come on, bro, it's gotta be around here somewhere.'

As Pepper leaned over to search near Kozak's head, Kozak glanced past him and saw the two shadows flutter overhead. Those shadows materialized into men leaping into the hole.

He opened his mouth, wanting to warn Pepper, but no words would come, just a half-strangled hiss and groan –

But Pepper had heard them hit the ground, and in one fluid motion he drew the FN Five-seven pistol holstered at his waist and sighted the first of two FARC soldiers coming over the pile of dirt.

Pepper, knowing that his first shot would give up his location and draw fire from one or both of the soldiers, changed his mind and threw himself behind the Warhound's legs before he took that first shot – and that's what saved his life.

While one soldier took Pepper's round in the head and lolled back, the second opened up, spraying rounds all over the hole until Pepper could steal a moment to pop up and drop him with a pair of rounds, one in the neck, the other to the shoulder, and that was good –

Because two more men were rushing through the tunnel, having come from the opposite direction.

He heard the grenade first as it bounced off the Warhound and struck the dirt a meter from his boots.

Purely on reflex, Pepper jerked forward and kicked the grenade, sending it arcing away, then he dove back behind the Warhound once again as the frag exploded, showering them with dirt, the shrapnel chinking off the Warhound's heavy armor.

Now, with his hearing gone, replaced by an explosive hum, he rolled back toward the tunnel. He sighted the two soldiers, getting off two rounds before tugging free a frag of his own and letting it fly. He thought he'd shot one man before the frag exploded, consuming them both, and then, just as he raised his head, he spotted movement from the corner of his eye – more combatants jumping into the hole . . . three, four, five, maybe six in all.

There were just too many of them.

He tore free another grenade, shifted back toward Kozak, and thought, *We go together, bro. Together . . .*

After leaving 30K in the hands of the Navy corpsman, who assured Ross he'd do everything he could to stabilize 30K, Ross took off running for the collapsed section of the tunnel. Were it not for the adrenaline coursing through him, he doubted he could have gone on.

He'd spotted the squad of FARC troops leaping into the hole, rushing up behind Kozak and Pepper as they did so, and the moment they hit the ground, Ross lowered his HK into the pit and held down the trigger, dropping the unsuspecting bastards from behind, the last man rolling to face him, only to be hammered back into oblivion.

'Pepper! Pepper!' Ross cried.

No reply.

Ross winced and leaped on to the mound of dirt about two meters below, his wounded legs giving out as he made impact, sending him rolling down to the bottom. He rose to his hands and knees and saw Pepper trying to dig a furrow around Kozak, whose head appeared from beneath the Warhound.

After Ross stumbled to his feet, Pepper craned his head, pointed to his pistol, then sighed and mouthed the words *'Can't hear you,'* as he gestured to his ear.

In the dirt, just behind Pepper, and just barely visible, was the Warhound's remote. Ross scooped it up and studied the display. If he could flex two of the UGV's legs, he could raise its torso a quarter meter or so. After a deep breath, he fought to steady his hand and tap in the command. The Warhound creaked, servos whining, then rose – just as Kozak moaned and Pepper tugged him free.

Kozak's face was twisted in agony as Pepper assured him he'd be okay. Damning to hell medical protocol that dictated they immobilize the patient right there in the pit, they hauled him unsteadily to his feet, and he clutched his chest with one arm, the other draped over Pepper's shoulder. They started down the tunnel, toward the ladder beneath the hut, and Ross dragged himself after them. The pain shooting up and down his legs came as electrified needles now, his arms growing heavier.

He helped Pepper get Kozak up the ladder, and then as he climbed and neared the top, the night sky faded for a moment. His heart raced. Sweat poured from his temples. He clutched the ladder even tighter and fought against it. No, he would not pass out. No.

He took a long, deep breath, as Mitchell's voice buzzed in his earpiece: 'Delta Dragon, this is Guardian. The Seahawk has disabled the APC. I don't see Valencia but assume he's still inside. Hamid and Delgado look injured. They're still trying to escape on foot. I'm tracking them now with your drone, over.'

'Roger that, Guardian. They won't get away.'

Sixty-Nine

Hamid and Delgado were heading toward the fishing boat rental place on the north coast, and Ross called for the Seahawk to land on the beach. He and Pepper headed out to board the chopper.

Meanwhile, Rugg called to say that his Marines had captured eleven men who'd surrendered and that the others were either wounded or dead. Sadly, he also mentioned that five of his Marines had been killed, while another fourteen had been wounded.

'You sure you're okay?' Pepper shouted above the rotor wash as they climbed into the Seahawk.

Ross gave him a vigorous nod and thumbs-up, and once they were off the ground and had donned their headsets, he issued his instructions to the pilot.

Meanwhile, the wounded were being evacuated on to the Sea Stallion, and Rugg called to say he was making sure that Ross's people were taken good care of for the trip back.

'Guess it's up to us old guys to finish this off, huh?' asked Pepper.

'Age and treachery,' said Ross.

Pepper smiled, thought a moment, then said, 'Going back for 30K . . . that was something.'

'You didn't think I had it in me.'

'I won't lie.'

'It's okay. So now you know.'

'Yeah. I sure as hell do.'

Hamid was limping, and Delgado was clutching his left elbow with his rifle slung over his shoulder as they came out of the mangroves on the east side of the beach and stepped on to the rickety wooden pier leading out to the score of fishing boats.

Their escape involved more than just stealing an old boat. Mitchell reported that a helicopter had landed on a tiny sand island less than a kilometer off Rupat's northern coast, and surely Hamid and Delgado would fire up one of the outboards and race out to meet it.

But before they reached the end of the pier, they froze and squinted in horror through the darkness —

As the air shimmered and fluctuated to expose Ross and Pepper, rifles trained on them, eyes burning.

'Don't move, Hamid,' Ross ordered in Arabic.

'And you, too, Señor Delgado,' Pepper said in Spanish.

Hamid took a step forward and leaned toward Ross, straining to get a better look at him. 'Who are you?'

'That doesn't matter. Why we're here is more important.'

Hamid contemplated that, his face stoic. He glanced back to Delgado. 'Do you know who they are?'

'Yes, he does,' said Ross. 'Don't you remember us,

little man? Back in that coke lab in Colombia? We saved your ass, and you told us you were a taxi driver.'

Delgado's gaze drifted past them, as though he were already searching for an escape route. 'I don't know you.'

'All right, listen to me,' Ross began. 'Put your rifles on the dock. You do it right now; otherwise I'll make the pain a lot worse.'

Hamid kept his rifle trained on Ross.

Standoff.

'Well, I thought it was gonna be a gunfight,' said Pepper, who slowly set his rifle on the pier. 'I surrender.'

'Sergeant, I wasn't talking to you,' Ross said in disbelief.

Pepper raised his palms, looked at Ross, winked. 'It's okay.'

And before Ross could react, Pepper charged toward Hamid, the man opening fire until Pepper reached him and tore the rifle out of his hands, bringing it around to clock him in the head with the AK's heavy wooden stock –

While at the same time, Delgado brought his rifle around and was about to fire, but Ross shot him in the hip, knocking him back into the water.

'I got him,' cried Pepper as Hamid crumpled on to the dock and Pepper reached into his web gear for a pair of zipper cuffs.

Ross ripped off his pack, set down his rifle and jumped in the water after Delgado, whose head had barely broken the surface. Ross reached him, grabbed the back of his collar, and began a modified combat sidestroke back to the sandy shoreline, and once he could stand, he continued to drag Delgado all the way to the beach.

The man was barely conscious, leg bleeding badly, as Ross got on the radio and called back the Seahawk for an immediate evac. Seeing that the little man wasn't going anywhere, he crossed on to the dock and dragged himself over to Pepper, who was resting his back against Hamid and just breathing.

'Chopper on the way?' Pepper asked.

'Yeah.'

'Good.' Pepper grimaced and suddenly stiffened in pain. 'He shot me up pretty good. Plates caught a few, but I got one in the shoulder, maybe the leg, too. Yeah, I can feel it . . .'

'Dude, what were you thinking?'

'I don't know. I just got no patience for that shit.'

Ross was so dumbfounded he had to laugh. 'Next time you give me some warning.'

Pepper was about to reply, but the Seahawk had swooped down toward the beach and landed.

Ross leaned over and cried in his ear, 'We got him, old man. We got him!'

Pepper nodded and forced a smile as the crew chief, along with Rugg and two of his Marines, came jogging up the pier.

Seventy

A squad of Marines retrieved Valencia's body from the disabled APC. He'd slowly bled out. He was a doctor unable to save himself, and this was justice served to a man who'd turned his back on his oath to save others.

30K, the most seriously injured of the Ghosts, was stabilized back on board the LCS, as were Pepper and Kozak, the latter of whom had suffered some broken ribs and a punctured lung.

During stabilization and triage, Wagner ordered the Sea Stallion to be reconfigured for medevac. The CH-53 was capable of carrying twenty-four stretchers, eight more than the number of wounded requiring critical trauma care. Singapore's two trauma care centers, Gleneagles Hospital in Tanglin and nearby Mt Elizabeth Hospital in Orchard would split the casualties to reduce overload at either center.

Ross stayed with his men, having been told that he'd need to have the shrapnel removed from his arms and legs. All Kozak could think about was whether or not the Warhound had been retrieved, and Ross assured him that yes, the big boy was back on the hangar deck, looking about as battle worn as they were.

Pepper was resting easy, the morphine drip keeping

him in a good place for now, and 30K was completely out, eyes slammed shut, face ashen.

With a deep lump in his throat, Ross reached out and took 30K's hand in his own. 'You can be a real asshole, you know that? Yeah, I guess you do.'

During the next few weeks, while he and the team recovered, Ross kept tabs on Hamid and Delgado, learning what he could through Mitchell and Diaz. For his part, Hamid would not talk no matter how many times he was interrogated and didn't seem to care if he spent the rest of his life in prison.

Delgado, on the other hand, knew the game all too well and was already working out his deal before federal prosecutors ever came to him with one.

Because Hamid's partner Amir Bahar had been seen on the island but not captured during the raid, those prosecutors wanted to locate him. They also wanted everything Delgado knew regarding Hamid's operations with Bahar, and they wanted the truth about what Delgado had done after he'd been kidnapped. The little man spun quite a tale:

Once he learned his cover was blown and ten years of work in Colombia as the Agency's most valuable asset was shot to hell, he got desperate. He knew the Agency would punish him for his failure, assign him to a desk for the rest of his tenure, so he did something radical. He hacked into his personnel file and altered the photographs as part of a plan to go underground with some money he'd socked away. Unfortunately, the FARC caught up with him before he could vanish, and it was Mitchell's friend, Adamo, who'd learned of the kidnapping through his own contacts and called it in to the Agency.

The FARC troops who captured Delgado and the cabdriver decided on their own that they'd make a switch in order to get paid twice: Hand over a cabdriver for some ransom money, then hand over the real guy, which was why they had dragged the cabbie out to the submarine.

Ross's team got caught up in that mess, Delgado escaped, and then, instead of going underground, he decided he'd go for broke. He struck a deal with Valencia and Hamid, who went for it because Delgado's European drug contacts were valuable to them and Delgado threatened to expose the group if they didn't take him under his wing. To ensure against any retaliation, Delgado proved that he had a partner who would blow the whistle on Hamid if he wound up getting killed. His partner was Tamer, whose family Delgado promised to take care of so long as the man remained loyal to him. Despite killing himself, Tamer knew that Delgado would keep his promise. Delgado was going to further open up the European drug markets for Hamid and Bahar, as well as tip them off to any known American intelligence assets. For this, he would be paid handsomely.

Ross had never known a more opportunistic, conniving, treacherous son of a bitch, and to top it all off, Delgado said the Agency had driven him to this. They'd put too much pressure on him and made him risk his life for an insulting paycheck.

He would spend the rest of his life in prison, but his deal kept the death penalty for treason and espionage off the table.

Every military base had its local sports bar, and every sports bar had its regulars, which in the Liberator's case included men whose work was never discussed. These were the Special Forces operators like Ross whose motto, 'Liberate the oppressed,' had given the bar its name. Their conversations ran the usual gamut from sports to beer to family and girlfriends.

It'd been nearly eight weeks since Ross and the others had all been together, so this night out was a reunion of sorts. He sat at a long booth, realizing what a dork he was for showing up so early. Pepper finally arrived, giving him a hearty handshake and warm pat on the back.

'They done picking the metal out of you?' he asked.

'Not quite.'

'I hate that shit.'

'Me, too. How you doing these days?'

'Serving with you left me feeling bloated and emotionally scarred, but the bullet holes healed.'

Ross nearly spat out his beer. 'You been rehearsing that all day?'

Pepper grinned. 'Kinda. You here for the early bird special, Grandpa?'

'You're two for two and on a roll.'

'They tell me I'm a crack shot.'

'They don't lie.'

'And here they are,' said Pepper, rising from his seat to allow Kozak to slide in, while 30K ambled over with an aluminum hospital cane in his right hand. He cursed, flumped into his seat, then looked up and asked in utter disbelief, 'Who stole my beer?'

'Easy now, Sergeant,' said Ross. 'Just ordered a warm-up for myself. Pitchers are coming.'

'You know the GST doesn't like us drinking booze,' said Kozak.

'And when the hell has that stopped you?' asked Pepper.

Kozak flashed his guilty-as-charged grin. 'I heard Mitchell can toss back quite a few . . .'

'Why don't you ask him?' said Ross, cocking a thumb over his shoulder as Mitchell approached, wearing jeans and a sweatshirt simply labeled: ARMY.

The team was about to snap to when Mitchell said, 'Relax, boys, I just heard you were all getting together, and I wanted to stop by.'

'We appreciate that, sir,' said Pepper.

Mitchell's gaze grew distant. 'You know every time I went downrange, I came back with new stories and new scars – and sometimes a heavy heart, but you know what the best thing was?'

The major waited . . . a dramatic pause.

'Shit, the best thing was I came back! So enjoy your

nonalcoholic beverages tonight, and as soon as the doctor clears you, I've got plenty of work. Are you in, gentlemen?'

'Hoo-ah!' they all shouted.

'Very well. See you soon.' With that, a living legend strode away from their table.

After they'd eaten their fill, traded jokes and relived the more hair-raising parts of the mission, they said their good-byes, and Ross made it a point to escort 30K out to his car, a red Mustang Cobra, of course.

'You didn't come out here to give me help, did you?' said 30K.

Ross shook his head. He closed his eyes for a moment and began to choke up.

'Sir, what's wrong?'

'Nothing.'

'Sir . . .'

'Look, I just . . . I want to tell you about my son . . . I want you to know . . . I guess I need you to know. Do you have a minute?'

'Sure. I got all the time in the world.'

TOM CLANCY

THREAT VECTOR

Jack Ryan has only just moved back into the Oval Office when he is faced with a new international threat. An aborted coup in the People's Republic of China has left President Wei Zhen Lin with no choice but to agree with the expansionist policies of General Su Ke Qiang. They have declared the South China Sea a protectorate and are planning an invasion of Taiwan.

The Ryan administration is determined to stop these Chinese ambitions in their tracks, but the stakes are dangerously high as hundreds of Chines anti-ship missiles thwart the US Navy's plans to protect the island. Meanwhile, Chinese cyber-warfare experts have launched a devastating attack on American infrastructure. It's a new combat arena, but it's every bit as deadly as any that has gone before.

Jack Ryan, Jr, and his colleagues at the Campus may be just the wild card that his father needs to stack the deck. There's just one problem: someone knows about the off-the-books intelligence agency and may be ready to blow their cover sky high.

'There's hardly another thriller writer alive who can fuel an adrenaline surge the way Clancy can' *Daily Mail*

TOM CLANCY

LOCKED ON

The Ryans – father and son – are fighting on two fronts . . .

When a deadly terrorist alliance creates the potential to blackmail world power into submission, it's got to be stopped before it is too late. That's just the trigger Jack Ryan Jr needs to take his work for shadowy intelligence agency The Campus from the back room to the sharp end: black ops.

Meanwhile, his father, Jack Ryan Sr, campaigning for re-election as US President, is up against a privately funded vendetta to discredit him. Caught at the heart of the conspiracy is former Navy SEAL, John Clark. And Ryan Sr soon discovers that being his friend could have deadly consequences.

With the breakneck speed and military action scenes that have made him the premier thriller writer of our time, Tom Clancy delivers a novel of high-tech warfare in which the enemy within may be even more devastating than the enemy without.

'Truly riveting, a dazzling read. A virtuoso display of page-turning talent' *Sunday Express*

'A brilliantly constructer thriller that packs a punch like Semtex explosive' *Daily Mail*

'The action comes thick and fast' *The Times*

He just wanted a decent book to read ...

Not too much to ask, is it? It was in 1935 when Allen Lane, Managing Director of Bodley Head Publishers, stood on a platform at Exeter railway station looking for something good to read on his journey back to London. His choice was limited to popular magazines and poor-quality paperbacks – the same choice faced every day by the vast majority of readers, few of whom could afford hardbacks. Lane's disappointment and subsequent anger at the range of books generally available led him to found a company – and change the world.

'We believed in the existence in this country of a vast reading public for intelligent books at a low price, and staked everything on it'
Sir Allen Lane, 1902–1970, founder of Penguin Books

The quality paperback had arrived – and not just in bookshops. Lane was adamant that his Penguins should appear in chain stores and tobacconists, and should cost no more than a packet of cigarettes.

Reading habits (and cigarette prices) have changed since 1935, but Penguin still believes in publishing the best books for everybody to enjoy. We still believe that good design costs no more than bad design, and we still believe that quality books published passionately and responsibly make the world a better place.

So wherever you see the little bird – whether it's on a piece of prize-winning literary fiction or a celebrity autobiography, political tour de force or historical masterpiece, a serial-killer thriller, reference book, world classic or a piece of pure escapism – you can bet that it represents the very best that the genre has to offer.

Whatever you like to read – trust Penguin.